Pond Hockey

Brian Kennedy

argenta
press

© 2013 by Argenta Press
First printed in 2013 10 9 8 7 6 5 4 3 2 1
Printed in Canada

The Publisher: Argenta Press is an imprint of Dragon Hill Publishing Ltd.

Library and Archives Canada Cataloguing in Publication
Kennedy, Brian, 1962–, author

Pond hockey / Brian Kennedy.

ISBN 978-0-9866546-5-7 (pbk.)

I. Title.

PS8621.E6315A64 2013   C813'.6   C2013-903710-1

Project Director: Marina Michaelides
Project Editor: Kathy van Denderen
Cover Illustration: "Winter Solstice" painting by Elizabeth Lennie © 2013; reproduced with permission

Produced with the assistance of the Government of Alberta, Alberta Multimedia Development Fund.

Alberta
Government

PC: 24

Dedication

For Mom, with one regret: that you haven't been here to enjoy any of this

Acknowledgments

I have a sign in my home office that says, "Nobody's going to write these books for you," the motto I adopted for myself several years ago. It reminds me of my duty to sit down and write every day. But what the sign doesn't say is that without the tolerance and encouragement of a soul mate, nothing would get done. So, Gaby, thanks for everything you do to make me believe in myself.

My editor, Kathy van Denderen, is magic with words, but she's no pushover. She has challenged me to be precise, making every syllable count. I owe her whatever artistry has resulted.

My friends in hockey include Josh Brewster, Gann Matsuda, Dennis Bernstein, Charles Smith, Doug Stolhand, Eddie Garcia, John Hoven, Dave Joseph, Jimmy Bramlett, Jonathan Davis, Keijo Jolli, Ted Sobel, Jon Rosen and Kevin Greenstein. All are excellent students of the game, and each has, in his own way, helped me. Thanks, colleagues.

The LA Kings and Anaheim Ducks have been kind enough to grant me media credentials, and many of the games I see and the people I have met at them moved this project along. Thanks to media relations people including Alex Gilchrist, Mike Kalinowski, Jeremy Zager, Mike Altieri, Jeff Moeller and Courtney Ports.

This book was completed during a sabbatical year, and I must thank Pasadena City College (PCC) for that time and my Dean, Professor Amy Ulmer, an unfailing supporter of my work. During the year I was on leave, I was a Research Fellow at the Centre for the Study of Sport and Health at Saint Mary's University in Halifax. My gratitude goes out to Professor Colin Howell, who made that possible.

Friends and family members may recognize their names in this book; it's my way of paying tribute to them. My dad is the character of Hugh Alexander. The father represented as Todd's father is purely fictional. Joyce was my mom's name, and I've used it for Mrs. Graham. Sandra, my sister; Phil Reimer, her husband, and Daniel and Sarah, their children; my cousin Gregg Thomson; my friends Tod Patric Hamilton, Tim Reid, Andy Holman and Jamie Dopp; among others, have inspired me. Mel Donalson and Beverly Tate have supported my work, as have all my colleagues at PCC. Thanks to all of them for their encouragement.

Introduction: Between Innocence and Experience

In a time when every toy you remember from childhood is as close as the click of the "Buy" button on an online auction site, nostalgia is a compelling pastime. Ebay has changed everything, as far as the past goes. G.I. Joes, Hot Wheels, Barbie dolls and accessories, authentic Cabbage Patch Kids—they're all there. Taking advantage of this, I recently assembled the complete 1971–72 Topps and O-Pee-Chee hockey card sets, because the Ken Dryden rookie card was the most coveted prize in the world when I was in elementary school, and the one I had was creased. I'm not alone in exercising my nostalgia muscle.

At the same time, the world of sports is much less innocent than before. In the past, hockey fans went to see a game at the Forum or the Gardens; now they go to a commercially sponsored arena with the name of a bank or an automobile company adorning it. Media members are cautioned, when they write their stories, to use the appropriate nomenclature for the rink. Sponsor money demands it. Professional sports have been taken over by the lure of the dollar, as evidenced by the NHL's recent lockout, during which, as it is commonly said, millionaire players and billionaire owners forgot about the rest of us, the real lovers of the game.

The contemporary moment, in other words, comes at the intersection of innocence and experience, to borrow the words of William Blake. Perhaps this explains why people are drawn to games like pond hockey, which holds out the promise of childhood innocence restored. Through the beauty of contesting for goals in an often-magnificent outdoor setting, players of all ages bond with friends the way they used to when they were kids.

But with the rise of the World Pond Hockey Championship, which takes place in Plaster Rock, New Brunswick, each February, it might be that the game has become the province of grown-ups. When an event gets a "world championship" label attached to it, you might fear that experience takes over, casting innocence aside.

Not so. The very names of some pond hockey teams that contest the tournament are the guarantee of that. The Mighty Quacks, the Polar Pond Club and Tougher in Alaska are just some teams you might find either in Plaster Rock or at the U.S. version of a pond hockey championship that takes place in Minneapolis, Minnesota.

Pond hockey remains fun, despite the intensity of competition that accompanies its various tournaments. And the rules are simple—no checking, no slap shots, no goalies—and sportsmanship is expected of everyone.

In many ways, pond hockey these days represents a modern version of the first contests for the Stanley Cup. Before the NHL took over the right to award that trophy, it was a challenge cup that was defended by whoever held it whenever another team demanded a crack at it. The smallest town ever to send a winning team was Kenora, Ontario. Some teams defended it as many as five times in a single season. Imagine that today—and imagine a city of around 15,000, which is how big Kenora is now, winning the trophy.

The World Pond Hockey Championship gives small towns such a chance once more, because anyone with a team can apply to play. It's amateur sport at its best, and perhaps one of the last vestiges of when the pure love of the game mattered more than whose pockets were lined, and whose emptied, in the attempt at sports supremacy.

This novel attempts to capture that feeling of innocence and the joy of playing for glory and bragging rights alone. Yet while the story is based on the Plaster Rock tournament, I've taken some liberties with the details of the actual tournament.

None of the events in these pages happened, nor are they reflective of anyone's real experience. Details of games are meant to be authentic, but they're formed out of my imagination alone. Scores in pond hockey tournament games are often in the range of 15–10, unlike what I portray. Other details are also taken from real life but have been fictionalized. For example, the Peterborough Bantam Classic is based on the Peterborough Liftlock Atom tournament, which has a history going back more than fifty years. The World Pond Hockey Championship in Plaster Rock is portrayed as taking place in late February, but the actual tournament occurs early in that month. The bids to participate in the tournament used to be submitted in May, and the teams were announced on June 1. In 2013, the deadline was June 30 for the 2014 tourney, not near Christmastime, as in the story.

It's my hope that readers who know Plaster Rock's World Pond Hockey Championship intimately will forgive the liberties I've taken. For those who have only a vague familiarity with the world of pond hockey, this book is meant as an introduction to an exciting adventure that is within the reach of almost anyone.

After reading Todd Graham's story, I suggest you go grab your skates and stick, or your running shoes and tennis ball, and head outside. Become a kid again through the magic of hockey!

–Brian Kennedy, PhD

CHAPTER
one

Todd Graham eased his two-year-old Lexus IS 250 off the highway at Exit 77, cruised down the ramp and took the left turn onto the rural road that would lead him home. Ten minutes later, he entered Queenston, Ontario, from the south. This side of town had once been home to Mackey's—local lingo for Mackey Motor Assembly, Incorporated. Mackey's had been the main employer in the town from the 1950s, when GM started using them to put together engine sub-assemblies, until Mackey's went out with the old century.

With that work gone and the plant abandoned, nothing much existed south of the town's main east-west street except relics of the boom times—buildings standing in scrubland of the type familiar to people who travel in the upper Midwest of the United States. Though it was a town of under 10,000, Queenston resembled places like Flint, Michigan, or Toledo, Ohio, where the great manufacturing dream that had ruled over most of the twentieth century had also died. The houses near the old factory, too, had deteriorated into barely inhabitable messes, where once they had been homes to families with dads who made a decent living working the line.

Todd crossed a bridge and then turned right onto King Street, which locals joked was the "King of Queens" long before the American sitcom by that same name existed.

He took a left toward his mom's house, then remembered that he needed to buy groceries. He did a quick U-turn.

When he saw the sign for Joseph's SuperFresh, he pulled into the lot and looked around. A small-town grocery store parking lot, with pickup trucks taking up many of the spaces. Carts were scattered here and there, with no indication that anyone cared whether or not they were free to roam the pavement, knocking into the sides of vehicles at will. He got out of his car and slammed the door hard enough to give emphasis to his feelings, a mixture of disbelief and unhappy familiarity with the surroundings.

He was home, though he was loath to call this town four hours northeast of Toronto by that name. Being anyplace but where he'd lived since finishing his MBA was to admit failure and defeat.

Sixteen years of living away, first in university, grad school and then working in Toronto, had come to nothing. He would be here for a while, but he didn't relish the fact. For the first few days, at least, he intended to lie low, get settled in a little and figure out how to deal with his new reality.

He grabbed the cart that was most likely to dent his driver's door and wheeled it in front of him, heading into the SuperFresh to grab enough groceries to get him through the weekend. He'd return on Monday, when it was less likely that he'd run into someone he knew, or he'd go out to the Superstore next to the 401 and really load up. Tonight, it was just going to be cereal and milk, and maybe some lasagne that he could pitch into his mom's freezer. Since she wasn't living at the house right now, he didn't have to consider her tastes as he made his choices.

Not that he could avoid seeing people forever. Sooner or later, he would run into a high school classmate, or maybe the parent of one, and he would have to diffuse their awkward surprise at seeing him. Everyone in town knew that he'd left a long time ago, and that there was really no reason for him to have returned, except maybe to sell the house. But they'd also know that it wasn't for sale, because his mom was still alive.

They wouldn't have any clue why he was living here again, unless he let it spill that he had to stay until he could regroup, get his head straight and find a job in Toronto, Winnipeg or any other big city that was "not here." Until then, Queenston was going to be his encampment, a place to lick his wounds, figure out how to deal with the fallout from being fired from his corporate gig and put a revamped resumé together that would help him restart his climb up the corporate mountain.

He walked into the store with his cart. Not much had changed in the time since his last visit. Soup on the right. Dairy at the back. Drinks as you headed to the checkout tills. The arrangement made it easy to get in and out quickly. He headed to the produce section and picked up a couple of apples, throwing them into a plastic bag as he whizzed on to the frozen food aisle and then to the cashier.

As he exited the store, relieved that the women working the tills weren't people he knew, he looked at the sky. Fall was coming. The light at this time of year was different. Softer late in the day, with sunset coming on without the long, slow burn that happened in the heart of summer. Pretty soon, the air would change, and winter would be on its way. The prospect made him shudder, not in anticipation of the cold, but because of the bleakness and short, dark days that always came when the seasons changed.

He put the bag of groceries in the passenger seat, got in the car, dropped the gear lever into drive and eased out of the lot toward the house he'd grown up in. As he drove, he peered out the windshield at the two-story buildings that ran along King Street, the town's main drag. More empty storefronts existed than there had been in the past. He drove by a group of young boys walking along the deserted sidewalk, baseball mitts hanging on their hands after a pickup game. As the kids walked, they scuffed their running shoes on the ground and kicked at imaginary cans. Their world was complete. They had no idea that their town, for some people, cultivated the desire to escape.

He'd been like them once, not all that long before. Summer was glorious then, the days long, school nowhere on the horizon. On those August evenings, his dad often told him to go get the mitts for a game of catch. He'd go, always with the same sense of anticipation mixed with dread. Summer, for his father, meant attempts to bond with his son, but the season also offered hours of extra daylight spent out on the porch chugging down beers. By the time the game of pops and grounders was suggested, the old man would already be pretty well sauced.

Todd could never say no to his dad. That would invite the wrath. But even as he fetched the mitts, he would feel the grip of anxiety start to tighten his stomach into a knot. Sooner or later, he'd miss a throw or let a ball get between his legs. Sometimes, it would roll as far as the street.

"Keep your eye on the ball," the rebukes would start. "Don't look up at me or where you intend to throw." The advice seemed sensible enough.

The next time, the comments would be harsher. "Come on, son. Watch the freaking ball!" But "freaking" wasn't the word the old man would use.

If Todd muffed the ball again, things would get ugly. "You sieve." He'd pause for effect. "That's right," he'd almost snarl. "That's right. Sieve." That he had merely repeated his first insult never occurred to him as being ineffective. He would glare at Todd, ready to blurt out more hurtful, angry words. Sometimes he would utter them; other times, Todd's mom would appear from inside the house to make peace. Sometimes, the old man managed to control himself. Sometimes. His mood depended on how many empty beer bottles were lying around.

However the encounter ended, Todd would slink into the house, glove dangling from his left hand and the ball he'd had to retrieve from the edge of the road in his right. If he was lucky, the cuff that the old man directed at the back of his head would miss, with Todd feeling only its breeze and his own terror.

The next morning, everything would return to normal, the game of catch not mentioned as father and son munched their cereal. Anyone observing the scene would view them as a happy family, but for Todd, the truth made it necessary to find a way out. But it was more than his dad's drinking that had driven him away. The bigger world had pulled at him, the hope that he might be the success story that populated local myth when parents talked about how their kids had traded their small-town roots for splashy jobs in other parts of the country.

Todd turned left onto Beechwood Drive, where his mom's house sat, one among a few hundred suburban ranch homes built in the 1970s, when Queenston was still in growth mode. Since his old man had passed away several years before, he hadn't thought of it as his mom and dad's place; it was his mom's place now.

When he got to his block, he looked around but saw no one. Everyone was probably inside, mesmerized by what poured out of the TVs glowing in their living rooms. This gave him a reprieve from human contact, but the next morning, he would have to face the neighbors. The shiny sports sedan would be a beacon for curiosity, set apart as it was from the Chevys and Fords normally found in front of the houses on this street and the others surrounding it.

His mom's car was not in the driveway, which surprised him even though he knew she wouldn't be at home. He parked the Lexus up near the garage door, got out and grabbed the groceries. He opened the front door of the house and quickly ducked into the living room, as if trying to avoid prying eyes. Once it was dark, he went out and unloaded the suitcases and boxes that filled the back seat and trunk. Anticipating a stay that could stretch into the fall, he had brought clothes for the change of seasons, along with his winter jacket, which could be needed in the evenings as early as the first part of October.

CHAPTER
two

The town wasn't the worst place in the world to live. As small towns went, Queenston had its charms—a little downtown near the river, a huddle of stores that had survived the advent of online commerce that made everything from vacuum cleaners to baby wipes readily available and cheap. Recently, rumors had circulated that a coffee shop where the word "latte" wasn't foreign, like it would have been during Todd's childhood in the 1980s and '90s, might open in an old library. The grocery store he had stopped at earlier wasn't the best, but a Superstore at the edge of town near the highway offered everything from books to hummus. An urban archeologist might have described the town in 2012 as sitting midway on the continuum between the heyday of its industrial past and a future that looked more promising than it had in 1999, when Mackey's had shut down.

Still, anyone with ambition tried to escape, whether that meant going away to university, working in the oil patch or heading to urban spaces like Toronto or Vancouver where life seemed more glamorous. The ultimate goal was to earn more than a steady union wage, an option now gone in any event. Todd's exit route had been university at Western in London, grad school at Queen's and a corporate job in management in Toronto. All through his twenties and into his early thirties, the last thing anyone expected was for him to come back to Queenston. He was one of those who had made it.

His parents had encouraged his dreams. They were not happy to lose him to Toronto, especially when he told them that his hopes to someday reach VP level would likely be followed by a move to the U.S. for bigger opportunities, but they were glad he was making his way in the world. His dad, despite hitting the bottle hard as he got older, still had loving feelings for his only kid, and he'd often told Todd he was proud of him.

"Don't come back," his dad had said on the phone during one of their conversations shortly before he died. "If you stay here for more than a weekend visit, you've failed."

Sure, his dad had exaggerated, but he got the old man's point. The town was a kind of vortex that pulled people in and didn't let go. Many of Todd's high school classmates had had the same plans as Todd and had left in a blaze of glory. Many returned, their dreams unfulfilled. A few of them had university degrees. Some even had a reason to be in Queenston. One guy had taken over his dad's pharmacy. Another was an accountant, about as big-time a career as you could get in small-town Ontario.

But others had struggled in the larger world. They hadn't made it, or they'd been in Toronto or Calgary for a few years and realized that the big city life wasn't for them. Most of them tried to paint their return home as a rediscovery of the simple life, the values they'd grown up with. This logic did not square with Todd's way of thinking. They just couldn't cut it against stiffer competition.

And here he was, exactly like them, his efforts to create a life outside of where he had grown up having stalled. At least some of them had the excuse that they wanted to raise families in Queenston, portrayed in this scenario as the idyllic small town. These people had married high school sweethearts before leaving, and when life elsewhere hadn't worked out, they returned, some with kids, others to have them. But Todd didn't have that excuse.

The morning after he got home, Todd wandered around looking at the stuff that cluttered the house, reacquainting himself with the items that formed the architecture of his childhood. The tall vase filled with dried sunflowers that sat next to the couch; the Royal Doulton figurines, one in a pink dress, another in a green dress; the white everyday dishes stacked in the kitchen cupboards—all were familiar relics of when he'd lived there, as if the house were frozen in time.

He sat at the kitchen table and finished his cereal— Lucky Charms, bought for old time's sake and in memory of the old man—then headed outside into the Saturday morning sunshine. The sooner he met the neighbors, new and old, and explained who he was and why he was at the house, the sooner they could process his failure, gossip to other people and move on.

Since his dad had died three years prior, a neighbor's son had done the yard work and snow shoveling. But this being Saturday, the natural thing for Todd to do was cut the grass, though the mid-summer heat had limited its growth. He got the mower out of the shed, doing the exact same chore he'd had to do when he was a teenager. Back then, he could have done the task another day, but his dad hadn't allowed it. Early on, he needed to supervise his son to make sure he was using the mower properly. Later, when Todd was a little older, he demanded that the work be done on the weekend only because he needed something to pick at. He'd watch from the porch, holding a beer in one hand as he gestured with the other, and yell across the yard above the whir of the motor. "Your rows are crooked. Get them straightened out!"

It was always something.

⸻

The only person who presented himself while Todd spent the morning in the yard was the neighbor across the street and a house down. Hugh Alexander had seemed middle-aged even when he was little more than Todd's present age. Mr. Alexander's beard was now gray, still trimmed neatly, nerdy-engineer style, but he hardly looked any older otherwise.

Mr. Alexander had lived in his house with his wife, Marcy, all the time Todd was growing up. They had a son, but he was older than Todd and had left town by the time Todd reached his teens. As far as Todd knew, he lived in Halifax or somewhere out east, another escapee from Queenston.

Seeing Alexander out front fussing with his garden hose reel, Todd wandered over. They chatted while the man adjusted the handle used to wind the rig. They talked mostly about Todd's mom and how she was getting along.

"We had to put Marcy's mother in a care facility," Hugh Alexander said. "Tough, tough decision. We tried keeping her here, but it didn't work out. Too demanding—on us, I mean. When she started refusing every meal, no matter what we offered, I had to put my foot down and find her somewhere to live. I know that's not what happened here," he said as he nodded toward Todd's house.

Mr. Alexander's assumption was correct. Todd's mother had gone into the same nursing home a couple of weeks before, but not because of an ongoing medical condition. She'd fallen at home and broken her right hip. She was going to be sidelined for a few months undergoing rehab, but her doctors expected her to make a full recovery. Todd told Alexander this, and that he was home for the duration of her treatment, news that the man met with a surprised "Oh" as he raised his eyebrows.

"I would have thought that you'd have a hard time getting that much time away from work," he said, a clear invitation for Todd to elaborate.

The truth was, his mother's hip injury offered a convenient excuse for him to leave Toronto. Todd's life had been coming apart for a while. He'd been out of a job for months, and nothing new was turning up. The relationship with his girlfriend, Sarah, had reached a point where they had both agreed to move on. In short, a change of venue was needed, so when he got the call about his mother, he decided to head home, even though he saw the downsides of that option.

Todd kept the details to a minimum. "I'm home long enough to get the place in shape and, hopefully, see Mom back from Bayside. It'll take a while for her to recuperate. She'll start rehab in the next couple of weeks, actually. And she's terrified of falling again."

"That's what happens," Mr. Alexander said. "Then they're so worried all the time that they get too cautious and hurt themselves again."

The man's frankness was surprising. Todd's plans did not include a second episode. "I hope not. I sure hope not," he replied. "I'm going to visit her tomorrow. She doesn't know I'm home yet." He wasn't ready to see her in what he assumed would be a vulnerable condition. He planned to make his first appearance at the nursing home for Sunday lunch.

"You get some supplies?" Mr. Alexander asked, almost as if they were planning a camping trip. "Grocery store out near the highway's better than that little one in town," he added.

Todd replied that he had. He half-expected the man to follow up with a dinner invitation, but he didn't. Todd had never stepped foot inside the Alexanders' house. Even at Halloween, their doorway was draped with a black curtain, with spooky music coming from behind it. They gave out candy, but they never allowed the kids a peek into their living room. Their odd behavior made their life as much a mystery as was possible in a town where secrets were hard to hide.

Todd looked around, thinking he might spot the bubble of a surveillance camera peering at him, perhaps hooked up to something that recorded the movements it saw. But if Mr. Alexander was on the forefront of surveillance technology, he likely had much more sophisticated equipment than that. Not that such security was needed in this town, on this street. But Alexander was known to be a tinkerer, installing gadgets to make life more convenient in his home. He had been the first person on the street to get an electric garage door opener, which had created a lively scene the day he first demonstrated it, when Todd was still living at home.

Todd circled back to his neighbor's question about the supplies he'd bought the night before. "I have enough to get by for a couple of days," he said. "I've been to the Superstore one other time I was home. I plan to head out there on Monday to stock up on meat and whatnot."

Alexander's face did not betray whether he had put two and two together and recognized Todd's reluctance to run into anybody he knew.

"Well, if you need anything," Alexander said, nodding toward the house, "we'll likely be home. Car will be in the garage, though, so you'll have to knock to find out." All these years later, and he was still jazzed about that door opener.

"Sure, yes sir. I'll let you know." Todd waved a hand toward his mom's house as a signal that he was leaving.

He wondered at his own formality at calling the man "sir," which seemed unnecessary at Todd's age. He crossed the road without checking for traffic. It was quiet on this dead-end street.

With the lawn mowed, he weighed the boredom of sitting in the house all day against the possibility of encountering an old acquaintance if he went for a drive. Although he didn't have any curiosity about the local happenings, getting out would move the day along. It also gave him an excuse not to unpack. Putting his clothes into the drawers of his childhood dresser and the closet he'd used as a kid had a definiteness to it that he wasn't ready to face.

His worry about being seen made him realize that the town was making inroads into his consciousness already. Long experience had told him that in Queenston, people filled in information gaps when they talked about what they'd been up to the day or weekend prior because not to do so invited questions. Pretty soon, your life was an open book. In Toronto, you shared only what you wanted to, and for someone to ask anything else was beyond the boundaries of taste.

He walked up the driveway, picked up the broom he'd been using to clear the sidewalk and started to make a final pass with it. Wisps of grass still were wedged in the cracks of the sidewalk and lying next to the edges. His father had always taken the time to corral these stray bits. Working on the cleanup triggered another memory of the old man.

When Todd was eight or ten, his dad had insisted on buying an electric mower. Everybody in the neighborhood still used gas ones, Lawn-Boys and Toros. One neighbor bought a Honda, but that did nothing for his reputation. "Honda? You gonna mow with that thing? You gonna drive it or ride on it?" he was asked half-derisively. It wasn't a riding mower, but until that point, nobody knew Hondas as anything but motorcycles or compact cars.

Todd's dad set himself apart from such controversy by running a cord from the garage to power his mower. It was less noisy than the gas machines that spewed out fumes as they smoked along in two-stroke glory. No matter that it cut a narrower path than the gas machines did and so took Todd all afternoon to finish a lawn that could have been done in half the time.

The quietness of the electric mower was a disadvantage on this particular day. Todd was pushing along the rows, hoping like heck they were straight, when he heard the bark. "Todd!" He turned in time to see the old man burst out of the front door. His angry tone was not about the lawn, but something else. "Get in here!"

Of course, he obeyed. When Todd entered the house, his dad led him to his bedroom. He'd gone in, his dad said, to check the window because it was supposed to rain later that day, but he noticed yesterday's school clothes still hanging over the arms of the desk chair. This was his latest campaign, launched under the guise of keeping the house neat so Todd's mother wouldn't have to clean up the mess.

Todd knew from experience that if it wasn't his room, his old man would use something else to initiate an argument. Just when Todd got one area of his behavior straightened out, his dad started to pick on another. As an adult, Todd learned in an Al-Anon meeting that his father's behavior was a product of the parent deflecting attention from his or her own heavy drinking. But when he was a kid, all Todd knew was that trying to please his father was a futile effort, like the story he learned in school of the man trying to push a rock uphill. Every time he got it to the top, it would roll down the hill, and he would have to start at the bottom and push it up again.

"Look at this mess, those clothes. We've talked about this." The words tumbled out of his dad's mouth in a rush. "Your mother will not, I repeat, *will not* be responsible for putting them away."

Todd nodded. Saying anything would risk escalating the confrontation. He waited to see what would come next, knowing that daring to interrupt his father would bring down the house.

"So, are we agreed? You'll keep your clothes picked up?"

Todd looked up as he heard his dad's voice mellow. Maybe this time things weren't going to build into a storm.

"Yes, Dad. I mean, I was going to do it. I just wanted to get the lawn done first. You know, it's going to rain, like you said." He paused. He wanted to look away from his dad but didn't dare shift his gaze.

"Okay, son. That makes sense. Now get back on the lawn, will ya?"

That's what I just said flashed through Todd's mind, but he kept his mouth shut. It was about the best ending to the encounter that he could have hoped for. No raised hands. No real yelling. His dad backed out of his bedroom and headed off to do something else, and Todd walked out to the yard, where he'd left the mower. He flicked the switch. Nothing.

"Damn it!" he cursed. He had unplugged the mower before he had gone inside, as he'd been told to do. His dad insisted on this, worried that a neighborhood kid would come along and turn it on, then stick a hand or foot underneath, where the blade was. "It's not like a gas mower," he frequently reminded Todd. "No kid's going to pull the cord on one of those hard enough to start it. With this electric machine, it's as easy as turning on a radio."

So Todd had always strictly followed the rule: step away from the mower and unplug it. No exceptions, no matter what the circumstances. The demand was understandable, but now, Todd looked toward the garage where the plug was. It was only twenty-five feet away, but it angered him that he had to walk over, reconnect the plug, and then trudge back here, all because his dad was on a cleaning campaign that had interrupted the job.

"Stupid idiot damn shit," Todd muttered under his breath. He and his friends had invented the secret combination of swear words sometime so far in the past that none of them could trace its origin. They used it when a situation got them really mad.

He came back from the garage still fuming, tripping over the cord as he did so. "Stupid idiot damn shit," he said again as the mower whirred to life. "Why can't we have the same mower everybody else does?" It would only be years later that electric models would become the standard as people became concerned with emissions. He repeated the curse words, louder this time. He was almost shouting them when he saw his dad on the porch once more, his raised hand signaling him to kill the mower.

"Stupid idiot what?" the old man asked. Todd's heart tightened in his chest. He had no idea how to respond.

"What?" he asked, offering a blank look in return.

"I thought I heard you saying something. In fact, I heard you all the way in the dining room, but I just couldn't make out the whole thing," his father said in a low growl. He stood in his usual spot on the porch. He wasn't a large man, but he had arms toned solid by years of working with tools, and none of the softness around the face that men in middle age often show. When he was angry, he clenched his fists, the cords of muscle stood out in his forearms and his eyes burned a hole in whoever he was looking at.

"I said what?" At this point, Todd had no other defense than to plead ignorance and hope that his dad would let it drop. He stood in the freshly cut row, both hands gripping the mower's metal handle, his eyes held steady on the old man's.

"Just get the job done, Todd, okay? How many times do we have to talk about rain today?" He turned and walked into the house.

Todd was saved, but barely. He kicked himself because it hadn't occurred to him that the lawnmower was so quiet that he could be heard over it. A stupid miscalculation. A Toro, by contrast, would have drowned out his voice.

Long Pond in Nova Scotia is one site where hockey as we presently play it is said to have begun. Other ponds and rivers also make this claim, such as Great Bear Lake, Northwest Territories, which Sir John Franklin mentioned in his diary in 1825. Before that, though, versions of shinny or shinty were played in Scotland, and Ireland had hurling. Both of these sports, played on ice, are precursors of the modern game.

The incident was one of many where his father's behavior would be volatile. On other, similar occasions, his dad would yell and maybe give him a whack or two. He would never cross over into abuse more severe than that. Todd learned to rationalize the few licks his dad laid on him as normal behavior that fathers displayed toward sons. He assumed it was the same thing his friends' fathers did to them.

Assessing his family's dynamic with the perspective of time, he realized that perhaps the neighbors had known what was going on. The Alexanders were close enough to hear the scenes his father created. Back then, Todd assumed that what happened in his home was private. He believed, like other people in similar suburban neighborhoods, that the house guarded the family's quarrels, but the flimsy aluminum-framed windows and hollow-core doors probably let out more secrets than either he or his parents ever imagined.

Todd picked up the rake to put it away. He had swept the grass into the mandatory green waste collection bag. He went inside the house, cleaned up, made a sandwich and reaffirmed his decision that he had to go out for a while. In the quiet living room, even the mantle clock was silent. Nobody had been around to wind it.

As he climbed into the Lexus, with no destination in mind, he considered a trip either west or east on the main highway. The nearest town was fifteen minutes away, but it offered even less amusement than Queenston. The car idled while his mind clicked through a set of images of places he could head to. Only one spot in town had the pull of memory for him, and he pointed his car toward it. The Pond.

three

Years earlier, the boys and girls of Queenston had adopted a special place to skate, just like kids in cold countries everywhere did. Out here, hockey was mostly the province of the boys; the girls figure skated when they got a chance between pickup games. From the time kids were old enough to set out alone from their house, they were drawn to what came to be called "the Pond." Actually, it was less a pond than a backwash that just happened to drain into an area large enough to form a good-sized skating surface. Still, it was commonly understood that if the name were ever written down, it would be spelled with a capital "P," to signify that it was the one and only, the Pond. Whether the practice of revering it in this way had persisted down to the present was local knowledge, outside of Todd's recent experience.

The Pond was close enough to walk to when he was a boy. But today the car gave him a kind of sanctuary. He could pull up to the spot just off the road above the Pond, sit by himself and think. He'd keep the Lexus running for its AC. Summer was by no means ready to release its heat-filled grip, despite the shortening days.

A quick right turn and two lefts took him to the familiar spot, its gentle downhill slope leveling at the bottom, with an earthen bank built up on the back side. The high bank allowed water to pool in the fall and start to freeze once winter came. It had never occurred to Todd that the bank had been made by someone who intended to create a rink. But that didn't matter. What counted was the result—a sheet of natural ice about 40 feet wide and 110 feet long, smooth enough to skate on. The almost-official rink was made by piling up snow at the sides and allowing it to freeze into "boards," though not ones that would ever carry advertising like those in an indoor arena.

Todd parked and then decided to get out of the car to explore. Nobody was around, and it was unlikely someone would show up, since this spot wasn't on the way to anywhere except the countryside. Exploring in the woods as a teenager had shown him and his friends that nothing but trees lay beyond. It was a good place to take a girl or to have a fire and drink if someone managed to sneak a case of beer, and it served as a good hiding place for certain items not welcome at home. Once, someone had showed up with some pot, but Todd didn't try it. He never knew whether his friends had smoked it or hidden it to use later.

He walked down the slope, the grass dry underneath his feet. It hadn't been the best summer for rain. Soon the local *Investigator* would be full of stories about how bad farm yields were this year. The familiar rant was always supported with quotations of alarm from the agriculture minister.

When Todd got to the base of the hill, he paused to take in the scene. The area where the Pond would form, providing there was sufficient precipitation during the fall, stretched out before him. The Pond was smaller than he remembered, just like the old cliché said, but it was still large enough to contain a lot of dreams and memories, mostly good, a few not so good. Snatching a kid's extra hockey stick or having someone make off with your NHL logo puck was a frequent occurrence, though most of the time, peer pressure would force the offender to give the item back.

To his right was "the Shack," a wooden warming shed built a couple of decades earlier but now a semi-falling-down wreck. He walked over. Some of the roughhewn boards, which hadn't seen paint since the Shack was completed, were rotting away from the bottom. Here and there, one was crookedly nailed back into place after pulling away from the framing. Some boards were warped, curling upward and jutting toward the grass that grew untended all around the Shack. It was a sad reflection of lack of care.

Pond hockey tournaments are held in the winter all over North America. The Alberta Pond Hockey Association holds a tournament every year on the Family Day long weekend in February at Lac Cardinal. British Columbia has a series of pond hockey tournaments each year played in Rossland, Prince George and Invermere.

The Shack had been the labor of love of one man, who had become the granddaddy of pond hockey at this spot. Bob, who was old to the kids then, was seen here more than any other place by this point in his life. He watched the kids play, breaking up tussles when they got out of hand and eventually coaching them to improve their game.

The Shack had been Bob's idea, something that he often told people just came to him one day while watching a scrum of players out on the ice. He started to build it the next weekend, using lumber he bought himself. At the time, none of the kids appreciated the value of such a structure, but when it was finished, they all recognized that putting on their skates inside the Shack was much better than sitting on the snowbanks that surrounded the rink.

The U.S. Pond Hockey Championships are held in Minneapolis, MN with at least 116 teams participating. New England hosts 3 tournaments, the largest of which is the New England Pond Hockey Classic, founded in 2009, held on Lake Meredith, New Hampshire, and hosts over 170 teams. The Lake Champlain Pond Hockey Classic hosts 50 teams on Lake Champlain at Colchester, Vermont, and the Monarch's Manchester Pond Hockey Classic goes on Dorr's Pond at Manchester, New Hampshire, with 32 teams. But by far, the most important tournie, is the World Pond Hockey Tournament held in Plastic Rock, New Brunswick, with teams from Canada, the U.S. and other countries around the globe.

Todd walked into the Shack, squinting in the semi-darkness of the interior. He sat down on the bench, running his hand along the splintered boards. Initials of kids from his time and, he presumed, the years after, marred the surfaces. He rested his head against the wall behind him, as he had done in years past when he was waiting to warm up or catching his breath from the spirited shinny games that they played on the Pond. At times, when it was really cold and lots of kids sought spaces inside, there could be more than a dozen of them sitting on the benches.

Being inside refreshed Todd's memories of the day they had first used the Shack after a dedication ceremony Bob had planned. The early winter day had been sunny but cold, and he and his friends had gotten to the rink early, since it was a Saturday morning. Nobody went on the ice, by Bob's direction. Waiting for the activities to begin, they joshed and pushed each other, their nervous energy and excitement spilling out. Todd and some others wandered into the Shack to see what Bob was doing. He was fiddling with something that looked like it belonged in the kitchen of an old farmhouse. That's because it did. It was made of black cast-iron, and to Bob, it was the last fixture the local kids needed to make the Pond and the Shack a second home.

"I'm not the only one who's going to appreciate this," the man repeated to every kid who came in to see what he was up to as he pointed to the round, black stove sitting on a slightly raised platform he had built to

Most professional hockey players have memories of the place they played the game as kids. Rick Kehoe, who was with the Maple Leafs and the Penguins for nearly fifteen years, can still name the guys he played with when he was growing up in Remington Park on the south side of Windsor, Ontario. Their outdoor suburban rink was equipped with lights and boards about a foot high. The skating and puck skills he learned there took him to the NHL.

accommodate it. "Aren't you sick of freezing your butts off, tired of having to go home early because your toes start to get numb?" He nodded in agreement with his own statement. "No more. Now, you just pop up here, take off your skates for a few minutes, prop your feet up next to old Betty and warm up. Before you know it, you'll be good to go again. Should give you hours more time on the ice." His voice sounded almost like that guy in an old TV commercial that urged moms to treat their families to steaming bowls of Lipton's chicken noodle soup on a cold winter day.

After a substantial crowd of kids and parents had gathered, Bob stood outside the Shack and made a speech. He talked about hockey in Queenston and how players all through the NHL displayed skills first nurtured in places like the Pond. Then they had all been allowed inside, "officially," for the first time. The dads had gone over to the stove, marveling at the heat it generated as the fire crackled inside. The moms had sat on the benches, imagining themselves as kids again, the excitement of skating on outdoor ice shining in their eyes.

Of course, building the Shack was partly to Bob's advantage, something that became apparent only later. He had an interest in the kids scrimmaging as long as possible because he'd taken over some of the coaching duties of the local Bantam team, the level of minor hockey that drew teams to play in the big tournament in Peterborough every winter. It was the most famous tournament of its type, attracting teams from all over Ontario, the rest of Canada and the northern U.S. It was widely believed that winning the trophy was an honor that would remain in a town's history forever. Ice time at the local indoor rink had been hard to get, and so practices, both informal and formal, were held at the Pond.

Along with promoting fun, Bob passed on a hockey ethic that flew in the face of the conventional wisdom of the time, which said that kids needed to focus more on structure and basic skating skills than was typical in a Canadian hockey upbringing. The belief was that too much unstructured play characterized the professional game, and that this had led to the country's loss of superiority in the sport. Only good coaching, hockey clinics and repetition of drills at a young age would avert the tragedy of losing Canada's hockey supremacy in the world. This line of thinking stemmed from the Russians, who had surprised Team Canada in 1972 and then gone on to do well in other international tournaments during the decade and who thrived on this "school of hockey" approach.

Bob disagreed. He preferred to focus on unstructured play first and to add what he called "drills and skills" later. He believed that a kid learned hockey by playing the game, but not with a coach scripting his every move. Bob reminded anyone who would listen that the best players came up on the ponds, and their puck-handling skills and ability to read the play and have good hockey sense were honed on that bumpy patch of ice. Such skills couldn't be artificially nurtured, he thought, no matter how scientific the coaching. The team with the greatest ability to read and react, inventing plays on the fly, won games, and the only way to achieve that was by spending a lot of time on the ice, in crowds of kids all fighting for the puck. Drills could come later, and Bob had tons of those. But he asked kids to participate in them only after he had instilled in them the pure love of playing the game.

That's where the Shack came in. It gave the local kids a gathering spot, a home away from home that was theirs, and they had flocked to it.

Todd continued to look around as the memories flooded over him. Present-day reality was not so glamorous as the scenes in his mind's eye. Betty appeared a lot worse for wear. Her lid was askew, and the years of rain and snow had taken their toll on her black finish. The roof of the Shack had long ago given up to leaks. The planks of the floor, scored by skate blades, were starting to rot away from rainwater leaking in. Here and there, grass snaked up between gaps in the boards.

Years before, the exhaust pipe took a sharp angle out and away from the back of the stove, but it was now half-cocked, propped up with a sawed-off hockey stick so that it didn't completely fall over. Where the pipe had once exited the building straight and square through a hole that Bob had sealed with insulation, it was now falling out of the Shack. The angle was crooked, the old insulation now scattered to the winds.

After all the work Bob had done, it was next to inconceivable that his labor of love could be crumbling into ruins. Still, the decrepit condition of the Shack took nothing away from the memories that days and evenings spent at the Pond had created for Todd.

The image most clearly burned into his mind was of sitting in the Shack while Bob tightened his skate laces. Cold fingers on kid-sized hands couldn't do the job that the burly, thick-knuckled paws of Bob could do, so it quickly became his job to loosen or tighten the skates of any kid who came in to warm up. As he worked on the laces, he'd typically make small talk.

"How's school?" he might start. Sometimes, it would be a query along the lines of, "Your parents sign you up for hockey yet this year?" Other times, he played social engineer, saying something like, "You know, your folks pay a lot for those piano lessons you're taking. You need to devote some time to practicing." His knowledge about the local children appeared to have no limits, though his sources were never clear to the kids who benefited from his wisdom. He might have been guessing, addressing the common obstacles kids faced growing up. But his pinpoint accuracy suggested more.

> The hockey-playing Staal brothers—Eric, Marc, Jordan and Jared—had a rink constructed for them by their father at their family's sod farm in Thunder Bay, Ontario. It had boards around it and mesh instead of glass. Eric and his brothers would play until their parents shut off the lights around the rink. Fans who might have hoped to visit the rink will be saddened to know that with all the boys out of the house, the rink has been dismantled.

Some of the questions and topics that Todd and Bob covered were ones that, had things been better in Todd's home, he probably could have discussed with his dad. "You're having trouble with your math again this year, right?" That had been one opening inquiry.

"How'd you know that?" he had asked Bob, wondering if the old guy had called Mrs. King, his grade five teacher, for information.

"I don't know for sure. I'm just assuming. I remember how it was for you last year. You getting any help from your folks?"

It was like asking whether they were helping him to create nuclear fusion in the basement. Todd's parents were nice people, his dad's drinking problem aside, but they didn't know anything about "New Math," the label for what he was being taught. He had sat down at the dining room table and tried to explain to them how frustrated he was with his math homework, but the attempt had been useless. His anger became their anger. "Ask the teacher. Get her to help you," were the flustered words of his mother.

"What am I paying taxes for? Don't they even teach you the twelve-times tables anymore?" his dad said in frustration. His father didn't have the tolerance a better-educated man might have for current teaching methods. His judgments regarding school were based strictly on whether the lessons would someday be useful on the job.

Todd shrugged and blurted out, "Of course, but this isn't about the times tables." At that, the old man got up and walked out of the room, leaving his son to his troubles.

"No, no help from them," he told Bob in answer to the question. "It's the New Math."

Bob looked at Todd and blinked. He, too, had been raised in an era when school focused on the three simple R's. "I don't know what that means, but if that's what they're teaching you, then they must have their reasons. Can't you get extra help from the teacher? Or is there a smart kid who could help you figure it out?"

On thinking about it, there was a kid, and that's exactly the strategy Todd decided to use. Trevor was always ahead in math, and though he wasn't one of the cool kids in the eyes of their classmates, he could be counted on as an ally when difficult homework problems came up. Todd started sitting next to Trevor when they went to the library as a class. Soon, they were doing their homework together. They'd often rendezvous at Todd's house after school, books open on the dining room table.

The strategy worked.

Todd got to the stage where he could cope with math, the signs and symbols of algebra that had eluded his grasp no longer swimming hazily in the air in front of him. His parents, meanwhile, commented on his improved report card without remarking on his self-created strategy of finding a solution to his dilemma. Todd put their inattention down to being relieved that they didn't have to spend money for a private tutor.

It was Bob who had helped Todd deal with the back-lash of being Trevor's friend. The kid was widely known as a nerd. Up until this point in the boys' school career, Trevor had been essentially invisible, hanging out in the library whenever he could avoid going outside for recess and getting picked last for games of soccer when he was forced out onto the playing field.

Nobody particularly bugged him, but when Todd starting befriending Trevor, his classmates began to tease him for it.

"What are you doing with that dork?" asked Timmy Reid. He lived around the block from Todd and was his best friend. He said it while they were walking home from school one day during the same grade five year.

Todd initially pretended not to understand. "Dork?" He played it off like the question took him by surprise, though he had known the attack was coming.

"You know who I mean, Todd. Math boy." Timmy arched his left hand up in front of his chest as if it were out of his control and stiffened his body to mimic a spasm—the universal "spaz" gesture that kids of the day used.

"He's not a spaz," Todd countered. In fact, there was nothing physically wrong with Trevor.

"And what's with that name? *Trevor.* It sounds like Rover, as in 'Red rover, red rover, we call Trevor over.' Are his parents British or something?"

Todd had no idea. He had talked to Trevor's mom a couple of times, when their homework was done at the other boy's place, but never his dad. He had never been in his friend's house past five o'clock, the usual time when a kid had to go home for supper, so he'd never met Trevor's father. "I don't think so," he said. He nearly added, "His mom doesn't sound like it," but he stopped. Admitting that he'd been to Trevor's house would only give Timmy more ammo to use against him.

"Yeah, well, some kids noticed that you're hanging around the guy, and they're saying stuff."

"What stuff?" Todd knew, but he could not let on unless he gave away his worry about spending time with Trevor. As it was, he'd had to create excuses to feed to Timmy for why he wasn't hanging out with him as much as he usually did.

"You know, stuff, like how you're a dork, too."

Timmy's comment shouldn't have mattered, but at their age, everything mattered. Todd had no answer, so he just let the subject drop, peeling off at the corner to head to his house while Timmy continued straight down the road to his.

But when Todd was in the Shack a few days later, he brought up his dilemma with Bob. He would have broached the topic with his dad if he thought he'd get a sympathetic ear.

"Some of us are good at one thing, some of us at another," Bob said while he tugged on Todd's laces and looked at him for the sign that the skates were tight enough. "Take hockey, for instance. A team has to have a guy who can score, and they've got to have a guy who can check. The guy who scores usually gets all the attention, the girls, the headlines, whatever. The guy who checks, he's more or less invisible. But he's just as important. Which guy are you?"

"Probably the guy who's invisible, but this thing with Trevor is making it harder to hide."

"You're wrong. You're the good player, the scorer. People notice you. Trevor is the checker, the guy who plods along and is happy to get a handful of goals a year. He's not the guy the scorer wants to hang out with, but sometimes he's the guy the scorer *needs* to hang out with. What I mean is, sometimes you have to have a guy like Trevor on the team, and it's not cool to ignore him. He's got to feel part of the group, too, and that's your job. You need him. So treat him right. Anyone outside who doesn't understand just doesn't matter."

Todd understood what Bob was trying to say, kind of. But Bob didn't explain how to confront Timmy so that he would back off, so he asked.

"You know, Todd, there comes a time when you have to stand up for yourself. Maybe you're a little young for that, but since this is what's happening, it's time for you to learn."

"But what do I say to them?" Did Bob mean he had to fight? Having to punch it out with someone, especially a friend like Timmy, was a high price to pay for a good math grade.

"Just tell your other friends that Trevor's okay in his own way. And besides, you need him for math, and he needs you as a friend. He's probably kind of lonely." That was Bob. He managed to sneak in life lessons, even when kids weren't expecting them.

The insects buzzed in the grass around the Shack as the rays of the afternoon sun glinted through the gaps in the boards. The humidity was starting to soak the Lucky Brand T-shirt Todd was wearing, but he wasn't ready to leave. He continued to contemplate the days when hockey had been the most important thing in his life.

The Shack and the Pond had been the site of so many of Todd's winter afternoons. So many games, so many goals. Unfortunately, the fun of playing on the Pond hadn't always been followed by joyous games where they counted—on the town's indoor rink or in Peterborough for the Bantam championship in 1992, when Todd was fourteen.

In a town the size of Queenston, assembling a group of ringers to enter a hotly contested tournament wasn't possible, even in the days before folks had started to leave for greener economic pastures. Some places, like Oshawa or Etobicoke, could pick and choose from among dozens, if not hundreds, of boys who could really play. The difference between the best fifteen and the next twenty or thirty was hard to detect in a place like that. But the Queenston team had been different.

All the boys in town in the eligible age bracket totaled maybe three dozen, and of them, a few didn't play hockey. Some kids were barred from playing by dads who didn't want to get up early Saturday mornings for practices. Others were kept off the ice by parents who were afraid their kids would get injured or who had restrictions on Sunday games. That left just more than enough players to make a run at the Bantam cup tournament in Peterborough, which was such an important marker of hockey skills in the thirteen- and fourteen-year-old age group.

Bob had been the guy to get things organized, selecting a group of boys and talking the parents into forking out money for travel and tournament entry fees. He also transformed the Pond from a neighborhood gathering point to the center of the town's hockey life, in addition to the indoor rink. His mantra was that the Pond had been the place where the kids had learned to love the game, and during the run-up to Peterborough, it would serve as the spot where the team would learn to play hockey with technical precision.

Todd stood up to leave the Shack. From the doorway, he looked around once more. The combination of time spent on the outdoor ice and the memories he retained of the Pond and the Shack made the place almost sacred, no matter its present condition. The kids of the Peterborough generation were on the Pond more than they were almost anywhere else, besides their classrooms and bedrooms. It formed their history, constructed for them out of Bob's, and later the town's, dream. For Todd, that 1992 season had been both the pinnacle and the end of his competitive career in the game.

The summer afternoon was still, the grass high but brown, and tiny gnats dive-bombed his face as he exited the Shack. It was unlikely that anyone else in town had even a remote thought of the Pond at this moment. But in a couple of months, the place would once again start its life as the center of after-school fun.

Yet the physical evidence suggested that this might not happen. The Shack displayed the kind of neglect that took years to accumulate, not the decay of a few summers in the sun. It had weathered to the point where it almost appeared unsafe to sit in. Betty likely hadn't been fired up for years. Without a heater of some sort, winter afternoons would be chilly, repelling skaters rather than drawing them in.

Maybe the locals didn't play here at all anymore, the magic of the Pond having been lost along with the man who had brought it to life in the first place.

Todd walked to the edge of where the ice would form once it got cold enough, surveying the tiny plot of ground that had figured so large in his upbringing. He turned, walked back to the car and slid into the driver's seat. He twisted the key to start the Lexus, pushed the "Automatic" button on the climate control to activate the AC and sat there for a minute more, making his quiet time a mini-memorial for Bob, who had been gone a decade.

Todd had been away in grad school when he had learned from his mom that Bob had died. She brought it up almost as an afterthought as they struggled to fill a ten-minute phone call with more than banter about the weather and Chretien's performance as prime minister.

"I was at a funeral last weekend," she said.

"You were? Whose?" Todd quickly scanned his memory banks for any recent news of someone being ill.

"Your old hockey friend."

Todd thought about his childhood friends. They were too young to start dying off now. Maybe someone had crashed a car?

"You mean…"

Before he could offer a name, his mom replied, "Bob. Bob MacIntosh, the fellow who built that shed for you guys."

The news had rocked Todd harder than when she told him about his father's death a number of years later. Regret that he hadn't kept in close touch with Bob washed over him. Todd had rarely seen his mentor since he was fourteen, when afternoons at the Pond had been replaced by hanging out with friends and doing what boys of that age do—experimenting with smoking, talking about girls they were too shy to approach in real life, pretending to be grown up though they knew they weren't. But Bob's presence had been a steadying force for him anyway. He took it for granted that the guy would always be there. If things had gone really bad at home, he knew a talk with Bob was available as a refuge.

"What happened?" He ignored his mom's misnaming of the Shack in his anxiousness to get details.

"He had a heart attack. He called an ambulance, and they got him to the hospital, but there was a lot of damage, and he never recovered. He had another attack a few days later, and that was it. They said he was sixty-seven or sixty-eight. Nobody knows exactly. He was born on the Prairies, and the town hall that held his birth certificate burned down in the 1950s. They estimated his age by when he'd played hockey."

"Played hockey?"

"Yes. I guess he played in the professional leagues."

Todd was about to express his surprise on learning this, but his mom went right on talking. "They said at the funeral that he had played in a handful of games with the Boston team in the 1950s."

"The Bruins, you mean?"

"That was it. 'Having a cup of coffee in the NHL' was exactly how the preacher put it. I don't know much more than that about his hockey life."

Of course, she wouldn't. Todd had never seen his mom watch a hockey game in his life other than some of the ones he'd played in. While he,

"Having a cup of coffee" in the NHL is the term used to describe the career of a player who gets into only a handful of games in the big time. The most famous player of this type today is probably hockey commentator Don Cherry. His NHL career lasted one game, played in the 1955 playoffs with Boston. Cherry had no goals, no assists and no penalty minutes. He played for nearly 20 years in the American Hockey League, from 1954 to 1972.

and sometimes his dad, were glued to the TV watching the Montreal Canadiens games on Wednesday and Saturday nights, his mom was always doing something else. Preparing his lunch for school the next day or getting a roast ready for Sunday dinner. She probably could have done these tasks another time, but nothing about sitting and watching the games had interested her. Or maybe it was just her way of trying to let the boys have their time together.

There was little point in asking his mom how Bob had managed to play in the "professional leagues" because she didn't know how the minor league path to the NHL worked. She had only the vaguest idea of who the Original Six were. He pressed her anyway. "Nothing else was said about his hockey career? I mean, no mention of former friends in the game? A minor league team? What about his family?" More questions lingered after these, but he stopped to hear her answer.

"Well, he had a sister. She and her husband lived here for a long while, and Bob settled in town to be closer to them. But they moved when the factory shut down. That left him in Queenston alone."

Todd conjured up the image of a bachelor in a house with castaway shirts and unread newspapers on the floor and frozen dinners heated in the microwave, their empty packages filling the week's garbage.

Bob had lived within walking distance of the Pond, in a post-war house on the edge of the newer development where Todd's parents owned their home. Todd had been at Bob's home three or four times, always with other kids, to do something or other related to the Pond. The day that stood out was when Bob had bought a pair of regulation nets. He walked the kids over to his garage to see them. They had stood in his driveway in a group, watching as he pulled the large door open. Inside, the red pipes of the nets gleamed in contrast to the whiteness of the netting itself. They rushed into the garage, checking the heft of the pipes and standing between the posts as if they were goalies.

The next time the boys turned up at the Pond to play, Bob had already hauled the nets down there, apparently without any help. Having real nets changed everything; it made their games seem official. Until then, the indoor arena was the only place they'd seen a full-sized net. The ones Todd and his friends used on the street were poor replacements for the real thing, being square, aluminum-framed and without the B-shaped curves of the top and bottom that regulation nets had.

Todd quizzed his mom some more. "If he played in the NHL, then he must have had some memorabilia from that time, don't you think? But if he did, he never showed it to any of us."

"I don't know. Maybe some clues will come to light when they clean out the house."

This conversation, which took place in 2002, had helped Todd to make sense of who Bob was. For instance, it explained the gloves Bob wore when he went on the ice to scrimmage with the boys. They were old-fashioned, made of brown leather but marked with scars that showed they had been through the wars of a lot of games. If he had played pro years earlier, that would be the reason he was using them when Todd was at the Pond.

Then there was Bob's almost magical skill with the puck. When he wanted to, Bob could pick it up at one end of the Pond and work his way through to the other end, avoiding everyone in his path. He shot left, so he stickhandled with his right elbow held high, the puck seemingly attached to the blade as he shifted his weight back and forth to evade attackers. That skill did not diminish even when the kids got older and their skills at checking started to improve. Clearly, hockey was in his blood.

The most famous backyard rink in Canada is the one Walter Gretzky made behind the family's Brantford, Ontario, house. The most well-documented amateur rink was the late Jack Falla's Bacon Street Omni, which he constructed for years in his backyard in Natick, Massachusetts. The story of its creation is told in his book *Home Ice: Reflections on Backyard Rinks and Frozen Ponds* (2000). He followed that up with *Open Ice: Reflections and Confessions of a Hockey Lifer* (2008).

But the question at the core, irresolvable for Todd, was why Bob had been in Queenston at all. Obviously, after he stopped playing as a pro, he made a life outside of hockey, rather than staying involved with the NHL game as a coach or scout, as many ex-players did. But Queenston was not just outside of the game; it was as far removed from the NHL as a person could get. None of these facts added up to explain why Bob's prospects in the pros had disappeared, given his apparent skill.

If Bob had been an enigma to Todd and his friends, the knowledge that he'd played the game at the highest level did make sense of something else. In 1992, the year that the town had been excited about going to Peterborough to contest for the tournament trophy, it was largely Bob's doing that had gotten them there. He was not alone in the idea, but once the local parents bought into it, Bob was the one to organize the tryouts. He had also served as assistant coach, standing with the team's head coach on the bench during the games. His teaching had made their practices look and feel professional, taking the love of hockey the boys had learned on the Pond and adding to it a sense of the mechanics of the game.

Up until that year, hockey for the kids in the town's indoor arena had been essentially the same as the games they played outdoors. In contrast to the drill-heavy clinics happening in other places in response to the perceived lack of skills among Canadian players, the coaches in Queenston assigned positions, but there was no practice to speak of, just scrimmages. The only input from coaches was to blow whistles for line changes and to explain the more obscure rules, such as icing and offside, to first-timers.

But the year of the Bantam tournament, things were different.

From the first practice after the team was chosen, the routine became more organized. The squad was broken up into two groups, and they were given practice bibs to wear over their regular sweaters. As practice went on, lines were formed and adjusted according to skill level. Kids were moved from forward to defense until each one was playing the position most suited to him.

Drills were not just picking up the puck and moving in on the goalie. Instead, the players practiced their skating, improving their ability to stop and start with confidence. They took turns taking the puck behind their net and working it out by shooting or passing it up along the boards. They learned how to play their positions.

Jim Pappin scored the goal that won the Leafs the Stanley Cup in 1967. Long before he was in the NHL, he loved shinny. He played on a creek, a lake and a couple of outdoor rinks in his hometown of Copper Creek, Ontario. There was so much snow that, at times, the ice would be covered up for a week.

As a right-winger, Todd was told by Bob that his section of the ice incorporated the zone from the faceoff dot to the boards up and down the length of the rink on the right-hand side. His job on offense was to get the puck out of the corners and pass it to his centerman. Todd was instructed not to go behind the net—another player would cover that. In the offensive zone, that would be the centerman, and when he was there, Todd was to work his way from the dot to the slot in front of the net.

In his own end, Todd had to leave the area behind the cage to the defenseman. Todd's job demanded that he be at the boards next to the hash mark, waiting for a pass. He had to keep his feet moving so that he had the momentum to take the puck out of the zone at the right opportunity. When the other team had the puck, he had to be out high to cover the point.

The lessons remained as clear in his mind as they had been on the ice with Bob and the coach instructing the team, though the strategies Bob used were dated in comparison to the contemporary style of play that emphasized wingers "cycling" the puck in the other team's end.

The information Todd's mom shared with him about Bob playing in the NHL clarified why his old mentor had known so much about hockey and why he'd had the ability to get a bunch of ragtag kids playing at a level that they hadn't known existed. Todd also knew that whatever success they achieved owed itself first to their love of the game, which Bob had nurtured on the Pond.

Yet still unresolved in Todd's mind was why Bob had never said anything about playing in the NHL. The boys had often talked about hockey when Bob was around. Mario Lemieux was in his heyday, and players like Mats Sundin were on everyone's mind. Montreal fans had enjoyed the 1986 and 1993 Stanley Cups, which had bracketed Queenston's 1992 adventure in Peterborough. Bob had heard the kids talk about

Lemieux's winning the Stanley Cup with the Penguins twice in a row and about other important games, but he never said anything about having made the big time himself.

This silence hadn't made sense when Todd had heard of Bob's passing, and sitting in the car ten years later, AC blasting against the heat, it still puzzled him.

He took another look at the area where the Pond would form, the ice hardening when it got cold enough. He glanced at the Shack and remembered again the fantastic days of being wrapped tightly against the cold, nothing else mattering except getting as much time as possible on the ice. Regretting the loss of those good old days, and the kid he had been, he backed the car out, reversed the direction he'd taken earlier, and five minutes later, he was home.

CHAPTER
four

Back at his mom's house, Todd pulled his car into the driveway. The garage's main door hid the typical collection of modern suburban accumulation, making it impossible to park inside. At some point in Todd's stay, the mess would have to be cleaned out. He wasn't planning to stick around until the snow started flying, but then again, his future was uncertain. The job market had to improve, or at least his personal fortunes had to turn, for him to contemplate reestablishing himself in Toronto.

Once he was inside the house, he plunked down on the couch. It was vintage 1980, decorated in a floral pattern that still suited his mom's tastes. He looked around at the décor. Unlike in the homes of many senior women with grown kids and grandkids, the end tables were not covered in photos. The only one was the portrait he'd had done in his MBA graduation gown. There were no grandchildren to display, since Todd was an only child, and single, and he didn't see any pictures of his dad around.

It was easy to infer that his mom's choice not to showcase photos of her late husband was not born out of disrespect but of resignation. Todd's parents hadn't had the happiest marriage even when times were good. His father drank, and his mom tried to cope. The best moments were periods of truce where they essentially lived in silence. Todd's mom managed to make herself more or less invisible in the house, a defense mechanism that Todd himself had adopted and perfected. Once his dad was gone, she had simply moved on, without reminders that would tempt her into thinking of the past as being better than it had been.

He stood up and walked from the living room to the dining room right behind it. The china cabinet stood on the wall to his left, full of his grandmother's good dishes and her teacup collection. The items were a mute reminder that in a prior generation, this had been a prosperous family.

Todd's paternal grandmother was a Montreal socialite. Todd's dad was expected to marry well and take the family place in society. When he had, instead, bummed around town all during his twenties, then moved and settled into a job at a factory in Ontario, the family essentially cut him off. Years later, his mom died, and because Todd's father was the only child in his family, he received a shipment of what was always referred to as "the good china." They hadn't used the dishes often, but getting rid of them would have been the same as saying that the family's heritage didn't matter, so they sat in the cabinet, a reflection of a past no longer valued. Todd's mom had said the china would be his someday, though he didn't care what happened to it, even less so now that his condo in Toronto had been leased out until he found a job.

He sat at the dining room table, memories of Christmas dinners and Sunday lunches resonant in the room.

Roast beef, turkey, roast pork. The fare was never fancy, but the meals were made with love. Mrs. Graham made sure to bake the cookies her son liked at Christmas, and she never forgot to make a pumpkin pie at Thanksgiving. It was just the three of them on these holidays. Company wasn't invited over because of the old man's alcoholism, which rendered him unpredictable in social situations. Still, Todd's mom tried to keep their home life normal, giving her son at least the appearance of a family life that replicated the ideal.

As Todd got into his teens, his family drifted from the strict protocol of sharing at least one daily meal. A formal Sunday lunch was no longer a regular part of their routine. They didn't eat their weekday dinners in the dining room together anyway, and meals became a catch-as-catch-can kind of affair because Todd's schoolwork and extracurricular activities demanded more of his time. Todd's father also worked as much overtime as he could when work was available. Even then, in the mid-1990s, his dad knew the plant was on shaky ground.

Todd ran his hand over the smoothness of the mahogany dining table, his fingers leaving patterns in the fine dust. The room hadn't been cleaned in the weeks since his mom had injured her hip. Still, he noticed a hint of citrus in the air. Lemon Pledge had been the smell of Saturdays since it had been his job to spray and wipe everything in the room. The lingering scent was a sign of her continued presence and the fact that she'd return to her usual chores one day, though when that would be was still unknown. Her life, and now his, had a quality that was both uncertain and unfamiliar.

Todd's return home had been motivated by the dreaded phone call that all grown sons and daughters living far from their parents expect eventually. The caller was a woman from his mother's library book club.

"Todd, this is Sandra Reimer." She didn't need to say anything more for Todd to realize why she was calling. She had no other reason to phone him. He only wanted to know what the problem was, and how bad. He waited for her to continue.

"Your mom's broken her hip, Todd. She fell in her kitchen."

His first thought had been relief. The words "cancer" and "stroke" were among the ones he'd been expecting.

He was about to ask her whether his mom was in pain, but Mrs. Reimer kept talking. "She's in the hospital. She had surgery right away to repair it. The surgeon was available, and he's not in Queenston every day. She'll be there perhaps a couple of weeks, and then she'll have to go to a nursing facility for rehab. Are you able to come?"

"I can be there tomorrow and stay a few days," he said, feeling the need to deal with the situation firsthand rather than leave it to anyone else. "And then I can settle things here and come back for a little longer maybe."

"I don't think you need to rush down, Todd. The emergency is over," Mrs. Reimer said. "Why don't you see if you can get a week off so you can stay for a proper visit?" She stated her opinion frankly, and he thanked her for her honesty.

Mrs. Reimer had no idea that things were finished for him in Toronto. He'd been out of a job since early spring, and none of his leads were turning out to be fruitful. He had been at the point of frustration for a while and was considering going home to regroup. Her call gave him the final reason.

Once off the phone, Todd decided that his best strategy would be to wind up his life properly before he departed for Queenston. He'd be staying for much longer than the week she had suggested.

Todd had been fired after fighting with his boss for months because he insisted they move ahead with a new product to take advantage of a gap in the market. Todd believed that if they were going to capitalize on the new product, the time was ripe. He saw this as plainly as if it had been a business case study in his MBA program. Reality proved an entirely contrary phenomenon, though, and after the idea failed, he was forced out.

Todd had worked for a food production company. His job was in procurement logistics, not marketing, but he had seized on a chance to take advantage of people's sudden taste for little bits of exotic luxury that could be bought at local grocery stores. The new product, in theory, was hot, more so since the company had been featured on a couple of Toronto-area morning TV shows. The trouble was, the product was sitting on the shelves and wasn't moving.

His boss, Mr. Lydle, had not been in favor of the expansion. His idea of growth was "incremental," a word he used so often that Todd was sure he could see it hanging in the air above his head every time he walked into the office.

The company had been founded by Lydle's father. Their specialty was pickles, and for three decades, they'd done well. Over the years, Lydle Pickles built brand equity. Their products weren't sexy—sliced gherkins on hamburgers tend not to be. But they were good and priced for value. Consumers came to trust the Lydle brand. The company didn't have to spend much on advertising to keep their market share.

That being true, sales were small. Compared to Bicks and the other giant brands, Lydle Pickles almost didn't exist. Their 500,000-bottle capacity would just about do a Kraft subsidiary for a day's worth of production, rather than the month it took Lydle to bottle that much product.

Todd was hired fresh out of grad school. At first, he was happy to do his part to ensure the firm's slow but steady progress. But as he passed his five-year anniversary with the firm and was edging closer to ten, he started to become restless. In his MBA program, he'd learned that there were ways to grow a business and opportune times to do it. You had to marry the two to be successful. So when Todd had seen the niche for a more gourmet, upscale offshoot to their traditional offerings, he'd built the business case for it and presented it to his boss.

"Textbook case, right, Todd?" Mr. Lydle had said, his sarcastic words disparaging Todd's ideas for growth. Even the set of Excel tables and financial flowcharts that Todd had prepared did nothing to persuade him.

It wasn't like Todd was telling Lydle to recapitalize the entire company. In fact, his plan didn't involve heavy borrowing relative to sales. But he knew—and it wasn't only textbook—that the chance of making big gains was staring them in the face, and that their position as a smaller player in the market made a niche offering perfect for them.

He'd been on vacation in Mexico with Sarah when he had his revelation for a new product. The holiday had been a last-ditch effort to see if they could rekindle the spark they had shared when they were first together.

After spending a long, sunny day on the beach and with night yawning ahead, they'd taken a cab to a restaurant someone had recommended, Tia Rosita's. The place was supposed to have authentic, homemade food, not the kind of dumbed-down fare that was typically sold to tourists in the main beach area. Neither of them had been crazy about venturing away from the safety of the tourist enclave, but it was only a ten-minute drive from the hotel, and Todd wanted to experience something new.

While they ate, Todd looked around, Sarah's silence driving him to seek stimulation in the surroundings. The restaurant ambience was rustic, almost dingy. The adobe walls had water stains in spots from leaks in the flat roof above. The tables looked like they'd been hewn out of rough wood by a local carpenter. The kitchen was well out of sight, not like in some restaurants that followed the modern practice of allowing customers to see how the chefs prepared their specialties.

But when the food came, their surroundings were forgotten. Delicately seasoned meats lying on soft corn tortillas begged to be folded and devoured.

Before they could start eating, their waiter, who spoke no English, brought over a plate with half a dozen bowls on it. Each had a tiny spoon in it for serving. "Salsa," he announced.

Salsa wasn't entirely foreign to Todd. Most Toronto grocery stores had a selection of such stuff for dipping tortilla chips in. The big chip companies all made their own version. It had never occurred to him, however, to use salsa to enhance the flavor of meat. He was yet to find out that "salsa" literally translated to "sauce," and that it was versatile enough to be used with almost any food.

The waiter motioned to them to spoon bits of the salsas onto the tacos, and Todd tried two of them. The first, a red one, was hot. The second, a green one, milder. Both added a saltiness to the meat that made its flavor pop.

"Mmm, this is great," Todd said as he looked up at Sarah. She was not registering the same delight.

She half-smiled, half-grimaced. "Yeah. Too hot, though. Why can't they just stick to the basics?" Sarah was taking tiny bites, as if she feared that the meat would drop out of the tortilla and into her lap.

Todd was not interested in finding out what her statement meant. He silently translated it to, "I'm not into trying anything new," another sign of their incompatibility.

"Yeah, it's hot, but there's more to it than that, I guess," Todd finally replied. "It's a flavor enhancer. Taste the saltiness, the smokiness. It gives the meat another entire dimension." He was not an expert food critic, nor did he aspire to be. But he did have some familiarity with the way food was discussed from his time at Lydle, even if his job was more on the purchasing end than in marketing and advertising. Sarah, who had been at graduate school with Todd, was in the food business, too, but her interest was focused on financial analysis, not the adventure that food could be.

"This is, what? Green tomatoes, onion, a pepper of some kind. Garlic, too, I suppose. You know, we could make this," he said offhandedly. "I mean, we, Lydle. This is something we could do."

Sarah nodded, disengaged. They finished their meal in silence.

On the cab ride to the hotel, the idea picked up steam in his mind. "You know that recipe for salsa I mentioned? There's nothing in it we couldn't get, probably, and the technology in the plant is the same as what we'd need to bottle it.

Think about it, 'Tia Rosita's Gourmet Salsa.' We could have a sensation on our hands. Grocery stores love that kind of niche product right now, and we have no presence in the specialty market. It could be huge for us, and there's variety there. Two or three of those would make a nice little product line."

Sarah did her typical killjoy move. "Where are you going to get the *poblanos*?" She had used her rudimentary knowledge of Spanish to ask the waiter what the dark green bits in one of the salsas were. It had taken him a while, but with the help of a diagram drawn on a scrap of paper, the waiter had supplied the information. He then went to the kitchen and returned with a poblano for them to look at. The pepper didn't resemble anything Todd or Sarah had ever seen in a grocery store in Canada. It was shaped like a long, thin green pepper but had a darker-colored skin and a denser, firmer texture.

In response to Sarah's doubts, Todd simply said, "Hey, Lydle's in the food business. If there's a poblano chile to be had in Ontario, we can find it."

When they got home a few days later, Todd started to do some research. He bought a few jars of salsa made by the giant food companies whose products filled the chip aisles of Metro to compare them to what he remembered. But when he tasted them, he noticed no punch, no pop. These salsas were a watered-down, over-salted version of the real thing, as measured against what they'd eaten in Mexico.

Each time he did a taste test, Todd compared it in his memory to the salsa on that Tia Rosita table. The Canadian product always failed. He put it on beef and chicken; he even tried it with eggs, as he'd seen done in his hotel at breakfast time. Nothing brought him back to that evening when his mouth had come alive with the spicy savoriness of Tia Rosita's miracle sauce. He was convinced that if Lydle could replicate the recipe, or even come close, they'd have a huge sales success on their hands.

Todd was so sure of his idea that he did an end-run around his boss and got the concept approved. Everything seemed perfect. The name, after a little wrangling, was accepted—Tia Rosita. The bottle label showed an image of a fancily dressed Mexican salsa dancer in a flowing red dress with her arms whirling above her head. Cheesy, yes. But it was an effective icon of the exotic Mexico of people's imagination. The day the product rolled off the line, Todd was there to crack open a bottle and try it. It had much of the depth of flavor that the original had. He was convinced they had a winner.

But Tia Rosita had failed. Miserably. The reason was simple; it was a "textbook case," in the words of Mr. Lydle's jesting taunt, directed at Todd when he was trying to persuade the man to adopt his product idea. In Mexico, such salsas were as ubiquitous as ketchup was in Canada. Every home had a couple of jars in the fridge or on the table, and salsa was liberally spread on almost everything from tacos to omelets. But Canadian consumers were not ready to adapt their eating habits to using salsa in this way, no matter how tasty the results might be. To them, the product was a chip dip, which is how the big food producers marketed it, and nothing more.

Had Lydle done what one of the major food companies would have and backed up the product launch with a multifaceted marketing campaign, the salsa might have taken off. TV commercials showing moms spooning Tia Rosita's onto plates, happy dads putting the salsa on meatloaf, or on hamburgers after grilling—these were the images that would have made the product go. But given the lack of budget (to Todd, it was more a lack of vision), all the company did was take out a few ads in women's magazines and do a bunch of in-store product demos. With no sustained campaign, the momentum never got going, and cases of the product piled up on warehouse shelves.

Several months after the release of Tia Rosita, Mr. Lydle called Todd into his office. "You know, Todd, you've got a good education," he began. "You've probably read every case study out there." Although he didn't have an MBA himself, Lydle knew enough about the favored method of teaching in such programs to say this with confidence.

Todd just nodded.

"But it seems like you missed the class where they taught that you don't produce a product where there's no market." The sarcasm was evident in every word. "I recognize that sometimes, a new product comes along and changes people's purchasing behavior. But Todd, the pickle industry is a conservative business. We just don't jump at new ideas."

That conservatism was exactly what Todd had hoped to dispel, and what he chafed at in every quarterly review of sales. He started to reply, saying, "Well…I understand that—" but he was interrupted.

"This company's mandate may seem boring to you, our products uninventive, but our customers like them. They buy them, whether times are good or bad. They trust us."

Todd knew what was coming next.

"And they believe that a Lydle pickle is a good pickle." The slogan adorned every bottle. Todd looked around the office as he listened. It didn't in the least resemble the corporate ideal of *Mad Men*, with its glamour and glitz. There was no view of the glistening skyscrapers of downtown, no waterfront. Instead, Mr. Lydle's office looked out across the street to a freight company. His desk was crowded with paperwork, copies of food industry journals and junk picked up at the trade's annual meeting, which had been months before. What he was saying, though, did ring strangely of the lingo of bosses in films. Old films. 1940s films, like *It's a Wonderful Life*.

The pickle boss continued. "You know, Todd, we brought you on to do a job. An important job. We needed a guy like you to keep things fresh around here. No pun intended. But you overstepped with Tia Rosita. And if you head out to the distribution center, you'll see for yourself the results of that. Salsa on every shelf. Cases of it. And with every passing day, the "sell-by" date gets closer. More important, you'll see in the quarterly earnings statement that we've taken a big hit on this little experiment of yours."

Todd's mind flashed forward to the next Wednesday, when the Board would meet to go over those sales numbers. He refocused his eyes on his boss.

"Between capital outlay for packing equipment and ongoing expenditures for ingredients, we'll probably post a loss for the fourth quarter for the first time since 2002. And that was a period of pretty bad business for everyone." He scowled as he said this. The company prided itself on riding through recessionary times with steady profit, part of their ethos of conservatism. "I can't justify that loss to the Board, Todd. In fact, I won't. *You're* going to do it." He shifted his weight in his chair.

Todd knew why it would be up to him. He had been the one to go to the Board in the first place and present the case for Tia Rosita. He would be the one to present the bad news.

"And after you've explained the Q4 loss, you're going to apologize. And then you're going to resign."

And that was how he'd found himself out of a job.

He left Lydle's office to return to his own, then decided he needed to find someplace else to process what had just happened. He grabbed his car keys off his desk and snapped, "I'll be back," over his shoulder at the receptionist, who raised her eyebrows as he whizzed past her.

In the car, he turned the key in the ignition, but with nowhere to go, he just sat, the motor idling. "What the hell just happened in there?" he said out loud. Then, his anger at Lydle's small thinking and his own failure overwhelming him, he yelled even louder, "*What the hell!*" He slammed the gear lever into reverse and then jammed the pedal to the floor as he exited the company's lot, heading toward his apartment. Once inside, he ripped off his suit jacket and threw it onto the couch and changed into his running gear, kicking his shoes off and leaving his dress pants in a heap on the floor.

He headed downstairs to follow his favorite course along Toronto's waterfront. Instead of jogging, as was his normal practice, he sprinted until his lungs burned, the cold and his exhaustion forcing him to stop, bending over for air. As he straightened up, hands on hips, he saw Toronto's skyscrapers in front of him. Instead of being a sight that welcomed him, their enormity overwhelmed and alienated him. He returned home and called the office to say he would not be back until the morning.

For nine years, Todd had made more money than his dad ever had. He lived well—he had a nice place downtown with a view of the water, took an occasional trip to Europe, went skiing during the winter and sometimes lucked out to score a pair of Leafs tickets. But that level of success and the income his MBA taught him to expect were now, temporarily at least, beyond him.

Todd searched for work for months, starting with the big food producers and then branching out to smaller firms. Then he tried other industries. Packing and shipping, furniture manufacturers, wholesalers, importers—he networked with everyone he could think of, but he got no bites and only a handful of "informational interviews," the term people were now using for networking meetings. Times were slow, and mid-level corporates were not being hired; they were being let go.

His savings kept him afloat for a while, but they were starting to thin as spring turned to summer. It was highly unlikely that anyone would hire over the summer, and he decided that it was time to give up the condo and live somewhere cheaper. That was when Mrs. Reimer had called to say that his mom was in the hospital. He had already put out feelers with a property manager, so when they found an immediate taker on a lease for his furnished sixteenth-floor apartment, the only option was to go home.

He told himself that it was only short-term. Plus, nothing said he had to be in Toronto to get a job with one of the companies in town. He could drive down anytime he needed to, stay in a hotel and do the interview the next morning. Potential employers wouldn't even know, since he planned to keep his 416 area code cellphone. He explained his decision to Sarah, who kept in touch even though they'd decided after Mexico to end their relationship.

"Sure, and if you need to have people mail paperwork, you can have them send it to my place," she'd offered.

"That way, they won't know that you've gone home." She might as well have added, "With your tail between your legs," because that was how both she and Todd saw the situation.

His mistake had been in settling for the job at Lydle right out of grad school. Many of his classmates held out for spots in bigger firms, where the interview process for positions was intense and often took months. Todd's job had come to him much more easily than that—a single interview with the man who would later become his boss and one other person from the company. Part of what Lydle Pickles liked about him, they said, was that he came from a small town, that he understood simple values. Had they had any idea of his family mess, any credit they gave him for hometown values might have been negated.

Todd had relished the thought of having a job waiting for him when he finished his MBA, though it was never in his plans to stay at Lydle. Once he got out in the professional world and gained some experience, he would find something else with more growth potential. But the comfort factor took over, and he stayed where he was.

First jobs, according to the mentoring in his MBA program, should be something you did for a couple of years and then moved on from if the goal was to climb the corporate structure to the CEO spot. Todd had been at Lydle for eight-plus years when he came up with Tia Rosita, which he thought would bring him the success he'd need to make a big jump.

But the long journey had led nowhere, and now he was back in the house he'd grown up in, with the same old stuff crowding the closets and his mom a ten-minute drive away, cared for by strangers.

He opened and shut the kitchen cupboards, trying to discover where his mom kept the Comet. He found it and set to work cleaning the sink—it was a task that had the virtue of showing an immediate result.

He should have gone to see her instead of going out to the Pond, but he was feeling too overwhelmed at being home. Tomorrow had to be the day. After he finished cleaning the sink, he wandered to the phone mounted on the wall across from the stove and called Bayside Manor.

"Hi, Mom. How are you? I'm home." It came out in a rush. "It's maybe too late to see you today," he apologized. "But tomorrow, okay?" He barely gave her time to get a word in.

"It'll be good to see you," she replied.

five

Sunday morning, Todd was showered and shaved by eight, though he wouldn't leave the house for hours. Bayside didn't have strict visiting hours, but the nurse on the phone said that it was best to not interrupt Mrs. Graham's morning routine.

Staff started to get residents up at around seven o'clock, but the seniors were free to sleep in if they wanted to. His mom would be one of the early risers, up by six-thirty as she had been all during his youth. But that was hours before she would be ready for company. She would not relish being greeted in bed by her son, let alone anyone else. She had always been a private person.

Breakfast was at seven-thirty for those who could make it to the dining room on their own feet. Residents who were not mobile without help, like his mom at the moment, were served in their rooms starting at eight. That took half an hour, then it was bath time. By ten o'clock, most folks would be dressed.

But on Sunday, there was a chapel service at ten. A lot of the residents liked to attend, if only for a break in the usual weekday routine. "When you're in here," the nurse told Todd on the phone, "every day seems to feel like the last one, even for those of us who work here. So they love the hour on Sunday when there's singing and a little sermon. Plus, it's never anything intensely religious." Had it been, Todd's mom wouldn't have gone. God, she once told him, left her behind when she married a drunk.

Todd puttered around the house until just past eleven, ironing a shirt and digging his dad's old shoeshine kit out of the basement. His dress shoes didn't need cleaning, but it gave him something to do. Although it was summer, and hot, he decided to wear his black, Jaeger linen blazer to see his mom. The Massimo Dutti shirt he paired with it would show her that he hadn't left his taste behind in the city.

He ate some cereal, having noted that his mom didn't have much food around, fresh or stale. The chest freezer in the basement that had been full of meat and baked goods all the time he was growing up now had Tupperware containers with dried-up food. Clearly, she had not been eating properly before her accident, which had probably contributed to her hip breaking. Todd felt a stab of guilt.

He rolled out of the driveway at half past eleven, planning to visit his mom for half an hour before they shared lunch together in the facility's dining room. She'd be in a wheelchair, and likely embarrassed about it, but lunch was one of two meals residents were allowed to host a guest at each week. Having lunch with her would help to break up the monotony that was his mom's life right now.

On the way to Bayside, Todd stopped at the gas station to pick up a couple of magazines for her. Her reading interests ran to things like *Women's Day*, *Chatelaine* and *Canadian Living*, but no title like that sat on the rack. Just a couple of car mags, some glossies with mixed martial arts as their subject, and a *People* and *Us Weekly*. He grabbed these last two, the exploits of the TV and movie famous splashed over their covers. She had never been into star gossip, but he didn't want to go into her room empty-handed.

He walked into the front door of the too-grandly named Bayside Manor and headed for the reception desk on the far side of the lobby. On the opposite wall was a calendar. "Today is August 19, 2012. It's Sunday!" it read. The letters were huge, the subtext clear—the residents needed reminders to keep them anchored in space and time.

As he signed in as was required, he asked the woman behind the desk about his mom.

"Mrs. Graham? She's in room one-one-four. She'll just be getting fixed up for lunch," the woman said as she handed him back his driver's license. "You're her son, right? You probably don't remember me, but I worked with your dad some years ago at the plant. I was a secretary about the time he got promoted to foreman."

Todd squinted at her. Her face didn't ring a bell. He bluffed it. "Sure, you're, uh, Debbie?" The name was a common one for a woman her age, which Todd pegged to be about mid-forties. "Jennifer. I married Gary Bramlett. Back then, I was Jennifer Davis."

The names she threw out were like a mini roll call of local royalty, people whose lives had been mired in the goings-on of the town since before Todd's family had moved to the place.

"So you lost your job when the plant closed down?" It was a natural question for Todd to ask, since almost everyone who had worked at the plant had been let go at the same time. He was aware that the subject might touch a sore spot, though.

"Yeah, lots of us. It's hard, you know? They don't pay as well here as we got over there." She grimaced a little. "But the work here's good. I mean, people like your mom make it more worthwhile."

The compliment was the kind that people usually delivered in a situation where niceties are called for. Todd had never thought of his mom as a particularly bright and cheery person, and especially not now, with a healing hip. She was not unpleasant, but neither was she a woman who showed her emotions. At least, she had never been an expressive type of person before. Todd had never seen her cry when he was growing up, even when things with his dad had reached their lowest levels. He didn't know what she'd be like in these new circumstances, though.

He headed across the lobby and down the hall to his mom's room, thinking that even with her current condition and the other aches and pains that might accompany growing older, she was possibly better off than she'd been when his dad was alive. The emotional turmoil that came along with having an alcoholic husband was no longer part of her life. He kicked himself for not spending more time with her during the years he had been living in Toronto. But between work and Sarah and getting on with the business of escaping Queenston, carving out weekends to drive home and hang out hadn't been high on his priority list. At thirty-four, Todd felt himself to be a stranger to his mom in many ways.

He walked into her room, the magazines held out in front of him almost like a shield. He feared she would be surly and angry about having to stay in the facility. He dreaded the moment when the only subject they would have to talk about was his job or his relationship, both failures. Her greeting wasn't what he expected.

"That jacket is splendid, Todd," she exclaimed. She smiled and reached out her arms, leaning forward in her chair in a "come hug me" gesture. Her hair was dyed the chestnut brown it had been her whole adult life. It was teased up into a helmet-like bowl, the same way she had styled it forever.

Todd was surprised that she could hug him as strongly as she could from the wheelchair. She was only five-feet-two, and a self-described "lightweight" at just over 110 pounds. It was her size that put his dad on a constant quest for pillows with just the right amount of lift and firmness to keep her high enough in the driver's seat to see over the steering wheel of the family car.

He tossed the magazines on the bed next to her and looked around to find a seat. "Don't get settled, Todd. It's lunchtime." He glanced at his watch. Eleven forty-five. Meals were the clock to residents. He smiled at her, feeling more relaxed than nervous now.

"How ya feeling?" he asked. "You look good." He tried to think of the name of the woman who had greeted him at the desk. It came to him after a moment. "Jennifer says you're quite the bright light around here." He looked at her for confirmation.

"Oh, I don't know. I guess I'm better off than some of them. I try to keep a smile on. What else can I do?" She paused and adjusted the buttons on the front of her sweater. The light wool suggested it was cold enough to slip from summer wear into fall clothing. Yet outside, the heat and humidity still lingered. In the room, the air conditioner hummed.

"Anyway, you know, there's a longer story to how I feel these days, Todd. Being here, with this," she said as she gestured vaguely to her hip, "I've had time to think. I've got things to be happy about, I've realized." She paused and then went on, "We haven't really talked since you lost your dad. I mean, about how our life was together."

Her sudden directness about his dad stunned Todd, and contrary to her suggestion not to get comfortable in the room, he started to settle into the sweet spot in the chair he had taken. Then she shifted direction. "But let's talk about that another time. Right now, you need to wheel me down that hall to the dining room." She pointed to where they needed to go. "Sunday is always a roast."

She hadn't been in the facility long enough to act like her memories of Sunday meals stretched that far back in time, but clearly, Bayside's routines had become hers. He pushed her wheelchair out the door and down to the wood-paneled dining room. Each table seated four. On Sundays, residents who had guests sat two to a table, each one with a son or daughter, or whoever was visiting, positioned next to them.

As soon as they entered the room, Todd's mom motioned to a table with just one person at it. "Over there, with Mary," she said, almost like Todd knew which gray-hair she meant. His mom had been thirty-seven when she'd had him, an older mom, especially for the time. But at seventy-two, she was the spring chicken of these ladies. Mary looked to be close to eighty. Most of the other people were about the same age. Todd took comfort knowing that his mom wouldn't be living in the place for long, but he also appreciated that she'd managed to find some people she seemed to like.

"Mary, this is my son, Todd. Thanks for letting us join you." Mary didn't say whether she had a visitor coming, but nothing on her face suggested anticipation that someone was about to walk in. Todd did not ask.

He parked his mom's wheelchair after moving the dining chair that had been in her spot. "Well, you've figured that out pretty fast," he said as she put on the two brakes. Commenting on the obvious and making light of what might otherwise seem tragic would become his strategy for dealing with her confinement here over the coming weeks. It would help him cope with the trauma that every grown child has to face when a parent crosses from being self-sufficient to needing care.

She launched right into a typical proud-mom speech for Mary's benefit. "Todd's just up from Toronto. He's got a condo there. He graduated with his MBA from Queen's."

Some of that was true as of this day, and some was close to not being true any longer. But Mrs. Graham only knew the half of it. That he'd gotten sacked over Tia Rosita and was currently "in transition"—in the polite euphemism of the unemployed—this much she was familiar with. She didn't know that he was not living in Toronto, but in Queenston, in her house. Todd had not found a moment to tell her that he'd decided to stay in town for a while until he got back on his feet. In the weeks since her fall, things had been too complicated, for both of them, to get into his problems.

"So you've settled in Toronto?" Mary asked. "Do you have a family there?" The question was a natural one for an older person to ask. Family, work, these were the thoughts seniors had of their own kids, if they had children.

Todd glanced at Mary just as the server came with their dinner plates. "Prime rib? Wow. You ladies have it far too good," he said with enthusiasm, trying to duck Mary's question. "Right now, I'm here, and that's what matters," he said after taking a bite of the meat. "Looking after Mom, getting her past this mess she's in. Not that this place is a mess. I mean, the hip and all." He was narrowly scraping by with this banter. He'd also dropped a clue that maybe he was staying longer than just a weekend.

Mary was generous in her response. "Oh, I know, Todd. I know. This isn't where a young lady like your mom is supposed to be. I'm sure she's surprised to find herself here, too, with a bunch of old people." As she talked, she tried to scoop up the food on her plate. Clearly afflicted with arthritis, her gnarled hands had trouble manipulating her fork. The kitchen staff had cut up her beef, and the green beans, too, had been sliced in half. She stabbed at the meat and lifted it carefully to her mouth, her hands now suited only for gross motor skills. Her struggle struck Todd as pitiable, but his mom appeared not to notice this portrait of the physical difficulties that came with aging. He glanced over at her. She was concentrating on her own plate. He wasn't sure if either woman had caught his admission that he was going to stick around town for a while.

"But I'm fine here," his mom offered. "I'm free from all my responsibilities. I haven't washed a dish in weeks, and if I want a cup of tea, all I do is order one up!" She accompanied her words with a flourish of her fork and a smile. The levity was staged but proved that she was doing her best to find the bright side of her situation.

The meal continued, with the conversation staying on familiar topics. They talked about the hairdresser who came in on Thursdays, the recreation leaders they liked and the ones they didn't and how nice the preacher's sermon had been.

After they finished their meal and coffee, Todd wheeled his mom outside to the patio. The sun was bright, the humidity slightly oppressive. But the space was boxed off with neatly trimmed evergreen bushes, so they could talk privately. Most of the other residents had returned to their rooms for some quiet time or a nap. His mom didn't seem bothered by the sweater that she was wearing, so Todd didn't offer to help her take it off.

"Mary's very nice, you know, and she's been a good friend in the dining room," his mom said. "Some of the others do nothing but complain throughout the whole meal. It's just that I don't want to talk about family matters in front of her, or anyone."

"You know what a wise man once said to me?" Todd replied. "People are going to talk about you anyway. Might as well give them something interesting to talk about." But he was only teasing her. He shared her desire for privacy.

"It's a small town, Todd, and people gossip. You probably don't know who Mary is, but her niece is the girl who does my hair. When I'm not in here, that is."

The connection seemed pretty harmless, but her point was valid. Once someone got branded with a reputation in Queenston, it stuck. Mostly, the talk was benign, with family habits and foibles following people down the generations. Todd assured her that some conversations would be kept between the two of them.

Before his mom could get onto the topic of her rehab, Todd shifted his attention to breaking the news that he was going to stay in Queenston to regroup. "Mom, you know all about Lydle and what happened there. And you know that I've been hustling for the past five or six months to find something else. Well, nothing's turning up. I don't know if it's the time of year, the economy or what." He didn't mention his real suspicion, that Tia Rosita was going to follow him around for a long, long time, and nobody wants to hire a failure. "So in the past few weeks, I mean, even the past month or so, before all this," he motioned vaguely to her wheelchair and the residence behind her, "I was thinking about staying here for a while. Just to live a little cheaper. I'm still in the job market back there." He tipped his head in the direction of the highway, which he and his mom both knew pointed toward Toronto.

"And Sarah has agreed to let me use her address if I need to for job apps, so that it still looks like I'm living in town. Plus, I have the same cellphone number, so who's to know that I'm not there? If I get an interview, I'll be close enough to zip into Toronto, stay in a hotel and get up the next morning to go talk to employers."

As he laid out the plan, he kept one eye on her and one on the door, hoping nobody would walk out and spoil his momentum. And he didn't mention that his next opportunity might be further afield than Toronto.

"You might as well live in the house, then," his mom replied. She didn't criticize the plan's substance, nor did she mention his failure in the job market. "I'm not there, after all."

"It's just for a while, Mom," he replied. "I mean, someone should be at the house to look after it for now, but you'll be out of here in a couple of weeks, right? And when that happens, if you want, I can get an apartment. I mean, there aren't a ton of people competing for rentals here, I don't suppose. I can probably even find a furnished place for cheap." It was the polite thing to say, though he was counting on living at his mom's place to keep his expenses as close to zero as possible.

"A broken-down dump with someone else's old furniture, more like. No, Todd. You're not going to do that. If you can stand living at home with me, when I get there, that's where I'd like you. Anyway, for me, the time frame is not a couple of weeks, more like eight or ten. I'm starting rehab next week. I could go home, I guess, but I didn't know you were coming. And the one thing that I was left with after your dad's layoff was his long-term-care insurance. I've been approved for up to ninety days of rehab, and they only start counting after they figure I'm ready to do exercises to strengthen my hip."

He expected a declarative "That settles it!" to end the discussion. Instead, she said, "I know this is hard for you. You like Toronto." She looked at him for affirmation. Todd nodded in agreement and to prompt her to go on. "I bet when you got out of here you never thought you'd return. And now that you're here, and I understand that it's only temporary, you're not too excited at the idea, eh?" She understood the feeling he'd had since his teen years that Queenston wasn't where he wanted to live when he grew up. To his mom's credit, she'd never done anything to hold him back. Quite the opposite, in fact.

He answered her questions in turn. "No, I didn't. I thought I'd gotten away from this town forever. And, no, I'm not all that crazy about it, but it just makes sense." He paused, digesting the unpleasant feeling that came over him, almost like the words "I've failed" were emblazoned across his forehead. He looked at his mom, worried that she might think he'd been anxious to leave her behind as well, out of his life. She waved her hand, indicating that he didn't need to apologize for what he said.

"But you know, yesterday, I was bored, so I drove to the Pond where we used to skate," he said. "I'm not even sure why I did it, except that I didn't want to go anywhere where I'd see anybody." He winced at the confession that he'd been in town early enough that he could have come to visit her the day before, but she gave no sign that this concerned her. "It felt good to see it again. Have you been out there lately?" He half laughed at the absurdity of the question. "I mean, before the hip?"

He knew she would answer no. Even he, despite his feeling of ownership of the Pond, had stopped going there long before he left town.

She shook her head to say she hadn't. She had been to the Pond only a handful of times when Todd was a kid. She was there when they dedicated the Shack because Bob had insisted that the kids who had helped to build the place invite their families out to see what they'd accomplished. In truth, Bob had done most of the work. Their role had been to haul a few boards from his truck and put on a coat of paint. The day they celebrated its completion, Todd's mom and a couple of others had supplied hot chocolate and donuts. After that, the Shack became a place that was more or

These days, suburban parks and other outdoor rinks have replaced ponds for a lot of players. But the scrabble of sticks, the shouts of "next goal wins," and the skills developed by playing shinny still give meaning to childhood in winter climes. In warmer places and during the summer, street hockey fills in for the pond, but the excitement is the same and the memories are just as rich. Former NHL great Luc Robitaille remembers his childhood, when a tennis ball would last for two years until the fuzz was all worn off from playing on the streets of his town in Quebec.

less kids-only, a clubhouse of sorts, not somewhere adults were welcomed. Except for Bob.

Todd's mom had turned up at the Pond a couple of times when he was late for dinner. She had never been in a bad mood because she had to go looking for him, and she wouldn't yell at him in front of other kids. One of their cardinal rules was that if he didn't embarrass her in front of his friends, as might happen if he talked back to her in public, she would be kind to him in front of other people, too. His dad hadn't shared that pact.

He recognized by her silence that her memories of the Pond were vague. He filled her in. "The Shack, remember that? It's almost ready to fall down. You know the stove that Bob put out there, the wood-fired contraption with the exhaust pipe out the back wall? That's all crooked now, and the seal's gone. I can't see how anyone could use it today in that condition. It'd probably end up with poisonous fumes inside."

"I remember how proud you kids were of your Shack," she reminisced. "Bob, too. It was like he'd built the Taj Mahal." To them, it had been like that—it was grand, and special. The kids were responsible for getting the stove lit and keeping it stoked while they were there. If anybody left anything behind, the last ones had to clean it up. They cared about the tiny cabin more than they cared about how neat their rooms were or how tidy their desks and lockers were at school.

"I don't even know if I could find it now," she said. The Pond was a five-minute drive from the house, but her sense of direction was almost nonexistent. Ever since Todd's dad had died, she had restricted her driving to going to the grocery store, the hairdresser and the library, a tiny circle of familiar spots. It wouldn't have occurred to her to drive to Toronto to visit him. Even going out to the edge of town to the Superstore was a big adventure.

"Yeah, well, it's where it used to be, out on Trulls Road. But it's a mess. It doesn't look like anybody's using it. If they are, they sure aren't doing anything about keeping it up."

"They're probably not, with Bob gone," she said, though she had no means of knowing. As kids grow up, they go through various phases. When they're in hockey, their parents know all the other parents. If they take karate lessons, their families become familiar with terms like *dojo*, *kata* and *gi*. But when kids move on to new interests, whatever community they might have formed with others dedicated to their earlier hobbies is left behind. There might have been a rink at the Pond for the past couple of decades since Todd had finished with hockey, or there might not have been. Mrs. Graham wouldn't have taken any notice either way.

"I was going to ask you about Bob, actually," he said since the topic had come around to him. "It's been years since we've talked about him." He didn't bring up his father, discussion of whom had been left lingering since Todd first arrived in Mrs. Graham's room.

"Let's wait for that, Todd. I do have a couple of stories to tell you about him. But right now, it's time for tea. Then a nap, and a couple of hours after that, dinner. That's how you learn to tell the time around here. How long until the next meal."

The fact that she could describe the routine suggested that she hadn't unconsciously fallen prey to its rhythms, which gave Todd comfort. He got up, released the brakes on her chair and wheeled her inside. Tea was served in the large sitting room next to the reception desk. When they got there, half a dozen others were sitting in big armchairs or on the couch. Mary was nowhere to be seen.

"That's okay, Todd. You can leave me here. They'll take me to my room to rest up after. I don't usually sit this long." He didn't know if it was a subtle rebuke. He leaned over, got another surprisingly strong hug and straightened up to head out.

"I'll see you tomorrow, Mom. There are other details we need to talk about." He needed to know where the mail key was and what to do about paying her bills.

She waved at him as he walked away, her attention already diverted by the TV, which had a picture of a sun-drenched cottage with the temperatures for the next few days displayed along the bottom of the screen. The irony was that it didn't make any difference to her how hot it was. The thought saddened Todd in a way he hadn't expected. He was not ready to think of his mother as an invalid. He walked past the desk and nodded to Jennifer.

He climbed into the car, fired it up and headed out of the parking lot. He needed to find out more about the rehab program she was going to be on. If she was in the mood, on his next visit they could talk about Bob. Maybe they'd even venture down the alley to the past.

CHAPTER
six

Todd got up the next day knowing that he had to chance seeing someone out at the Superstore, because a look in his mom's supply cupboard revealed that he needed more than food. The house was starkly devoid of shampoo, laundry soap and spare toilet paper. He wondered how she got along, though one little lady didn't need much, particularly the huge quantities of merchandise sold at a warehouse store.

At Superstore, he parked the car far from the main doors, as was his habit, choosing a spot in a corner where door dings from carts would not pose a problem. The long walk to the store didn't bother him. Always conscious of his fitness, he saw the walk as a chance to sneak extra physical activity into his day.

He got a buggy as he entered the store and then started for the produce section. The late strawberry crop was in, evidenced by the amount of berries sitting in the cases as well as their low price. He had just rolled into the bakery section and was scanning the shelves when he heard a voice ahead of him.

"Don't shoot!" It sounded like an adult's voice mimicking the mocking tone of childhood. He lifted his head.

Standing in front of him was an older, more puffy and weathered version of the kid who had made most of his early teen years close to miserable. Kenny Horton still sported the haircut he'd had back then, a semi-mullet that snaked over his shoulders. When they were in grades five, six and on up through high school, the guy had towered over the rest of the kids, at least in the attitude he took, which conveyed that at any moment, he might decide to rough up someone, just for the fun of it. Now, he stood in front of Todd with his lips curled into an expression that was half snarling wolf and half clueless dumb-ass, waiting for him to say something. Todd's immediate reaction was to register how un-adult-like the other man's behavior was.

Had Todd looked back on his interactions with Kenny from a rational, adult point of view, he would have realized that the guy had never laid a finger on him, and probably wouldn't have. But the threat that he could have, and that he let you know at opportune times that he had that option, had kept Todd and many boys cowering in fear of him. Now, almost two decades later, what could Todd say? "Don't shoot" was the nickname he had gained after the notorious failure of his team in the Peterborough Bantam tournament. He thought he'd left the moniker behind by virtue of earning a graduate degree, moving from Queenston and finding a job in big-city commerce. But Kenny Horton hadn't forgotten. His throwback look suggested that he hadn't been much of anywhere in the intervening years, either.

Todd nodded a hello, still not quite finding words.

"I mean, hey man, you back?" Kenny spoke first. Whatever memories the guy had of Todd's hockey failures, he wasn't going to get into the topic right then. Kenny peered at Todd through eyes dimmed by too much partying, awaiting his reply.

"Visiting. My mom, uh, you know, she had a fall." He didn't divulge any more specifics. Although they were adults now, the old fear of the bully, the memories of Kenny taunting him, weren't buried deep enough to put them on familiar terms, especially given what he'd just said.

Todd deflected a question back at Kenny to avoid further comment on his own situation. "You off today?" he said. He peered into Kenny's cart, which had nothing but two loaves of bread and some packaged food from the deli.

"Man, I'm off every day," Kenny replied, his eyes glancing over Todd and then down at the floor. "I had a job, you know, at the plant. That didn't last. I was one of the last guys hired. Then they shut down, you know?" Todd knew. "Drove truck for a long time, but I hurt my back. I've been off for almost a year." He looked up once more, his vacant eyes suggesting that these two jobs had been the best of his prospects.

Todd knew that he ought to feel sorry for the guy. His own life, even with his current troubles taken into account, had already been better than Kenny Horton's ever would be. Plus, Todd had a future, where this guy plainly didn't. Still, he didn't feel pity.

He straightened his back, squaring up instead of trying to shrink down, as he might have done when he was younger. Kenny was the first old friend, if the term could be stretched to define their relationship, that Todd had run into, so his impulse was to ask him about the Shack, maybe get into Bob. But he ended the encounter without further conversation.

"Yeah, Kenny, well, I'll see you, eh?" He'd need to process the "Don't shoot" comment before he was ready to build a bridge to his former tormenter. He pushed his buggy past the guy, who was standing with his mouth open, ready to say something else, one hand holding onto a bread rack, the other one on his cart.

The afternoon came and went with a visit to his mom. Todd found out how she ran her house, where the checkbook was and what had become of her car. It had been in the garage for an oil change the day she had fallen, she reported. Daryl, the mechanic, had sent word that he was keeping it parked in one of his service bays until someone was able to pick it up. Todd's mom also said that her rehab would not begin until after she had her hip x-rayed. The surgeon wanted to ensure the bone was healing properly before she started therapy. As he and his mom talked, Todd mentioned he had bumped into Kenny.

"I've seen him around, Todd. Same place—at the grocery store. He actually said hello to me. Called 'Mrs. Graham.' He's a sad fellow, really. Thirty-four, and he looks forty-five if a day. It's hard to believe he was a decent athlete when you guys were kids. I know you never really liked him, but he was an important part of your hockey team. You used to tell me that he was the only defenseman who had what you called a 'booming slap shot,' and you'd say it with pride." It was true. Despite his outsider personality, Kenny had been part of the local hockey scene.

"It wasn't that I didn't like him. The reason none of us thought of him as one of us was because he was a bully. Plain and simple. It was a good thing that he was on our side. But in school, none of the hockey stuff carried over. We were all just scared of him."

Kenny lived to intimidate, and once, he'd gotten into a fight with a kid who was visiting for the summer. That act alone had earned Kenny his reputation. That and his big mouth and belligerence toward everyone around him.

"Childhood's like that, Todd. These days, they've got anti-bullying programs in schools. All that tells you is that nothing has changed. I suppose it's the law of the jungle that certain kids are going to try to be number one." His mother was actually citing an axiom of the business world, though she wouldn't have recognized this. Todd turned the conversation to more mundane concerns for the duration of his visit.

As the week went on, the need to revisit the past began to solidify in Todd's head. He decided to go down to the basement and dig among the boxes that contained the relics of his childhood, including his hockey career. He found the box with mostly hockey stuff next to the furnace, the dust thick on its top. Obviously, his parents had never had any reason to disturb it in the years since he'd stashed it.

The most recognizable award given to NHL players is the Conn Smythe Trophy, presented to the most valuable player in the Stanley Cup playoffs. The newest award is the Maurice "Rocket" Richard Trophy, inaugurated in 1999 to honor the player who gets the most goals in the regular season. The great Montreal player was the first NHLer to score 500 goals, though ironically enough, he never won the overall league scoring title. That is still signaled by the awarding of the Art Ross Trophy.

He opened the box, excited yet fearful, knowing that it held the best and worst memories of his childhood, all of which revolved around hockey.

The top layer of the box was trophies. The "Milkshake Award" was a puck mounted on a small, black, wood base. His name and a date on a plaque affixed to the wood were proof that he'd once played for the Queenston Rebels.

The trophy was awarded at the end of the season to the player who had consistently performed well in practice. Each practice, the player who did the best "earned a milkshake," which back then cost a buck, as a weekly award. The coach would give him the dollar on his way out the door. Todd had won so many "milkshakes" that he was handed the trophy at the team banquet. The coach didn't do this every year. But that had been the year of the Bantam tournament, 1991–92, and everything was magnified in importance that season.

In the box, Todd found other trophies, or, as the kids liked to call them, "cups," using the word for the greatest one of all, the Stanley Cup. In fact, none of the trophies was actually a cup, because he'd never been on a team that had won a league championship.

Instead, each trophy was adorned with some version of a tiny brass or silver plastic hockey player in a pose that made him look like he was about to take the shot that would score his team a huge goal. The trophies were won throughout Todd's hockey-playing years, which had gone from when he was seven up until the time that checking got too scary for him, right after his second Bantam season. Midget hockey—he knew before he got there—would be far too rough for him. And after Peterborough, hockey had fallen apart for him anyway.

He dug further into the box, finding a couple of school yearbooks and the first fish he had caught—a stuffed lake bass—a misfit in this collection that got in the way of what he was really looking for. Finally, from underneath his grade eight yearbook, it surfaced: the silver medal hanging from a red velvet ribbon. It looked the same as it had the day he'd received it after losing the final game of the Peterborough tournament. After he left the ice, he had taken the medal off, as had his teammates. The medal had sat in his T-shirt drawer for years, never worn again.

He picked it up, remembering the moment the Sarnia Cyclones players got their gold medals. Silver meant Todd's team had lost, though the adults in his life, even his dad, tried to console him after the medal presentation. "Silver, Todd, that's something to be proud of." The words meant nothing.

The truth, and everyone on his team knew it, was that the medal should have been gold. It would have, but for Todd's fatal flaw. His inability to shoot the puck in tight situations. He considered putting the medal on, to see how it would feel after all these years, but the sense that doing so would remind him of the bad times stopped him. He packed up the box and went upstairs.

Hockey practices at the indoor arena had been as frequent as they could be in the year Queenston raised the money to send the Rebels to the Peterborough tournament. But when it looked like the team could benefit from extra work, their assistant coach held practices on the Pond, where their love of the game had first been fostered. The ice surface was too small for whole-team scrimmages, but Bob had something else in mind. He divided the guys into groups of four or five and worked with them on developing the skills lacking in their game.

At first, Bob's demand that the players show up for practices, as well as kicking the other kids off the Pond when he had drills scheduled, had been a source of mild irritation to some parents whose kids used the ice for fun. But Bob prevailed with the same logic that he also used on the team. "We're going to go to Peterborough and show them that this town's alive," he would say. The par-

Serge Gagne, who works in Anaheim as the NHL Official Scorer, played at a suburban Montreal rink while he was growing up. There, each kid always took two pucks. One was the good one—in his case, a Montreal Canadiens logo puck. But he would only use that himself, because if a puck went over the boards, it would be lost in the snowbank. That was why he always carried a spare. And when that puck got lost, he'd make careful note of where, so that in the spring when the snow started to melt, he could arrive first to retrieve it.

ents would end up nodding in agreement. Although the real decline of the town through losing Mackey's was still some- where in the future, Queenston residents sensed their community was at risk, that people were moving to places of greater significance than this one. Winning the tournament would allow the town to make a mark, to say that it wasn't going down without at least one sign of its existence having been registered.

So the drills began. Todd usually worked with the two other boys who made up his line. Dave Joseph, his center, was a big kid—or "husky," the term most often used to describe him in those days. Dave had the size to fill the slot, if not quite the speed to keep up with his two wingers, Todd, on the right, and Timmy Reid, on the left.

"Your job is to buzz into those corners and get the puck," Bob would tell the wingers. Feed it out to the slot. Dave will bang it in from there, like Phil Esposito used to do." The boys had only a vague idea who Esposito was, but they understood the concept.

Bob would throw the puck down the left or right side of the ice, where it would generally be stopped by the low boards he had installed behind the net area on each end of the Pond. He'd done that, he explained to them, because otherwise their practices wouldn't be anywhere close to realistic.

Todd's dad had seen the boards when he drove by the Pond one day, and he asked his son about it. Todd explained Bob's reasoning, only to hear, "Who does he think he is, an NHLer?" Years later, Todd would find out that was exactly the case. But when Todd was a kid, Bob was just a slightly gruff but kindly fellow who had everyone's best interests at heart, particularly when it came to hockey.

Todd would chase the puck if it was going down his side, with Bob's "Hard, hard, Todd! Come on! Remember, there's a defenseman there, too," ringing in his ears. If the puck went down the left side for Timmy to chase, Todd's job was to trail the play slightly, waiting for the puck to come to the slot. If Dave got it, Todd had to go hard to the net for a possible rebound. If the puck came to him, then Todd was expected to shoot it from the slot, with Dave crashing the net to get to the puck if the goalie made a save. They practiced this endlessly.

Todd felt like he was learning something. He had played hockey for seven years prior to this season, and mostly, the games were group efforts at chasing the loose puck. There wasn't any organization involved in their play. He had tried to mimic what went on in the NHL games he and his dad watched on TV, but the speed and skill of those players, and their almost magical abilities, made it hard to use *Hockey Night in Canada* as a learning tool.

Bob simplified the process by giving Todd and his linemates a formula to follow. He did the same for each of the three forward lines the Bantam team featured. Bob also used his hawk eye to pick up on the skills his players needed to work on as individuals. For Todd, that was his skating, which he knew had major flaws.

"You turn well going toward your right," Bob said to him one day. "Your cross-cuts to the left aren't so good, though." In truth, they barely existed. Todd could go right beautifully, his blades flashing over one another just like Pavel Bure's did. Maybe it was because he shot right, and therefore carried his stick over to that side. But if Todd tried to go the other direction, he felt off kilter, like his feet would slide out from under him. Instead of cross-cutting, he cheated, gliding on his left skate and pushing with his right for a couple of strides before crossing over, then going back to his pushing technique.

"Let's work on that," Bob said. "Stay after, okay?" Todd just nodded, aware that this weakness was going to make it hard for him to get to the slot in a hurry every time, whether he had been the one to feed the puck out front or not. That was the other part of the lesson. When the puck went into his corner, it was not enough to put it to Dave in front, with Timmy going there also for a rebound or in case the centerman missed it. Bob wanted all of them to be what he called "hungry for the net," and so even the player who had made the pass out front had to go to the goal and hope a rebound bounced toward him.

For Todd, just getting an assist on someone else's goal was good enough. A point was a point, and he had never scored more than a few goals a season. But Bob disagreed, and he made it clear to Todd that his way was going to be *the* way. It was one of the few times Todd saw him in anything but the happiest of moods. "Aggression…" he said, leaning close to Todd's face as they took a break in their drills, "is learned behavior. When I say be 'hungry for the net,' I want you to think like a tiger. The puck is meat." Todd nodded his understanding.

So they drilled his skating, Bob setting up a couple of wood blocks for him to go around. He forced him to cross-cut left, not allowing Todd to glide. "You won't fall, Todd; it just feels like you will. But that edge is just as good as the one on your right skate. You just have to believe it." Todd skated circles until he felt like his legs would collapse under him. Then Bob changed the drill to figure eights. Then it was turns going in a right-hand direction. "You can't let that side get soft working on the weak one," he explained. Todd just did what he was told.

After they'd been at it for a couple of weeks, every second day or so, Todd could feel the difference. The puck went into his corner one evening at their "Pond practice," as they liked to call it, and he charged after it. He picked the puck up and was about to cut in a circle to his right, which was what he'd always done before, when he realized that he felt strong enough to go the other way, so he did that. His head up, he fired the puck directly onto Dave's tape. It got there so fast, the centerman wasn't ready for it. He got away a weak shot.

As the line skated toward Bob to review the play, Dave was smiling through his cage. "You've changed," he said. "I mean, I was waiting for you to cut the other direction. You always do that." It was part compliment, part excuse for why Dave had muffed the perfect chance that Todd's new-found skill had afforded the centerman. Todd didn't say anything, looking down at his skates.

"Yeah, everyone's getting better," Bob cut in as the boys reached him. Then he looked at Todd. "If you can fool your own centerman, you can fool the opposing defenseman as well. One time, go right. The next time, cut left. Leave him guessing as to when and where you're going to thread that pass out front." Todd nodded.

"And you," Bob continued, tapping Dave on the helmet, "Stay awake." The older man then turned to Timmy. "You learning something here, too, boyo?" The left wing answered that he was. "Your turns have always been okay, both ways. That's why I haven't had you drilling them."

Todd felt a little embarrassed by this tacit mention of his extra drills with Bob, which once again pointed out his weakness. "But you see what you can accomplish by mixing it up, doing something different now and then, right?" Timmy was a smart player, even for a fourteen-year-old. He nodded that he got it, and Todd was pretty sure that he'd be seeing some changing up of his turns the next time they got out on the ice for a real game.

The night that Todd's newly strengthened skills at wheeling both right and left with the puck were discovered, Bob had something else to say to him. "You know, none of this is going to do much good if you don't shoot the puck if the situation calls for it," he stated. "I've been telling you guys to pass it to the slot, and we've talked about you having options of going left and firing it out directly, or right and shoveling it on the backhand." His comment made sense with what he'd said earlier, so Todd nodded. "But you have another choice, and that's to shoot for the net yourself after you come off the boards."

Todd tried to envision doing this. At fourteen, he was still not confident that he could propel the nearly six-ounce puck with enough speed to be dangerous. He could put one on net from the faceoff dot, on his forehand, but not hard enough to blast past a goalie. In any case, that was the shot he would use if he shot after whirling around to the left. But using his backhand, if he turned out of the corner to the right, would result in a wobbler that wouldn't even get past the defense. That was part of the reason why he preferred, in every case, to pass it into the slot to Dave or Timmy. He said as much to Bob with the admission, "My shot isn't really all that strong, Coach," which was what they had started calling the older man.

"We'll work on that next, Todd, but sometimes it's not about how strong your shot is. It's about your willingness to shoot in the first place. Think about it. You have three options, even with a weak shot. Come out right or left and pass, or come out, say, left, and then take the puck directly to the net. When you're close enough to shoot with some power, shoot."

Bob's advice sounded simple enough that Todd could imagine himself doing it. But out on the ice, he had to deal with the other players, the tangle of arms and legs and the bodies in the way. The target of Dave's stick as he stood waiting to unleash his shot, which was much better than Todd's, made the pressure too great. Nine out of ten times, Todd ended up passing.

Still, he didn't want Bob to think he was ignoring his advice, so he gave him a weak nod. "You're not completely convinced, I can tell," Bob said. "We'll just have to work on that part of the game, too."

After practices, Todd usually hung around, helped to clean the ice and waited until the kids who had been skating were gone. Sometimes, when he had put everything in order in the Shack, he would go back onto the ice for a final skate. Wearing his toque rather than his hockey helmet, he felt the cold air rushing over his face as he guided a puck in front of him. When he got to the net, he would shoot, putting all his muscle behind the puck, and then watch as the twine bulged. It was always the most glorious goal ever scored.

It would have been dark for three hours by then, but not late, maybe eight or half past. He would get a ride home in Bob's big Chevy truck, jumping out at his curb just as the coach cruised to a stop. The porch light would be on, and his mom would be standing in the kitchen paging through the newspaper. With any luck, his dad would be there, too, having a cup of tea. Other nights, it was something stronger. At those times, Todd rushed to his bedroom, using the excuse that homework called him, regardless whether he had schoolbooks in his backpack or not. If he didn't have anything else to do, he turned on his radio, tuning it to a Major Junior game from Ottawa or Kingston on the AM dial.

─────────⟨⟨⟨⟩⟩⟩─────────

Todd sat in his mom's living room checking his email on his laptop, his treasure box of hockey memories left behind in the basement. The nighttime use of the ice had been made possible by another Bob move: installing lights around the rink. Maybe the lights were still there? He hadn't thought to look when he was at the Pond the other day. He would do that the next time he drove by. There was no way to know if they worked, though, even if they had survived the years. It was unlikely a live power connection was hooked up.

CHAPTER
seven

Getting into a routine in his new, albeit temporary, life didn't take Todd long. The first week, he surveyed the house to see what needed fixing up. Whether or not his mom would end up staying in her home long term wasn't known, but he had to get it in shape for the upcoming winter.

As days passed, the list of chores grew even though Todd crossed off what he completed as he went along. Clean the gutters. Seal the leaking one at the front left corner of the house. Paint the garage door and the trim around the windows. The paint had long since faded and was starting to peel. Fortunately for him, the house's exterior was essentially maintenance-free otherwise. But he needed to cut back the rose bushes and trim the old evergreen in the front yard before it got completely out of hand. The beige carpet in the front hall was also starting to look dirty. He'd need to rent a steamer from the local hardware store to tackle that job. Also on the list: replace the bathroom tap. He'd have to hire a plumber for that. Then there was the need to look at the furnace, change the filter and figure out if it required more work, which would only be a guess on his part.

He recognized his own limitations when it came to repairing things. Although his dad had been a hardhat type of guy with a workbench in the garage and enough power tools to build a cabin in the backyard had he ever thought to, handyman skills had not been passed from father to son. Todd had come to accept that not sharing guy stuff with the old man as he grew up was another consequence of his dad's drinking. When he was sipping, he had no patience whatsoever, and at those times it was best to stay well out of his path.

A few weeks went by, and kids now wandered by the house in the morning wearing backpacks full of schoolwork, rather than carrying footballs or soccer balls on the way to their friends' houses or the park. Summer was officially over.

Each day, Todd tried to attend to some task and to balance his work around the house with visits to his mom. After the first Sunday, he didn't bother buying magazines anymore, but at her suggestion, he started to bring books from the library. She liked the Maisie Dobbs mysteries and the detective books of a writer from Scotland. He could never remember his name. The librarian knew, though, and she was happy to recommend titles.

Mrs. Graham had started rehab a couple of weeks after he got home, and she spent most afternoons with her physical therapist, a young woman called Andrea. Todd had not known that such a job existed in a care home. He always thought of "PT," as he had learned to call it, as something athletes did after they had surgery on a knee or shoulder. During one of his visits, he peeked through the window of the therapy room, which looked like a cross between a hockey team's training room and a torture chamber, though the equipment was updated to modern, surgically clean standards.

"What do they do to you in there?" Todd asked his mom, curious about the complexity of the apparatus.

"I'm learning to walk a new way," she replied. "My hip's healing, but I have to be careful with it. I can walk all I want, but the last thing we need is a stress fracture." She sounded just like her doctor because she was repeating his words, verbatim.

"So, what kind of things do you do?" He was fascinated by the balls and pulleys and machines that filled the room.

"We work on my balance. Andrea teaches me to walk straight, not to bend over, which is what I was starting to do. I guess that's a habit that comes with age."

"Or with carrying the burdens of the world on your shoulders," he said offhandedly, but halfway meaning it. She just smiled.

"These are things you just take for granted when you're healthy," she added. "But once you've had a fall, it takes time to put new patterns in place." This was Andrea-language. But his mom seemed to enjoy the challenge of therapy, and she was starting to look like her old self, not the tiny waif he had first encountered at the nursing home in mid-August. The consistent, proper diet was showing results.

"When you get home, you need to keep eating properly," he said to her.

She smiled again. "Are you calling me fat?" She raised herself up in the chair she sat in, now a regular one, not a wheelchair.

"Hardly fat, Mom. But you weren't looking healthy when I first got…" He hesitated using the word, "home." He was making it sound as if he was admitting he belonged in Queenston. He grimaced and finished the sentence with "here."

"You know, Todd, it's not easy to cook for one. When your dad was around, it was different. Now, you try to find a single pork chop at SuperFresh. They just don't sell them like that. And anytime I buy multiples of anything, I end up throwing half of it away." The dried-up food in the basement freezer was testament to that.

"I'm not sure if I'll be around for a long time after you get home, okay?" he said in response, phrasing it like a question. "But for as long as I'm there, you're going to eat nutritious meals, like the ones you're getting here. Maybe I'll ask them if they can send you home with some kind of a menu. We can cook together."

She smiled but didn't ask him how the job search was going. His mom was living day to day now, more so than she had in the past, even when dealing with an alcoholic husband. Maybe the walls of the care facility did close in on a person, as had been his suspicion the first day he'd visited. He hoped that returning home wouldn't be too big a transition for her.

Had Todd's mom asked him how he was moving along with his career hopes, she would have discovered that as summer turned into fall, Todd had stayed busy sending out job queries, mostly to firms in Toronto, but he found it more difficult to network from Queenston than he had imagined it might be. It wasn't like he could toss off invitations to coffee when he did make a contact via email. But he managed to get some momentum going when one of his MBA classmates mentioned that he was working at a large food processing company and that a management position could possibly open up sometime in the future. Just not immediately, given the state of the economy.

The recession that had driven so much industry in Ontario out of business—or more correctly, down to the States—had made everyone nervous, from mom-and-pop operations to big corporations, and hiring was being deferred. Todd had learned to accept that the situation was out of his control. All he could do was plug away, watch the job ads online and in the industry mags and use the Queen's alumni network to try to turn up leads.

When he visited his mom, most of their chatter was about the news on TV, the goings-on in the facility and her prospects of going home at some point, as well as other trivial matters. But one afternoon, after exhausting all other topics, they got onto the subject of Todd's dad. His mom had promised to embark upon the conversation since Todd first visited, though even at that, the talk came three years after it probably should have, because the old man had been gone that long.

When Todd's father died, they did what most families do, which was to have a funeral where everybody said all the things they were supposed to say. After the service, Todd had stood in the lobby of the old house that had served as Payne's Funeral Home, staring at the carpet and shaking hands with people who muttered the usual, "Sorry for your loss." Those kinds of sentiments weren't hard to take. It was the "Reg was a great guy. We used to work together. I never saw him down," kind of comment that was so confusing and difficult to comprehend. Maybe his dad was a great guy at seven in the morning when his shift started—his alcohol consumption having not yet begun—but later on, at home, he presented a different side, the side Todd and his mom were forced to deal with.

Hearing those remarks, Todd had muttered his thanks, his mind wandering to the times when his dad was passed out on the couch in front of the TV by nine o'clock in the evening. When Todd was old enough, he would pull a blanket over him for the night.

That was all behind him, with the old man lying in a box in the next room.

The funeral was a whirlwind of activity, the funeral director guiding them from moment to moment in what was, for him, a carefully scripted dance. Todd and his mother were numbed by the routine. They didn't discuss anything else.

He then returned to his life in Toronto; five days, including the weekend, was all he could spare from work.

His mom was left to pick up and go on, and she did fine. She had handled the financial affairs of the house rather than leaving them to Todd's dad, so, as she had explained it, she was aware of aspects of life that widows, at least of a certain age, sometimes aren't. Where the life insurance papers were kept, what to do about the banking. She'd even had the car and house put into joint ownership some time before.

Her explanation to her son had been simple: "With a disease like your father's, you never know what's going to happen, so I prepared myself." She said it with a clinical tone, whereas Todd had expected melancholy.

They had talked about him on occasion since, but they had never gotten past a surface discussion of memories of the good times, probably because neither of them knew how to bring up the negatives in his legacy. Todd knew his mom had been miserable much of her married life, but he also remembered how she had brightened when times were good—when his dad was working and keeping his drinking in check, which wasn't as often as when he was on the downside.

Now, as they finally had time to sit and talk, face to face, with nothing else pulling either of them away, they delved into what had not been said sooner.

"You took charge of everything pretty quickly after Dad died," Todd started, intending to broach the emotional part as the conversation went on.

"Actually, I did that a long time before, Todd." She moved swiftly to the level of feeling. "You know how I told you after he died that a disease like drinking forces you to face certain things?" Todd nodded. "Well, going over money matters and deciding to add my name to everything made me realize that whatever hopes I had for Reg and for our life together were long past coming true." She looked down at her hands, folded together in her lap, and pursed her lips.

Todd was surprised that she used his dad's first name. She never did that when she talked to him about the old man. He decided to go right to the heart of the matter.

"You loved him?" It sounded too much like the question a character in a Harlequin romance might ask a jilted lover. "I mean, I know you guys loved each other, but how did you deal with his mood swings?"

"I just did. In my day, you didn't think of a divorce. You just took life for what it was. And of course, I kept hoping that something would change. I thought when you were born, he'd stop drinking."

Todd was surprised to learn that his father's problems had existed before he was born. He blurted out, "So if you knew he drank too much back then, why'd you marry him?"

"I didn't really know how much he drank, or maybe I just didn't know what to look for. And your dad did have an appealing quality to him, Todd. He was a man in the way that men used to be. He was smart. He was good with his hands. Remember the shelves he built in the garage? He did that in one weekend, with just a few scraps of wood. I was impressed. It made me feel, I don't know, secure." Her eyes had darted up from her lap and back down several times. Now, she maintained eye contact once again.

His mother was talking about the values of a generation entirely different from his. Few of the guys Todd knew had sufficient skills with tools to impress a female, nor did the women that Todd had dated look for that quality in a partner.

"So you fell in love with him, and then what…? Had me?" The last question lingered in the air before she answered it.

"There was no 'accident,' if that's what you're wondering. And we did love each other. Think about it. If I had left your father as soon as I saw something was wrong, then you wouldn't be here now, with me."

It was a profound thought, but it didn't explain why she had given up her happiness for so long. Todd said so.

"Well, I guess I learned to cope. You take what's good, and you focus on that. There's no ideal life, Todd. Anyway, Reg was, I guess you could say, under control when you were a small boy. It was only as you started to grow up that he began to drink again like he had when I first met him. Part of the reason I supported your hockey was because I was hoping your dad could be involved with it," his mother replied. "I thought it might give him a reason to stay sober." She shrugged her shoulders as if to indicate that she hadn't known what else to do.

Rogie Vachon, who won three Stanley Cups with Montreal before suiting up for the LA Kings for most of the 1970s, played his hockey outdoors in Palmarolle, Quebec. Games took place either on the river near his home or the local outdoor ice rink. There was no indoor arena nearby. Rogie was a goalie, playing with Eaton's catalogs on his legs and no skates. The sticks he and his friends used were handmade. The Montreal Canadiens signed him as a prospect at 15. He is the best retired NHL player alive today who is not in the Hockey Hall of Fame.

"All the other fathers would be there, at the rink, yelling and encouraging their sons. Some not so nicely, in my recollection. I thought your dad might show an interest. Some of the dads even used to go stand out by the Pond when you boys were practicing with Bob. They wouldn't say much. Bob wouldn't allow it, and they respected what he was doing for you kids. They'd be there, though, watching, talking to each other, smoking."

"And Dad?"

"I don't know. Well, yes I do. By that time of the day, he was usually…preoccupied." The last word came out hesitantly, almost like it was in quotation marks.

"With drinking?" Todd's suggestion that she actually say the words made her face cloud over. She looked at her hands once again.

"He had to do that, most days, and even knowing that you would have wanted him out at the Pond or arena, if only to be a part of the group of dads, wasn't enough to make him stop. When I finally realized that, I knew that nothing was going to change. But by then, you were ten or twelve, and it was too late for me to leave. I didn't want to spend the rest of my life alone, in some apartment somewhere."

The fatalistic scenario she painted sounded old-fashioned, equating divorce with becoming some forgotten, lonely old lady in a dingy tenement. "Why alone, Mom? I would have been with you."

"Kids grow up, Todd. It seems like a long time from twelve to when you leave for university, and for the child, it is. Think of all that happens in those years. But for parents, it's barely a blip. Then you're gone. What was I going to do? Everybody I knew was married."

He noted that she did not use the word "single," or even "divorced," to describe her potential situation back then.

"So I did what the old saying said—I grinned and beared it." They both laughed at her grammatical tease. "Bore it. And when your dad died, I just picked up and moved on. Having the house and my memories of you there helped." She didn't mention her husband, which explained the absence of photos on the end tables. Neither had Todd seen the albums of family snapshots they kept while he grew up.

"Then I took that spill, and life changed again." They didn't refer to her fall often now, since her recovery and rehab were sailing along smoothly.

Until this talk, he hadn't realized how important his hockey had been to her, nor how it had given her hope. Maybe if he had been aware of this, he would have played harder, taken more risks, tried to make of himself the player that a father would have wanted to watch.

His big moment in the final game in Peterborough in 1992 had been a turning point. After that, he had stopped playing hockey until he was in graduate school, when he was persuaded to take a spot on his department's club team. He'd enjoyed it enough to continue with men's rec hockey on and off afterward, but he'd never played in a contact league again after Bantam.

As it was, he had been a relatively mediocre winger. His problem, the one that still haunted him in the form of Kenny's taunts at the Superstore the week he got home, was that he just wouldn't shoot the puck, even after Bob had worked with him individually on the skill. No matter the situation, no matter how clear the lane to the net was, he would freeze. His eyes would dart from the goalkeeper to the other players on the ice, and his brain would tell him that someone else on the shift had a better angle than he did. Most of the time, the impulse was right, and the pass would go off, giving another kid the opportunity to be the hero. Todd never wanted to risk muffing the shot and instead was happy notching the helper.

Would scoring a few goals have changed the dynamics between him and his dad, perhaps drawing his father into Todd's hockey world and giving him a reason to stay sober? That was the logic of the family member of an alcoholic, but he and his mom both knew that his dad had to take responsibility for his own behavior and that his drinking was not the result of any short-comings of Todd or his mom.

> The modern puck is one by three inches and weighs about six ounces. It is made of vulcanized rubber. Precursors include wooden pucks and balls made of wood or rubber, some wrapped in leather. At one point, wooden pucks were square. The rounded edges came in the 1880s. During modern NHL games, pucks remain frozen so that when used, they don't bounce as much as they might otherwise.

As the conversation continued, Todd's mom revealed the mess that her life had been, most of which she'd kept from him. A couple of car wrecks, money troubles after the plant shut down and the general sense of loneliness and abandonment she had felt. These were what she had been forced to survive.

The light outside started to change, indicating that suppertime was coming. Todd went to stand, but his mom put her hand on his, holding him in his chair while she summarized: "I loved your dad, Todd, despite his drinking. That wasn't who he was. I still saw him as a good man, and he tried his best with you. He really did. So all the problems I had to put up with, I just put up with. Maybe I didn't know any better at the time, but staying seemed like the right thing to do, and I don't regret it. But now, I see what I missed, all the time I lost. That part doesn't seem fair. Not fair at all."

She shared these thoughts on an afternoon when it looked like the opportunity for such talks in this setting, distanced as they were from the familiar surroundings of the house, might end. She was nearly well enough to come home.

Todd had the house in pretty good shape by the time his mom was ready to return to it. The survey he had done in the early days he'd been home helped him figure out how to prioritize his time and what expenses might be coming down the pike. He had almost finished his list of tasks for outside the house when he turned to the interior. He still had to organize and sort some of his dad's old junk.

There were tools in the basement and the garage, as well as camping gear from his father's fishing excursions with his work buddies. His dad had been an outdoorsman. Rods and reels, portable camping stoves and lanterns were the remnants of his pastimes, none of which his son had shared in. Todd had no plans to ever use any of what he found, but he couldn't bring himself to just pitch it, either. These trips had, after all, been meaningful to his father.

He had asked his mom if it was okay to go through his dad's belongings and identify a few things to keep. She said that was fine, but being alone in the basement with all his father's stuff made Todd feel uneasy, like the old man would come charging in any minute and demand to know what he was doing.

Todd and his dad hadn't been close by any means, though as he grew up, Todd hadn't recognized the distance between them as a loss. He just figured that this was how fathers and sons got along. When Todd learned about generation gaps in Social Studies class in high school, his life made more sense to him. But it wasn't until much later that he gained a full understanding of what a parent's alcoholism can do to a child, depriving him of the ability to trust and making him unsure of his own self-worth.

He shouldered an old metal ice chest up the stairs and through the door at the landing that led into the kitchen. He headed back downstairs for another load, wishing that instead of going through the detritus of camping gear, he was looking at hockey memorabilia, like what was probably found in Bob MacIntosh's house after his death. Most kids in hockey country dream at one time or another that their father had been an NHLer before they were born. If called upon, Todd would have gladly taken on the job of sorting through the old hockey sweaters and sticks he assumed Bob owned, not simply because of the intimations of a glamorous hockey life Bob might have had, but because of what the man had meant to him.

Bob had offered Todd the stability of a father figure, making up for some of the lack of closeness in Todd's relationship with his own dad. Being able to look up to an adult male and trust him, and his moods, had created a bond that Todd never shared with his own father.

Bob had been tough on Todd and the other players. Hockey demanded that. But he'd also been understanding. When he raised his voice, which was seldom, they knew it was because he was trying to get through to them. Bob's words mattered, more even to himself than to the kids, and his tone betrayed the intensity he felt about the game and drove them to be better players.

His passion was hockey, and Todd's knowledge that the old coach had been a former NHLer made sense of how he had criticized their game. Bob knew what to say because he'd experienced the game at its highest level. But he didn't care whether any of the kids he coached would ever make anything of themselves in hockey. His absolute belief in them wasn't about where they'd be in ten years. His focus was on their game right then and there, as thirteen- and fourteen-year-olds.

Todd tossed old blankets and towels into the discard pile he had made in the center of the furnace room, the memories of Bob flowing back to him, along with some regrets.

He hadn't appreciated the guy as much as he should have. Only from the distance of time could he recognize that the lessons Bob had taught the boys transcended hockey.

Todd lamented never taking the chance to knock on his door, walk in for a cup of tea and tell him how much his friendship had meant to him. Not for what he had done for him out on the Pond, but for being there when Todd needed him.

His cleaning chores forgotten, he was mulling over a plan to repay Bob, even though he was gone, when the phone rang. Todd ran upstairs. His mom. Her doctor had confirmed that she was coming home within days, a week at the very outside. He hung up and descended into the basement once more. He would have to increase his efforts to spruce up the place, skipping the garage, where she was unlikely to go, and concentrating on the TV room. The camping stuff that remained would have to be piled neatly and left for later.

As he gathered a stack of outdated magazines and started toward the garbage can to toss them, he realized that his mom wouldn't be able to go down the stairs to the basement for a while. He would have to move the TV upstairs. He knew she would hate that.

The one pet peeve his mom had all during his youth was that she absolutely did not want the television placed in the living room. "When you do that, it's on all day," she'd said. "Even when no one's watching it." She wasn't concerned about the high hydro bill. For her, the flowing babble of game shows in the morning and soap operas in the afternoon somehow equated to a lifestyle that she felt was beneath her.

He leaned over the TV and unscrewed the cable connection at the back. He'd have to figure out how to drill a tiny hole to the living room upstairs to string the wire through. For that, the old man's tools would come in handy.

Todd lifted the television off the table, balancing it against his chest as he made for the stairs. He could hear his dad's voice in his head. "Lift with your legs, not with your back." Although he would have barked out the advice, the old man would have had Todd's best interest at heart anyway.

CHAPTER
eight

Around Thanksgiving each year, Todd carried out the same ritual: he played his Tragically Hip collection from start to finish on his iPod, and nothing else. "Fifty Mission Cap," "We Are the Same," "Vaccination Scar"—all of these songs evoked a feeling that went with the season as much as Christmas songs reminded him of December.

As October days wound toward Halloween, the advent of cooler temperatures meant he couldn't go outside and skip a coat anymore. Fall also meant hockey was starting. In his mom's neighborhood, Todd saw the change in seasons in the growing number of street hockey games being played after school. When he lived in Toronto, the arrival of fall meant Leafs-mania would begin, a phenomenon that could not be ignored, even if you rooted for another team, as he did. In Queenston, some people were loyal to the Leafs, but others favored Montreal, which was his team, or Boston. It didn't matter which was your favorite—the desire to lace up the skates once again became overwhelming as the air grew colder.

As he was slinging on a jacket before jumping in the car to visit his mom, Todd's thoughts turned to the Pond. It wouldn't be long before ice formed there, but he had no idea whether anyone skated on it these days. All the evidence on his last visit suggested the area was neglected.

The air was a bit sharp, but Todd and his mom sat out-side anyway, on the same patio they'd been using since his first visit in August. Now, the trees around the grounds of the facility were yellow, orange and red, and some leaves had started to fall. The few that the groundskeeper hadn't raked up were swirling in tiny whirlwinds that made them skitter across the patio stones. "Do you want to go inside?" Todd offered. His mom sat on a chair opposite him, a small table between them. She'd brought a blanket out with her and had it draped across her knees.

"No, I'm fine, thank you," she replied. She had come to see herself as separate from "the old ladies in this place," as she called them when out of earshot. Going inside would be a con-cession to being like them, huddling against the cold far before winter descended and made staying indoors inevitable.

Todd zipped up his jacket and stuffed his hands in the pockets. "Hockey's in the air, I think," he said. "Do you remember how things changed around this time of year?" he continued. "I mean, for me and my friends?" We'd put the baseball mitts and bats away and get out our footballs. But deep down, we knew football wasn't going to last long. Hockey was coming."

"You boys never put your hockey stuff away com-pletely, Todd. You'd play baseball in the morning in the summertime, and by afternoon, I'd see you out on the drive-way with Timmy Reid taking shots on goal. If there were enough of you around, you'd start a game on the street. That went on all year round."

Todd didn't remember hockey being so all-pervasive in their lives. They also played in soccer leagues in the summer and practiced the game in backyards around the neighborhood. "You don't think we ever stopped playing hockey?" he asked his mom.

"I don't *think* so. I *know*. You'd argue over who was going to be Denis Potvin or Gretzky under the full blaze of a summer sky. I heard you from the kitchen window. It was always the same." When Todd was a kid, air conditioning was a rare luxury, so windows were left open for the breeze during the warmer months.

Often, street hockey players use old game sticks no longer fit for the ice. Sometimes, these sticks are used for so long that their blades become shaved down by the pavement. They become thin and pointy, their narrowness making it hard to stickhandle a bouncing tennis ball. Sticks like that, called "toothpicks," are highly prized, but they eventually break. At that point, a street hockey blade can be attached to the leftover shaft.

"But by this time of year, at least as I remember it, there was nothing else," Todd said. "Once the World Series was over, we'd pretty much forget about all the other sports and live hockey." He looked to his mom for confirmation, though he didn't doubt the truth of his statement.

"You'd start asking me every day before you went to school 'How long until the ice comes?' and you'd ask the same question again at bedtime. I guess you thought that, *poof,* from one day to the next, it would be cold enough to freeze that Pond of yours."

What his mom said was true. It was how it had seemed to him. It also felt like the more he asked, the slower the ice would form, the same way Christmas could be accidentally delayed because a kid bugged his mom endlessly about it. Still, he didn't let a day go by without making the query.

"Childhood isn't all it's cracked up to be, is it, Mom?" Todd mused. "I mean, if adults want something, they figure out how to get it. Or they realize there's a waiting period, and they find other ways to occupy themselves. Kids just obsess until it drives them crazy."

"You're describing yourself, dear. I'm pretty sure you were the kid with the most singular focus on the planet. Your dad used to talk about your one-track mind, remember?"

Todd's father had said that, but as a kid, he just put it down to general statements that adults love to say. He didn't give much credit to the old man for a truthful and accurate analysis of his personality.

In hindsight, however, he could see that he did have a one-track mind. When he was ten or twelve, his focus was hockey. Later, in high school, that focus had changed to getting good enough marks to get out of Queenston. Then, in university, qualifying to get into the MBA program after his BA. Once there, the job. And then eventually, the Tia Rosita venture.

"Do *you* think I have a one-track mind, Mom?" The question rolled out before he could decide whether or not he wanted to hear the answer.

"You do, Todd. But it's not a curse. It's a blessing, if you can focus it on what you want. You've done that—"

"Up until now," he interrupted her. "But over the last couple of months, it hasn't worked so well. Nothing's happening with the job search. And as for Sarah, well, you know, that's gone for good. I'm kind of stuck right now. Nothing's working."

"You're forgetting one thing. What would I have done without you here?" said his mom. "Withered in this place?"

He recognized a hint of desperation in her voice. Maybe being here and being a son wasn't such a lowly calling, after all. Still, feeling needed did nothing to quell his fear that if he didn't get back into a job soon, he'd be in Queenston for the year, and if he stayed for the year, he might be in town forever. What he'd do for a living was entirely unclear to him. How unhappy he'd be, however, was as clear as crystal. He could not admit that this fatalism was exaggerated.

Driving home after his visit with his mom, Todd looked at the fields next to the road. The crops were harvested, and the tractors were working their way around, plowing, getting the land ready for the stillness of winter and then the next growing season.

In an age of global warming, it was uncertain when winter would come. Even as far north as the town sat, where snow and a white Christmas were the norm, it didn't mean that the freeze would happen before Santa was out doing his work. But this year, winter arrived about the same time as it always had when Todd was a kid. It wasn't much past his birthday in early November that it started to snow.

His mom had been discharged a few weeks after Thanksgiving. At home, she was getting along fine, using a cane for stability and returning to the rehab center three times a week to keep up her strength-building program.

"I think they just like you in here, Mom," Todd told her one afternoon as he dropped her off at the door for her two-hour session. She smiled as she got out of the car, then scowled as a nurse wheeled her through the front doors. "It's regulations," she had been told at her first return to Bayside. Using a wheelchair was a blow to her dignity. She didn't say it, but it was obvious that she felt proud of how ably she'd recovered, largely because of her own efforts in physiotherapy.

Needing an activity for the two hours he had to wait for her, Todd generally brought a book and sat outside reading. But with the weather change, it was too cold to do that. Other days, he picked up the groceries, but this week, they had already done that together. So instead, he decided to drive out to the Pond and see if the ice had come in yet. The question had been jangling around in his mind since he'd felt the first snap of cold and seen snowflakes floating down outside the kitchen window.

When he got there, he saw that a thin sheet of ice covered the space between the earthen banks. He walked toward it. One end was thicker, maybe a half an inch. Not strong enough to skate on without being destroyed by the skate blades, obviously, but water was pooling in the low spots and freezing. It could be the start of a rink.

He looked behind him to where the Shack stood. Next to it was the tap that the city had installed years before to give a source of water to build up the ice. Left to Mother Nature, the Pond wouldn't get thick enough to skate on, especially with the number of kids who used it during its prime, nor was it large enough to accommodate all who wanted to play on it. Flooding remedied both problems.

He tried to turn the tap, which didn't budge. He went to the car to get the pair of garden gloves his mom insisted he keep for use when pumping gas. Coming back, he slipped them on and grabbed the spigot tight, giving it a firm twist. "Lefty loosey, righty tighty"—the mnemonic device was one useful lesson his old man had left him with.

With a squeak, the handle turned, the twisting action suddenly becoming easier. After a sputtering sound that came as the tap released some air, water gushed out. At first, it was brown, sediment and rust mixing because the faucet hadn't been used. It might have been as old as last spring, or maybe two or five or ten springs old. Soon, the water ran clear. If anyone wanted to make ice, all that was needed was a hose. The one that had been here when he was a kid was heavy and black. Not like the green garden hoses that people used in the backyard to water their tomatoes.

The water started to pool at his feet. He shut the tap off and looked around, the conviction forming that he could make skateable ice on the Pond once more.

His idea existed in the vein of "If I build it, they will come." But they very well might not. The proof was in the decrepit remains of the Shack that used to keep kids warm but now looked like a long-forgotten farm shed.

Who says a pond has to be a pond? Dennis Milligan, one of the NHL Off-ice Officials in Anaheim, grew up in California. But that didn't stop him and his siblings from turning their backyard into a hockey paradise. A neighbor put in a pool, but he could never understand why his kids weren't having the same fun as the Milligan children, judging by the sounds he heard coming from behind their house.

In some measure, Todd's notion resembled the desperate gesture of someone lost. By recreating the Pond, he would become the lonely single guy who, having failed in the big city, was now reduced to playing shinny with a bunch of kids every afternoon after school. Even worse, he might end up skating a puck alone, because the Pond had long fallen out of favor with the local children. Yet if nothing else, reviving the Pond would give him a place to get some exercise, since the weather was getting too cold to carry on jogging. He could work out some frustrations with hard stop-and-start drills.

He decided to dive in and do it. The worst that could happen was that he'd get the rink ready, skate around a couple of days, get tired of the cold, drive home and never return. All he'd be out was the cost of the hose. Yet, at its best, the plan to make a rink would be no different from what Bob had done. A few kids had seen Bob at the Pond, which at the time was cared for by their fathers. He'd started to turn up regularly to watch them. Maybe he had endured some strange looks, but it had been his idea to build the Shack, and his efforts turned the Pond into the town's unofficial practice facility and proving ground for its players. Bob's gesture hadn't been a desperate act; it had come from the heart and offered the kids who used the Pond a chance to excel at hockey that they wouldn't have had otherwise.

Todd discussed his plans with his mom when he picked her up, probing her to see whether she thought building a rink would make him look like some lonely, pathetic bachelor with no other life.

"That's nearly the silliest thing I've ever heard," she said. "No, you know what? That *is* the silliest thing I've ever heard." She smiled, then pronounced her verdict, "If you want to make ice and skate on it, then do it. 'Just do it right,' your dad would have said."

To make sure he was doing the job correctly, Todd searched the Internet for advice when they got home. Backyard rinks were a popular topic, and most people said that the best way to build one was to first lay down a plastic sheet as a base for the ice to form on. Hardware stores and online retailers sold huge sheets just for this purpose, but this had never been necessary at the Pond. The natural ice that formed from the water that pooled there gave a base. He decided to do things like Bob and the dads before him had done and just flood the area.

The next day, Todd was back. It was an hour before dark. He'd bought a heavy-duty hose from the hardware store downtown along with a nozzle-end sprayer. He slung the hose over his shoulder and hauled it down to the faucet. He had even remembered to buy a washer so that the tap wouldn't leak. That had been his dad's influence, too. "You get a puddle there, pretty soon it's frozen," the old man had said, talking about their own garden hose that he used to wash the salt off his car in winter. "You forget and go to turn it on, and you're on your ass." Directness was his preferred method of instruction.

Todd connected the hose, turning the coupling tight so that not even a single drip could escape. He turned on the tap, closed the nozzle end and walked with the hose to the far side of where the rink would soon be. It had snowed overnight. A light dusting covered the thin layer of ice that had formed naturally. Too much snow to flood over. He'd have to go home for the shovel. He reversed his steps and drove home, returning with an old snowplow-style shovel with an aluminum blade and wooden handle. Once the ice was cleared, he sprayed it. Working from the far side of the Pond, he used a rhythmic back-and-forth motion to make sure the water was evenly distributed. It took him less than twenty minutes.

The trick, he discovered, was to regulate the water flow. His first impulse had been to fully soak the surface, the word "flooding" seeming to suggest this course of action. Soon, he discovered that this method pooled excess water that would be too deep to freeze quickly. The key was to mist the water out of the nozzle so that it froze right away. That way, layer could be built on layer.

By the end of the week, with diligent work on his part every day, the ice was thick enough to skate on. The Pond wasn't large enough for a horde of kids to use, but for Todd, alone with a puck on the end of his stick, it was more than adequate. He planned to expand the rink surface to its original dimensions as time went on by gradually flooding further on each side of where the natural ice base had formed. The snowbanks that he piled up around the sides would act as boards that would define the ice surface, just like in the old days.

Marcel Dionne played on two rinks—one at the school across the street from his house and another in his backyard. He could look out his living room window and see who was on the ice at any given time, and as soon as the first few guys appeared, he would go out, too. His skills were noticed at the age of 10, and he eventually played for Detroit and Los Angeles, amassing 731 goals during his NHL career.

He stickhandled through imaginary defenders like he'd done practically every winter day during his childhood, whirling around like an NHLer on his way to scoring the OT winner that would secure him and his teammates the Stanley Cup.

As he turned and skated toward the Shack, the years since he had done this with Bob looking on were erased. He felt the same delight as when he'd been a child on the Pond, skating in the winter cold for nothing but the pure joy of doing it.

With his mom now back at home, the house was more alive than it had been in the nearly three months he'd been there on his own. When he felt the need for time alone, he could go downstairs, since his mom wasn't supposed to climb stairs yet. But with the TV moved to the living room, he really didn't have an excuse to be in the basement. His refuge was to continue sorting through junk, which allowed him some private space and time to think.

Being hip-deep in old boxes on a weekday morning didn't do much for his self-esteem, however. Everyone he knew, all his university classmates, Sarah and even the people at Lydle were probably sitting at their desks right now. They were on the phone, tracking sales numbers, or they were meeting with suppliers. All meaningful tasks, productive of something. The guys among them were dressed in Calvin Klein suits with complementing ties and Italian shoes, or at any rate, that's what he would have been wearing were he working at this moment.

In sharp contrast, Todd was grubbing around his mother's basement, sifting through treasures left over from childhood, wearing his jogging suit. It wasn't exactly good for the ego. The fear that he was becoming mired here, a Queenston resident with few prospects, wore on his mind, no matter how irrational the idea was. Christmas was coming, and hiring would stop until after the holidays. That meant another month or six weeks, minimum, before he'd even have the hope of an interview that would get him back into the corporate game. Once more, he cursed his faith in Tia Rosita.

Opening the top box stacked next to where his hockey memorabilia was, he found his old train set. His Transformers toys. A well-worn stuffed bear he had called "Gingie." Some Hardy Boys mysteries. None of it had been thrown away. Most moms pitched the junk when their kids were old enough to fly the coop. Or they sold the stuff at garage sales, watching eager buyers rifling through boxes of hockey cards hoping to find valuable rookies.

Maybe his mom had forgotten about the boxes, or maybe she had decided it was up to him to clear them when he had the chance. Or it might have had something to do with her wanting to hold onto those days when Todd was home and her family was intact. Although she had had to deal with an alcoholic spouse, she at least had her son to give her life focus. Now, however, that phase of her life was over, and she was free to make her own choices, without taking her husband's needs into account.

Todd's childhood was well behind him also. It was time for him to throw its remnants out with the weekly garbage. Todd knew he would never be able to part with all of these treasures, but he was determined to thin out the collection, discarding items he had no honest memory of.

He opened the box next on the pile, expecting to find the usual mix of old baseball caps, stuffed animals missing one eye and Hot Wheels cars with half their paint worn off. Instead, he discovered his scrapbook. A photo album, really, but his mom had turned it into a scrapbook by inserting construction paper pages in with the plastic photo pages. He flipped open the front cover and found an old report card with his mom's signature at the bottom. Next was a series of photos. Him, at ten, as a catcher behind home plate. His soccer team at twelve or thirteen. He and a friend stuffing their faces with chocolate bars while watching TV. Then came the hockey section, which was devoted almost entirely to the 1992 team.

There was a group photo taken next to the team's bus, the boys standing beside some unidentifiable roadside stop. The bus was a rental, a school bus painted white instead of the usual yellow. Next to it were fifteen or so kids, most of whom were wearing Queenston hockey jackets. On one end of the group stood Bob. On the other was their coach, Mr. Templeton. Todd was standing slightly left of center in the photo, next to his two linemates, Dave Joseph and Timmy Reid.

He flipped the page. Scene after scene from that magical year appeared in the form of local newspaper clippings.

He took the scrapbook into what had been the TV room to sit down. He steadied himself to contemplate the memories the articles held. The task would occupy much of what remained of the morning and take him places he wouldn't want to go, emotionally. But he felt he was ready.

The pages of the scrapbook revealed the story of what some people thought of as the greatest year in Queenston hockey. At first, the articles from the *Investigator* were just tiny clippings. One heading was "QCHL," for Queenston Community Hockey League. Under that, the word "Bantam" appeared, and then a brief story about a game that had been played sometime during that 1991–92 season. His mom had saved the newspaper stories that reported on his games, and on occasion, mentioned his name as a goal scorer. She hadn't kept whole pages, so none of the stories had dates on them.

But as he turned the pages of the book, the stories got larger blocks of copy, and their headlines were more spectacular, until "Local Squad to Contest Tourney" appeared. The story detailed that a group of local boys had won a playoff among a number of teams from the region to decide who would compete in the yearly Bantam tournament in Peterborough that marked the supreme level of achievement in hockey for their age group. It was the biggest sports news of the day, as signaled by the amount of space the story took up on the front of the B section of the *Investigator*.

The excitement of qualifying was firmly lodged in Todd's memory. The regionals had been held in Odessa, an hour's drive away. They'd traveled there on the bus, all of them as a team. That was Bob's idea. He thought that if each boy's parents drove him, there would be too many distractions, not enough focus on what they needed to do. So Bob had rented the bus, which they boarded at ten on Saturday morning to head out.

Bob didn't put up with any tomfoolery once they were on the road, and he didn't give them the usual adult "You'll distract the driver" speech. When they got on, he was already in the front row. Once they were out on the highway with the bus comfortably rolling over the asphalt, he stood up and turned around to face them. They grew quiet.

"You boys know why we're on this bus, and that's to get to the tournament. I wanted you here, together, rather than with your folks. I'm glad they're coming to the games; it'll be good for you to have them there. But right now, your focus can't be on the excitement of having them watch you play, and you shouldn't be dreaming of becoming heroes. You're here to play hockey the way you've been taught to play it. Each one of you needs to think about the skills you've worked hard to develop. Even more, you need to think about how we work as a team."

They had started out that year as a ragtag bunch, though by virtue of having survived a process of tryouts and cuts, they were the best of their age group in town. But they hadn't gelled as a team until just before Christmas, when the extra practices at the Pond started to pay off. It was now a couple of days after New Year's. Winning the tournament in Odessa would send them to Peterborough in three weeks.

"You guys weren't a group when you started. Nobody's passes connected. Nobody got back to help out the netminder. Your skating wasn't up to scratch. But you've learned." They all knew why—it could be put down to what Bob had done for them and his decision early on to form his lines and stick with them, rather than to continually mix and match various players in order to find the right combination. His philosophy was rooted, he had explained, in the old ways of hockey.

He always used the same example when describing his concept of team play: "You look at Boston's Kraut line— Schmidt, Dumart and Bauer—those guys could find each other with a pass in a dark tunnel with ninety-nine rats trying to get the loose puck. Why? Because they'd done it a thousand times. You don't have that kind of experience, but you play together consistently, and you'll get it."

Todd and his linemates had heard the speech a hundred times if they had heard it once. Everyone else on the team had heard it, too—from the first-line superstar center to the defense. It didn't matter that they had no idea when the Kraut line had played because Bob told the tale with such conviction.

As the bus driver exited the highway, Bob continued. "Now, we're going in there with something at stake." He paused to regain his balance as the bus lurched over a rail-road track, a signal that they were getting close to Odessa and would be arriving at the arena within a short time.

"We're trying to get somewhere. We're trying to put Queenston on the map, and getting invited to Peterborough will do that. Will we win there? I don't know. It doesn't matter today. Today, and tomorrow, we've gotta win *here*." He emphasized the last word as he slapped his palm down on the top of the seat he was facing.

He then looked at each boy to reinforce his meaning. They sat still, their eyes never leaving his as his gaze moved steadily from the front of the bus to the back.

"You can worry about being heroes after this is over. For now, it's all for one and one for all." He turned around and sat down. None of them knew what to do next. Staying silent and contemplating what they'd been told seemed like the right thing to do. Nobody stirred until a few of the guys started to whisper, unable to contain their excitement about the game they would play that afternoon.

Heading into the arena, Todd saw his parents standing in the lobby alongside the other moms and dads. His team wouldn't play until after lunch, but Bob and Coach had wanted them at the rink early. They piled their gear in the lobby for one of the dads to watch until it was time to get dressed. The moms had packed lunches for them, and they had to sit in the stands, as a group, and eat while they watched the Kenora team. Their coach said Kenora was the odds-on favorite to win the tournament and go to Peterborough, and for that reason, the Rebels would have to go through the Thistles. He wanted them to watch Kenora play, to try to learn what they could about defending against them.

Todd sat with his linemates. "Look at the goalie," he said as he watched the Thistles' netminder. "He's got a good glove hand." The kid had gobbled up several pucks with his mitt, which he also used to make saves that might have been made with his stick or a leg.

Perhaps the most famous contemporary "pond" is the Rideau Canal in Ottawa. It has a stretch nearly five miles long where people can skate their cares away. Some think that it would be the ideal place for an NHL Winter Classic game, with no official boards and just a couple of nets spread nearly 200 feet apart, like in an indoor arena.

"Yeah," Dave said, "maybe too good. He's getting everything shot at him with that trapper." He was thinking along the same lines as Todd. If the kid depended on his mitt that much, he was probably vulnerable elsewhere. Together, they studied the boy for a sign of what that weakness might be.

The game drew to a close with the expected result, Kenora solidly thumping the opposing team, 6–2. It gave them the right to play in the afternoon game on Sunday that would determine which team went to Peterborough.

Todd and his buddies headed to their dressing room. Their game was in half an hour. Most of them had a parent alongside, looking around self-consciously for something to do. Some dads chatted. Others just watched while their sons taped their sticks like they'd seen the NHLers on *Hockey Night in Canada* do. With less than fifteen minutes to go until game time, the coach yelled, "Skates!" meaning that any fathers who were there for the purpose of lacing up a kid's boots super-tight had better do it now. Five minutes after that, it was "Parents out!" The room cleared, and it was just the team, Coach and Bob, who addressed them.

"No more speeches, boys. It's just a game. Win this, and you play Kenora, but that's not for today. Right now, you need to concentrate on Apsley. They've got a few really big boys on that team. They hit. You need to keep your heads up."

Todd didn't enjoy this aspect of the game. Passing the puck, carrying it and making the occasional deke—all of these were okay. But the contact, the chance to get "leveled," as they called it, scared him. The fear of the big, crunching check that made the recipient's teeth clack together and made a foggy feeling run through his head like a fist pounding into a bucket of sand turned a fun sport into a nightmare for him. It was why pond hockey was so much better, free as it was from the violence of the indoor game.

Knowing the Apsley team was rough, Todd was glad he wasn't playing until the third shift. He'd have a chance to size up the danger and figure out if he could play it safe on the ice, avoiding the hits.

He stood up with the rest of the boys, put his stick in his left hand and gave the goalie a high five on his way out the dressing room door. Once in the hallway, he switched the stick to his right hand, blade down, the same way he always did. He'd heard while watching an NHL game that hockey players were a superstitious lot. Before he learned what the word "superstitious" meant, he had not known what to label the feeling he had to do certain things precisely the same way before every game. After he looked up the word, his behavior made perfect sense to him.

He got to the ice surface and jumped on. Already, the parents on both sides were cheering as they saw their boys coming out. Soon, the puck was dropped.

Apsley was big, but this advantage was forfeited by their lack of speed. Todd's team, relatively small in comparison, was able to get the opponent's two biggest players, both defensemen, turned around and chasing well before the first period reached its halfway point.

Bob's wisdom inspired them. "Look at them, boys," he said during the first couple of shifts. "They're big, but if you get behind them, they're not going to catch up to you. Get into the corners and get that puck. They can't hit you if you get in and get out fast enough."

Todd watched carefully from where he sat on the bench, observing his team's wingers weaving in and out of the corners in a flash, feeding the puck to the front of the net. The big defensemen for Apsley, after a while, stopped chasing them into the corners. Knowing that they weren't going to arrive first, they didn't want to leave the slot wide open. So they parked on the goal line or in the slot and tried to disrupt the shooters who were taking threaded passes out from the boards below the hash marks. In doing so, they gave the wingers free rein with the puck.

Todd decided while waiting for his first shift that if his teammates could go into the corners without fear, then so could he. He went out and lined up opposite the other team's left wing in his own end, for a faceoff. The opposite center won it, but he drew the puck back behind the winger, though not far enough for the defenseman on that side to grab it. Todd jumped around the winger and grabbed the puck off the boards. He chipped it past the defenseman and put on his best burst to get around him, planning to pick up the puck on the other side.

As he tried to accelerate, he felt the threading of a stick between his skate blades, and he crashed to the ice with a *whump*. His breath left him as he hit the ice, but he still had the presence of mind to swing at the puck to center it to Dave. He got only part of his stick on it, and the whistle blew as the defenseman touched the puck, then skated over to the box to serve his penalty.

Todd groaned while forcing himself to his knees, a couple of teammates coming over to help. He leaned on his stick for support as he got up, then he skated to the bench. He wouldn't be on the power play, but his contribution had been in hustling to get his team the man advantage.

As he leaned over on the bench trying to suck in some wind, Bob walked down to where he was.

"That's it, Todd. That's hustle. You sized up the situation and used your speed. Good play." Todd nodded, still not able to catch his breath.

"What did you plan to do if you'd picked up that puck while you were still on your feet?" Bob added.

It was the eternal question for him. Todd wasn't a risk-taker. Passing was always safer than carrying the puck himself. His strategy would have been to shovel the puck to Dave or Timmy at the red line, rather than taking it into the Apsley end. Bob was suggesting that he shouldn't do that reflexively, but try the alternative. From the safety of the bench, it seemed entirely logical that he could have carried the puck into the other team's end.

Todd played it out in his mind. He could have put the puck on his forehand and shoveled it in front of him as he scooted down the right-side boards. If the big goof chasing him caught up to him, he could have dumped the puck to the center. Otherwise, waiting with it, maybe even taking it deep into the corner and then pausing until Dave could find his way to an open spot in the slot, would have worked.

In reality, going into the corner would have been like turning on a neon sign that said, "Hit Me!" in big, bold letters, even though the Apsley defensemen seemed to be abandoning the corners to the Rebels' forwards. So, as nice as the idea of skating the puck was, he wouldn't have taken the chance.

He looked over the boards at the play going on, his team still with the man advantage. Terry, the first line center, and by far Queenston's best player, had the puck in the Apsley slot. Terry's back was to the net because he had just picked up the pass. He spun around, put his weight on his left foot and whistled a wrist shot past the goalie, who was already halfway down and couldn't stretch his oversized trapper out far enough to get it. The score was 1–0, and although Todd didn't really have a part in the goal, he considered that he had an unofficial assist, since his good work in drawing the power play had set the events in motion.

The Apsley team tried to get under the Rebels' skin as the game went on. They weren't openly dirty, but they played on the edge in a manner the Queenston team hadn't seen before. They slashed and hacked, and they trash-talked to make the opposition uncomfortable. Late in the second period, Todd was out again, once more facing the defenseman who had tripped him. As he skated out to take his winger's spot for the draw, the guy said, "Next time, Seven, I'm going to hurt you more than that." Todd was caught off guard and didn't know how to respond. He had no counterthreat in mind to throw back at the kid.

As Todd watched the third period tick away, with his team leading 4–1, the reality of the game sunk in. Hockey at the all-star level entailed hits, injuries, threats and a general sense that if a player didn't watch the other guys at all times, they would take every opportunity to flatten him. This wasn't fun. It sucked.

The Rebels headed to the dressing room after their 5–1 win and were in the process of taking their equipment off when Bob spoke.

"Boys, you did it! You won the game, and that gets you into the final against Kenora tomorrow. The good news is that the Thistles don't play like Apsley. They're not goons. They don't have a single guy nearly as big as those two monsters on defense today."

Todd looked around to confirm that his was not the only sigh of relief in the room. If the Thistles weren't scary like these guys, it would be easy.

"But that's not what we're worried about with Kenora," Bob added. "They don't have to hit you and pound you to beat you. They're fast. They're tricky, and they're smart. You're going to have to remember the skills we've worked on all this time if you want to win. And every one of you has to have a better game than you had today." He looked around the room, a mix of warning and encouragement etched on his face. The players sat still, equipment in their hands, but none of them reached for his hockey bag.

"Now go home, watch *Hockey Night in Canada*, and *get to bed*! I need you rested. We'll get on the bus at ten o'clock tomorrow, get here by eleven. You'll watch the consolation game between Apsley and Smithville. We'll do that together, as a sign of respect for the two teams that didn't make the final. Then, we'll get dressed for our game at one. Be ready.

And remind your moms tonight, not at nine tomorrow morning, that you'll need a lunch."

As they continued to pack up their stuff, Bob gave them one final reminder: "Don't leave those bags full all night. Air out your gear. You don't want to put it on all stinky and sweaty tomorrow afternoon!"

They filed out, got on the bus and headed for home.

The next day's routine was much like Saturday's had been, but as the Rebels' game drew close, the players were keyed up almost beyond control. They watched Apsley pound their opponents into submission to take the third-place honors, eating their lunch while the third period unfolded. Then they went down to the dressing room. Outside, a signboard had their name on it: "Queenston Rebels/Bantam Championship" it said, indicating that they were in the tournament final.

They dressed with some nervousness, throwing more than the usual number of tape wads around until Bob put a stop to it. "Save it. Save your energy for Kenora," was his simple warning. His speech before the game was a repeat admonition that Kenora was both fast and tricky with its passing.

The game was as intense as Bob said it would be. Each team played to its strength, using good puck control and precise passing. In the second period, with the score tied at one, Todd fed Dave from the right hash marks, a perfect pass that landed on his tape. Dave got off a weak shot, and the goalie had no trouble getting a leg on it.

Later in the second, the Rebels went down a man, and Todd was sent out to help kill the penalty, as sometimes happened. His intensity was what Bob prized, as he reminded Todd before he sent him out, and Todd was proud of that. He loved to be on the PK, charging out to the left defenseman, trying to block the shot, collapsing into the slot to chase down the centerman or fighting in the corner to turn up the puck and then fling it down the ice so the other team had to chase it.

He never expected to score a goal, but sometimes, the hockey gods offer up a surprise. Off a faceoff in Todd's end, the puck was squibbed back toward the blueline. The right D-man picked it up as Todd went out to cover the guy on the other side. Without looking, the right-side guy passed toward the side Todd was covering, but he didn't get enough wood on it. His half-fanned pass rolled slowly along the blueline.

Rob, the other guy playing forward on the PK with Todd, shot up the middle of the ice to grab the puck. He picked it up before the defenseman on Todd's side of the ice could get it, heading up the ice. Both defensemen made quick turns to pursue him. These were not Apsley's lumbering giants, but fast skaters whose specialty was tracking down speedy forwards.

Todd was wary of going with his teammate in case he lost the puck, since it was a man-down situation for his team. If Kenora turned it back the other way, they'd have a three-on-two. He followed a half-stride behind, pinching off the defenseman on his side of the ice as they both skated toward Kenora's net.

Rob continued up the ice, the puck in front of him. The defenseman on his left tried to grab the puck from him and missed. As the play developed, it was Rob, Todd and the remaining defenseman crossing the Kenora blueline together.

Following Bob's principle to keep it simple in such situations, Rob went right in on goal and shot, while Todd followed directly behind him as they went down the slot. Rob peeled off left as he got to the goalie, and as he moved out of view, Todd had a clear look at the netminder. He had gone down to make the save and was lying with his arms outstretched toward Todd's right side.

And there was the puck. It was rolling away from the goaltender, out into the slot and toward Todd's stick. The defenseman covering him saw it at the same time he did and reached to try to trap his stick so he couldn't get the shot. Todd picked up the puck and, using a move that he had learned while playing keep-away on the Pond, where nothing was at stake, hooked it in toward his body. He paused half a second and watched as the guy sailed past him, missing both him and the puck.

All he had to do was convert, and to do that, he didn't even have to shoot. He just had to shovel the puck on his forehand so that it rose up over the outstretched mitts. It did. He watched as the puck rolled up and over the goalie's arms, then dropped down on the other side and trickled, at one-quarter speed, over the goal line. It barely made it to the back of the net. Todd didn't care.

In the time-honored gesture of goal scorers every-where, he raised both arms above his head. He heard the roar of the crowd. A second later, his three teammates caught up with him, smothering him with hugs and pounding him on the helmet. "You did it! Way to go! You did it!" they yelled. He looked at Rob. "You just put it there, and I shoveled it in, that's all," he said, almost screaming the words.

Maybe to some it was a garbage goal, one that had been about ninety-eight percent the responsibility of the guy who had intercepted the pass, steamed up the ice, paused long enough to suss out what the netminder was going to do, and challenged him with a shot that he could stop but not control the rebound on. But to Todd, it was a rare and precious thing.

Sitting on the bench a few minutes later, Todd was completely absorbed in his goal, which was special for two reasons. He had never scored shorthanded before. And it could be the goal that would win them the game and send them to Peterborough. He watched as the seconds of the period ticked away, and then the third, Kenora desperately putting on the pressure. With every save his goalie made, he punched the boards in front of him. "One more, Michael! One more!" Todd yelled. "Hold on!" Todd's team collapsed down toward the crease to help their goalie, throwing themselves in front of the puck to keep the one-goal lead.

Coach, meanwhile, encouraged them. "Come on, guys, hold on. Get the puck out of your end. Get it out!" he yelled, his face red. Bob stood beside the coach. He wasn't yelling, but he came down the bench with advice. "Play some offense, guys. Hold the puck. They can't score if you've got it. And they're not going to score from their own end."

Todd didn't get as much ice time in the last period as in the earlier going, but he was okay with being a third-liner. He'd put in the goal, and he couldn't screw up the game from the bench. Time moved by. Three minutes became two, then one. The Thistles pulled their goalie for a final charge and took a couple of good shots as the ten-second countdown began. The final blast went wide and hit the boards behind the net as the buzzer sounded.

The Rebels charged off the bench to fling themselves into a pile on top of their victorious goaltender. In the stands, parents hugged each other and jumped up and down. Even the moms, who sometimes looked like they were only there to fill seats, understood the importance of the win and celebrated with everyone else.

Todd picked his parents out of the crowd as he got up from the pile of celebrating players and lined up to shake hands with the Kenora squad. His mom was beaming. His dad stood impassive, adopting the eternal pose of hockey modesty, pretending the day was no different from any other. The other dads were coming up behind him, grabbing him by the shoulders and then shaking his hand. When Todd skated to the boards and stepped off the ice, his father was there.

"I got it," his dad said. "The puck you scored with. I have it." He reached into his jacket pocket and pulled out the black rubber disk. He didn't explain how he had gotten the puck, but said, "When we get home, we'll paint the date on it. You've still got some model paint in your room, right?" One of their bonding moments was building a plastic model of a 1966 Mustang that Todd had received as a birthday present a couple of years before. Todd nodded to indicate he had and then went to join his teammates, their excited yells reaching out to him as he got near the dressing room.

"Todd. Todd." He heard his name being called as he held the open scrapbook on his lap and stared blankly at the wall where the TV had been. "Todd, it's time to get lunch started." His mom was always anxious to get going on this shared activity.

Todd's curiosity had been piqued by his memories, but he put his scrapbook away and went upstairs before he got to the section on the Peterborough tournament. His mom was in her now-familiar spot in the green recliner that had been his dad's. It was planted in a corner of the living room, where she could watch the TV and still keep an eye on what was going on in the kitchen.

Even with her at home, Todd was doing most of the cooking. Her doctor had expressly forbidden her to stand for long periods. Usually, Todd would give his mom a bowl of green beans to cut up or a couple of potatoes to peel while he prepared the rest of the meal. Today, he handed her some carrots, a bowl and the peeler and sat down on the couch next to where the chair was.

"Mom, you know, I was just looking through that scrapbook you made when I was a kid," he began. "And the Odessa and Peterborough stuff is in there." He looked at her, and her smile told him that she remembered, perhaps better than he did. "It got me thinking—you promised to tell me Bob's story. What was up with that guy?"

"He was a hero to you boys," she said, sounding as if she were using one of the clichés hockey players spout after games. "He knew hockey. And he didn't mind spending the time it took to teach you." Ring up cliché number two.

Todd was hoping for something more authentic, some details that would account for the man's motivations. "I know that if it hadn't been for him that year, we never would have made it to Peterborough," he replied. "Though, of course, it was my goal that got us past Kenora." There was no harm in mentioning his glorious moment. "What I don't get is why he did it. I mean, none of us were his kids. He wasn't even from here, right?" He looked at his mom again, who nodded to indicate he should go on. "So why would he spend all that time, every afternoon and the evenings, doing those special practices for a bunch of kids he really didn't have any reason to help out? I could understand it if this had been his hometown or if one of us had been his son or even a nephew…" He let the sentence trail off, leaving her to decide what to tell him, if she knew anything at all.

"Well, you know how your dad had a hard time fighting the bottle?" Todd held his head level, not interrupting her. "That was Bob, too. Only he got a hold of himself." Her selection of words betrayed her roots in a time when alcoholism was a choice, rather than a disease, and when recovery was seen as a simple matter of self-control. Of course, she had since learned better.

"But before he did, he let it ruin his own hockey career."

Todd wandered over to his laptop, which was sitting on the dining room table. "I keep meaning to see what Bob did in the NHL." He turned on the computer and waited while it flashed to life. Then he opened his browser and typed in "www.hockeytruth.com." Whatever Bob had accomplished in hockey would be there.

A second later, the details appeared. "Robert Daniel MacIntosh. Born August 17, 1935 (?)." The question mark was in reference to the loss of birth records Todd's mom had told him about. "Property of Chicago Black Hawks." There had been no draft back then. That didn't start until 1963. In Bob's day, a prospect just signed a form, called a "C Form," indicating his intent to play for a certain club. Bob's Junior days had been with the St. Catharines Teepees of the Ontario Hockey Association in the early to mid-1950s. His pro days, according to the website, had been from 1955 to 1959, and he'd played in exactly five NHL games, with the Black Hawks, as they spelled their name at that time. The rest of his career had been in the minors.

"Hey, I thought you told me Bob was with the Bruins? It says here it was Chicago."

His mom's forehead crinkled and she pursed her lips, suggesting that she couldn't quite recall the specifics of the phone conversation she'd had with Todd at the time Bob died. "Chicago, then," she said. "Yes, that must have been what the minister said."

Todd searched for a history of the Hawks, finding one at *Wikipedia*. It said, "Chicago was the model of futility in the NHL. Between 1945 and 1958, they only made the playoffs twice."

He repeated the information to his mom, adding, "So Bob was around twenty-one when he got his NHL break. He was in his mid-fifties when the Rebels went to Peterborough, so his playing days were behind him by thirty-five years." He looked up from the screen and continued, "How'd you know about the drinking?"

"I found out because at his funeral, a couple of older gentlemen who had known him in hockey in the 1950s gave eulogies. They talked about their days on the road, saying what a fun-loving guy he was. They meant well, but to me, given my experience with your father, everything they said was code for 'He drank. A lot.' I felt really sad for him."

"Did it make you wonder whether we were ever in danger, being so close to him, I mean?" The question reflected the fear contemporary parents have for their children, fed by news stories that make it seem like every kid is constantly in peril.

She went on without acknowledging Todd's question, those fears not being something she had ever thought about. "I learned his history from his sister, who also spoke at the funeral. I mean, the private information she told me after the service. I made a point of talking to her alone. She said that after hockey, Bob hit bottom. He ended up in Montreal, living in a rescue mission. He spent as many nights there as he was allowed to. Then he'd wander the streets, or crash at his girlfriend's apartment until his behavior became too unpredictable when he was drinking, and she would kick him out. He repeated this cycle for maybe three or four years, until his family decided they should intervene."

"You said he got a hold of himself. Was that because of his family?"

"His sister and her husband, who from what I gathered was a pretty big guy, went to Montreal one weekend and found him. They got him to agree to come back to their place, which was here. They dried him out, and I guess at that point, he'd had enough of his old ways. Sometimes that happens." What she really meant was that she wished her deceased husband had had a similar experience.

"But his sister said that by then, Bob's talent as a hockey player was gone. He was almost thirty, and he'd pretty much burned his bridges in hockey. So he stayed here. He ended up doing okay for himself. He was a smart man. He built a paving business, running a couple of crews. You remember that. When you were really little, you loved to watch them do the driveways around town, in the days when new houses were still being built."

Todd didn't remember, though it was the kind of thing that a five-year-old boy might find fascinating.

"When he started to get a bit older, Bob sold the business. But he was bored. He needed to get out of the house. Hockey, and the Pond, gave him a purpose. I think being involved with you kids helped him stay away from drinking."

The story added up. Lonely guy comes to small town at thirty. Since everyone knows everyone else's business, his failure in hockey marks him out for scorn at a chance blown, a chance that any man in any town in Canada would love to have. He picks up the pieces, learns a skill, and given that he's a big guy used to dealing with the rough play on the ice, he can command a crew and motivate them to work hard. He starts with one truck, ends up with two, and paves the driveways and parking lots of a town flush with success because of its thriving auto-parts factory. Whether by luck or good sense, he sells the business right about the time the boom peaks and retires with a little bit of money in the bank.

Hockey, which had been so important to him years earlier, had also created his worst scars. But he returned to the game in the pure form of a bunch of kids playing on outdoor ice, using Queenston as both his exile and his redemption, with the boys of Todd's generation playing a crucial role in his efforts to recapture his hockey roots. The culmination of this experience was Peterborough, which no team had made it to after the 1992 Rebels had. It was the prototype of the recovery story, every bit as poignant as TV documentaries that featured musicians who burned through their cash and bottomed out before making a comeback.

The one element left unexplained was why Bob hadn't told the boys he'd been in the NHL. Todd refreshed his browser and looked at the stats. One goal, one assist. Five minutes in penalties, which meant one scrap. The player he had fought, and whether Bob had won, were now facts lost to time. Todd couldn't quite see the Bob he remembered throwing down with anyone, but back then, the league was tough, and each player had to fight his own battles. This was true even for the Montreal Canadiens' standout superstar, Maurice Richard.

"Okay, so that's Bob's story," he said to his mom. "But why didn't he tell us that he'd been in the big league?" There would have been no greater sign that he deserved respect than that.

His mom shrugged. "Maybe he was embarrassed at how it ended. Maybe he didn't think it was so important after all those years. Maybe none of you guys were fans of the team he played for." She did not understand that this would not have mattered. He had been in the NHL. He scored a goal on an NHL goalie. In 1956, the league had only six teams. Netminders like Jacques Plante, Gump Worsley and Gerry McNeil guarded the pipes, brave men who faced the shooters without masks until Plante donned one in 1959. That era now lived only in black-and-white photos and a few grainy films, but Bob could have told his players about it—offering stories with firsthand weight.

"Well, if I had known he played in the NHL, I would have bugged him for details," Todd replied.

"I'm sure you would have. But would that have helped you learn how to play like Bob wanted you to?" his mom responded.

She made a good point. Bob's silence, if it had any benefit, kept the boys from being distracted from the lessons he tried to teach them. Not knowing about Bob's past allowed them to judge his advice by how well it worked on the ice, rather than because an ex-NHLer had dispensed it.

Todd put away his laptop and turned his attention to real life again. "I was going to make a meatloaf. You game?" he asked his mom. She nodded yes.

Moments later, being knuckles deep in hamburger, ketchup and Worcestershire sauce let him forget the past. For Todd, Peterborough had been both his biggest moment in hockey and the producer of his greatest disappointment.

"I like to put a little grape jelly in there," his mother said.

"So that's what made it so good." Salsa hadn't existed in Queenston when Todd was growing up.

nine

The days continued cold, and Todd's experiment with flooding the Pond was going better than he expected, except for forgetting to drain the hose the first time he'd used it. He had to take the hose home and store it in the garage overnight to thaw out, but other than that, he hadn't encountered any trouble, and the ice was improving every day. Using his misting technique, Todd ensured that the water would fill the tiny bumps and cracks that marred the ice and render a smooth surface, durable enough to hold up under use.

For the moment, the only cracks were those made by Todd's skates during his forays onto the ice. He was at the Pond around three or four o'clock most days, when his mom took her afternoon nap. He skated for a while, then scraped and used the hose until the sun started to hint that darkness was coming. He'd get home around five, in time to make their dinner. Staying later than that was impossible. The lights surrounding the rink did not respond when he threw the switch, leading him to assume that the power had been cut off.

One afternoon toward the end of his second week at the Pond, Todd was flooding when a car drove up and parked behind his. His first thought was that someone who now owned the land the Pond sat on was coming around to shoo him away for trespassing. A man got out of the car and started to walk down the bank. Trailing along behind him was a kid of about eight. When they were within about twenty-five feet, Todd saw who it was.

"Trevor?" Since he'd been in Queenston, Todd hadn't made any effort to reconnect with the people he'd known as a youngster. His routine of house fixing, heading to the nursing home, job hunting and now taking care of his mom at home had kept him too preoccupied to seek out old friends. Many of the people from his past were gone anyway, and he had assumed that the ones who remained weren't people he cared to keep in touch with. Trevor was different, one of those with ambition. He had gone away to school and earned an engineering degree.

"Todd!" he exclaimed as his arms stretched out for a hug. "I heard you were back—how are ya?" In adulthood, he was more gregarious than he had been as a kid. He had been a math nerd, a skill that Todd had taken advantage of when they were in elementary school. As he grew up, Trevor had broken out of his shell and even started in hockey, playing in the town's house league for a number of years and serving as the fifth defenseman when the team had qualified for Peterborough.

Todd smiled and stepped back after the embrace. Time hadn't done Trevor any big favors. He was rotund, though the familiar shy childhood grin came out from his now-pudgy cheeks. "This is my son, Brandon," Trevor said. Todd stuck out a hand, and the boy shook it, both of them with gloves on. Todd walked over to the faucet and shut off the flow.

"What are you doing in Queenston?" Trevor asked the expected question.

"My mom, she fell and broke her hip. Things were kind of winding up for me in Toronto at the same time, so I decided to come home and help out. I guess you heard that my dad died a few years ago?" Todd looked to his old friend for affirmation.

"Yeah, my mom kept me informed while I was away. Is your mother okay?"

Todd nodded. "Yeah, you know the old clichés—slow process, better every day. She's all right." He was on the brink of asking the next, most natural question—what was Trevor doing back? Instead, he turned to the rink. "I thought you were going to ask me what I'm doing out here. I decided to flood the Pond. Might as well have some fun way up here in the wild."

"You been skating?" Trevor replied, looking over Todd's shoulder at the rink. "Is it ready?"

"Heck, yeah. Actually, it's only been a week or so, and I've just been able to get on the ice in the past few days without doing too much damage. I skate, then I scrape and flood. I generally head home around suppertime and get my mom something ready to eat." It sounded like a simple, almost charming life, but hardly what someone with an MBA should be doing to fill workday afternoons.

"Why not let me help out? I don't think anyone's been on the ice here for a while. Several winters, I'd guess, but Brandon's at an age where outdoor ice might do his game a lot of good. They practice inside once a week. Anyway, maybe I can come by tomorrow about this time. After work."

Todd glanced at his watch, an Omega Speedmaster he'd bought when he was in Switzerland several years before. It was almost five o'clock. "That's a good idea, but it won't work. The lights are off," Todd replied. "You can't see a damn—er, darn—thing once the sun goes behind the trees." He looked at Trevor, apologizing for using the language in front of his son.

"He's heard far worse than that by his age. Different from when we were kids," Trevor said as he acknowledged the faux pas, then gestured to the rink with a wave of his glove. "You're in luck, buddy," he continued.

"Why's that?" said Todd, his breath coming out in a cloud of vapor produced by the cold. He wiped a hand across his nose, which was offering a steady drip.

"I work for the town. I can talk to people, figure out what's going on out here and get the lights turned back on."

Todd waited for him to explain what role he played in Queenston's economy. Being an electrician would have been quite a fall from having an engineering degree. He pursued the line of thought, but phrased his question casually. "So what's my mom's tax money buying when it comes to your services?"

"I'm the city planner. Not that there's a lot of planning going on right now. But call me the chief cook and bottle washer of the city's engineering department. Believe it or not, even though we're not exactly in growth mode, someone needs to be around who can read plans and site surveys. Mostly, I deal with issues like when and where to put up new power lines when Hydro wants to do repairs, and how to reroute water flow when a line breaks. You know, glamorous stuff."

"Well, you did a BSc in engineering, right?" Todd asked. "Did you get the professional engineering credential to stick after your name?"

"Yeah, I did that. Thought I was going to end up with a big architecture firm in Toronto or somewhere. Some of the people I graduated with are working abroad. One guy designs the electrical systems for skyscrapers in Hong Kong."

His dreams sounded surprisingly like Todd's. Hesitant to ask what had pulled Trevor back here because it would mean sharing more of his own story, Todd shifted his weight from one leg to the other. He needed to start the task of draining the hose and rolling it up to store.

"Gotta go," he said. "If dinner's not on the table by six, well, my mom really doesn't care, but I do have her following a kind of routine that works for both of us. Supper and clean up for an hour, then watching *Jeopardy!* and *Wheel of Fortune.* Then she reads for a while and gets ready for bed. That way, while she's watching the tube and doing all her other activities, I can get some of my own things done." That meant combing job ads and working on getting his resumé out, but he didn't go into detail.

Todd walked to the faucet, unscrewed the hose and drained it, then curled it up. Brandon, instructed by his dad to help, lent a hand.

"I'll give you a call at your mom's house when I figure out what's up with the lights," Trevor offered. Then they parted ways.

A few days later, Todd was at the Pond following his same routine when he heard the crunch of tires on gravel. It was Trevor. He hadn't called since they'd seen each other. Brandon wasn't in tow this time. Todd didn't have a chance to ask after the kid before Trevor burst out, "Flick the switch, buddy," as he came down the bank.

"Oh, wow, what happened?" Todd asked. "Let me get over there." He scrambled to the pole and pulled the breaker, and the slow fizzle of gas and flicker of light turned into illumination as three of the four lights woke from their slumber. The other one blinked on and off briefly, then went dead again. Their glow covered most of the rink's surface, darkness just starting to fall. Had the lights all been working, it would have been possible to hold a full practice or scrimmage, just like in the old days.

"That one on the far end of the ice isn't working. I'll have to get someone out here to check it," Trevor said matter-of-factly. "Hopefully, it's just the bulb." Todd waited to hear the story of how the magic had happened.

"I realized that if there was power here, it had to be metered somewhere. But I checked the records, and nothing showed up as being out this far. So I got thinking. Remember when we were kids, there was a house out here?" Todd nodded. "It was the last house on the road. Once you get down to the 'T' there," said Trevor, pointing down the road to a junction, "that's all county grid.

"In other words, that house was the last one being metered by the town. When it was torn down years ago, the power was shut off. But the box wasn't mounted on the house. The plans showed that it was mounted on the power pole that runs from the main road. Don't ask me why. I find all kinds of weird installations around here. We're constantly correcting that sort of hillbilly engineering." His wide grin indicated that he was proud of being able to bring the town into conformity with modern building codes.

Trevor went on. "So if the box was still there, I thought the Pond should still have power. I shot an email over to Hydro and had them re-up the meter. The account will have to be paid for by you and me, by the way, not out of city funds. But I thought you'd be okay with that, for old time's sake. Anyway, we can work out the nitty-gritty later. The bill shouldn't be more than about forty bucks a month, and that's only when there's ice in and the lights are turned on."

Todd nodded. His savings weren't exactly growing, though he was holding steady since his expenses were pretty much nil living with his mom.

"So here we are a few days later, and you've got power. That shed, or Shack, or whatever we called it, that's another story. Before you even try to fire up that little stove, we need to get someone out to have a look. That backwoods rigging was fine for twenty years ago. These days, we have codes that govern that type of installation, even if it's just on a forgotten skating rink on the edge of town. After all, by supplying you with the lights, the town has kind of put its stamp of approval on the place."

"Great, Trev. Thanks for doing that," Todd said. "I can't stay today, but maybe tomorrow or the next day, I'll do these chores in the afternoon." He gestured to the shovel and hose. "And we can meet here for a skate. Maybe do some passing drills. Bring Brandon," he added.

"Sure, bud. By the way, maybe you could stop by the city building one afternoon, just to square it all up with the powers that be?" Trevor suggested. "Besides, there are some people in the office who remember you. When I told them what I was up to, and that you were behind it all, I got a few interested looks. Come by. We'll have a coffee."

Todd nodded again, picked up the equipment and headed to the Shack, where he stored the shovel and hose under one of the benches.

The next afternoon, he was sitting in the lobby of the city hall, a combination office, workshop, truck depot and police station. He waited for Trevor on a hard metal chair outside the engineering offices, then stood up and walked around, looking at the local history displayed in glass cases on the walls. The damming of the river in 1924 to alleviate spring flooding. The new bridge that was put up in the 1950s to replace one that dated to the World War I era, connecting King Street with the area where the factory was. The drive-through visit of Queen Elizabeth in 1977, when she was celebrating her reign of twenty-five years. And the 1992 trip of the Queenston Rebels Bantam squad to the Peterborough tournament. Todd found himself smiling in the second row of the official team shot. There were Timmy, Dave and the rest. Bob looked like he did in Todd's imagination, which was nat-ural because Todd had just seen his photo in the scrapbook he'd discovered in his mom's basement.

"Glory days, eh?" Trevor had inched out of his office and snuck up behind Todd. "Look at us. The pride of Queenston."

"Trev, do you really think this is the culmination of the town's history? I mean, we're right beside the Queen, for goodness sake. Didn't anything else happen that mattered during that era? Or since?"

"Sure, the factory shut down, putting half the town out of work and landing us on the road to economic ruin that we're still going down." His tone betrayed a surprising cyni-cism considering that he had chosen to return and make a life in Queenston. "The truth is, these pictures were put here—what?—twenty years ago, and I guess they've kind of become part of the scenery in the office. Nobody even thinks about removing them. And if they did, there's not a lot to replace them with."

"How about pictures of you triumphantly riding into town to claim your place as city planner?" Todd matched his friend's ironic tone.

"I did that for the same reason you did. Family called. But you know what, now that I'm here, this ain't such a bad place to be," Trevor said, feigning a *Dukes of Hazzard* accent. Todd didn't have a chance to reply before his friend continued. "Forget that for now. I told you I needed you to meet someone. Follow me."

Trevor led him through the door that separated the engineering department from the police station. There, he quickened his step, walking up to a booth, glassed in like the teller cage in an old-fashioned bank. "Knock, knock," he said as he tapped on the glass. Todd couldn't hear the sound of the rapping knuckles because the barrier was so thick.

"Can I help you, Mr. City Planner?"

Hearing the voice, Todd stopped short, trying to focus through the window, his palms growing instantly sweaty. He locked his gaze on Trevor, his mouth a dry gulch of dust. Trevor sensed his nervousness and took over.

"Todd, you remember Heather?" It was a question they all knew the answer to. Heather Evans. His high school crush. His whole life, at least for the year they were in grade ten. Then she dropped him for Warren Clark, a muscular dude who played football and had his pick of females. Todd hadn't had another girlfriend until his second year of university.

Heather hadn't just broken up with him, she'd done it in the worst way possible. One morning when he was walking to his locker, he noticed a few kids standing around it. A piece of paper was taped to the door, below the vents. He grabbed the note as soon as he got there.

"Dear Todd," it said in typescript. "I know it's been a while, and I really like you, but I don't think it's going to work out." There was more, but he didn't read on. The news wouldn't get any better. His eyes scanned to the bottom, looking for her name. The note was unsigned.

As he was reading, three or four more kids gathered, drawn by the first curious onlookers. The letter's contents had been plain for all to see before he got there, yet he had snatched it off the locker as if he could still preserve its secret. He scanned the faces surrounding him to see who might have read it. Trevor and the kid next to him had guilty smirks. They knew what it said. He decided to go on the attack.

"Funny, Trev," he said. "Funny joke. Ha, ha. You post this for everyone to read. Make me look stupid. Cool."

Todd saw the strategy as his only hope of saving face. The lack of a signature made it barely plausible that Heather hadn't written the note. Playing it off as a grand joke might give him an escape route, or in any case buy him some time.

"Not me, Todd," Trevor said, his face registering confusion. "Why would I—"

Todd interrupted the question midstream. "Sure, you can't get a girlfriend, so why should anyone else have one, right? Nice move, bud. Real swift."

Trevor's blank expression revealed that he had no idea what was going on, but a few of the six or eight kids gathered had started to drift away, half-buying Todd's scam. He was determined to direct the focus away from the obvious truth that this was a "Dear John" letter. If it worked, he could stash the note away, go to class and figure out what the heck was going on when he got a chance to reread it later, alone. He faced Trevor, shoving the piece of paper in his backpack as he spat out his words. "So, way to go, man."

Todd spun around and busied himself poking around in the locker, and by the time he turned around again, everyone had left. The bell rang for first period, and the halls emptied as fast as if someone had pulled the fire alarm. He had escaped.

But he couldn't deny the truth. He and Heather were over. Being with her had been shooting above his level anyway. She wasn't the kind of girl who would be attracted to someone like him. They had been together on yearbook the year prior, and he managed to impress her with his creativity at taking photos, but they were an unlikely pair. Her type usually attracted the alpha type of guy, and when she figured that out, she had moved on. Todd could do nothing about this. His sports career had effectively ended two years earlier, after his great failure in Peterborough. After that, he had melted into the crowd, a yearbook nerd, a nobody.

He never got a firsthand explanation from her as to why she'd ditched him in a note. In the math class they shared, she wouldn't look up to catch his eye. After that, in the hallway, he started to approach her, and she turned away. Later that night, at home, he read the note over a few more times, deciding that maybe it was a good thing she hadn't signed it, after all. It would have been a dead giveaway as to its origin. As it was, nobody in school asked him about it. They hadn't been a highly visible couple. When she started hanging around Warren during the breaks between classes, any questions that anybody might have had were answered.

"Wow...Heather?" was all he managed to squeak out in the silence of the police station. He wanted to ask what she was doing there, and why she had chosen the public humiliation of the letter in grade ten, but both questions remained unvoiced. Todd looked at Trevor, imploring him to say something. He just smiled.

Heather jumped in. "Todd. Trevor told me he'd seen someone from the old days. I kind of heard you were home. How are you?"

As his head began to clear, Todd contemplated what to say so many years after the breakup incident. They were both adults, and what she did then had no relevance to now, though he was still curious.

"How are *you* doing?" was all that came out of his mouth.

He looked through the glass. She was the same Heather, her eyes smoky and mysterious in the best sort of combination. He could not tell if the rest of her still looked as hot as when they were in high school. The barrier of the information window she sat behind blocked his view.

"*What* are you doing, more like?" He had recovered command of his voice in the moments it had taken to try to check her out.

"I'm the dispatcher, paperwork queen and all that jazz," she replied. To Todd, her response was the equivalent of saying, "I'm another one of those people who looked like they had great prospects, but never made it out of here."

Trevor put a more important-sounding spin on it. "She keeps us all aware of what's going on and kind of pushes us around when she thinks we're not working hard enough." He was not afraid to joke with her. The days of her reign as the most desirable girl in high school were remote, not something that made Trevor shy with her anymore. He no longer had the attitude of the kid who tried to stay out of everyone's way and work on his math.

Trevor turned around and put out an arm to guide Todd back in the direction they came from. "Anyway, my boyo here has promised to pay for coffee," Trevor said over his shoulder as a goodbye to Heather. Todd didn't get out a goodbye, but he offered a wave as he turned around to go, raising his eyebrows in a gesture that suggested his surprise at seeing her.

Once out of earshot, Todd turned to Trevor with a quizzical look. "That's why you wanted me to come down here?" he asked.

"Just thought you'd like to know that Heather Hottie was still around, old friend. And as far as I know, she's on her own."

Todd was incapable of processing this new information, so he left it alone. The town was frozen in time in more ways than its reliance on the Peterborough tournament as its high point.

Trevor filled the silence by saying, "I don't know if you care about this, but that thing she had with Warren lasted until after we finished grade twelve, right? Then he left town and never came back."

"University?" Todd had no idea whether jock Warren had been on the scholarly track.

"From what I heard, he's a union meat cutter at a plant somewhere near Kitchener."

They headed across the street to the only coffee shop in town except the truck stop on the highway next to the Superstore. Phil's was what big-city people would describe as a quaint café, old-fashioned in a way that had become charming and hip in cities like Toronto. The kind of place featured in American TV shows about diners.

The counter had stools along its length. The front of the room along the window had booths. In between the two sat five Formica tables, each with two chairs on either side. They'd been there since before Todd and Trevor were born.

Phil, the owner of the restaurant, didn't see any reason to replace what was still functional. That the place had turned into a time warp didn't bother him. In fact, had he redecorated, the regulars would have strongly opposed it. One time, he'd removed waffles from the menu, and the outcry had gone on until he reinstated them.

Trevor had spent enough lunch hours eating club sandwiches and chicken burgers at Phil's that he didn't notice its shabbiness anymore. It hit Todd, however, as soon as they walked in the door. He almost said something but caught himself as the words were forming in this head. There was no alternative like a Second Cup or Tim Hortons anywhere nearby. If they were going to have a coffee in the heart of town, it was going to come from Phil's Bunn machine.

Trevor pointed to a table, and they sat down. He held up two fingers to indicate to Phil that they'd each be having a cup, and he nodded to the glass case behind the counter, saying, "Cake's pretty good. German chocolate, it looks like. It kind of depends on Phil's mood. Before you go, you gotta try the red velvet. He got the recipe from *Good Morning America*, he says."

Todd waved the suggestion away. "Can't do that at this time of day, buddy. I've got my girlish figure to worry about." He had maintained his college weight of 165 pounds into his thirties, a fact that made him proud.

Trevor gave his paunch a poke. "I don't think I've been doing quite enough thinking about my own figure," he said in reply. "Maybe you're going to rub off on me in a good way." The coffee arrived in white porcelain cups sitting on saucers that showed the marks of having been used a long time.

"So you're back. Here we are. I'm not sure I would have imagined it, for either of us," Todd's friend said as an opener.

"Me neither, but I gotta tell you, I don't really consider myself *back*. This is temporary, until my mom can get around on her own. And she's close. She's walking around the block now with just a cane. And that's only a precaution. I think she'd kick it to the curb first chance she got if I wasn't there to ride her about it."

"You got your MBA, right? You finished it?"

Until this point, Todd had not filled in his friend on what he'd done after university. He replied, "Yeah, I graduated from business school."

Trevor's next question was obvious. "So, why didn't things work out for you in the big TO?"

Rather than avoiding the subject, Todd came clean. He explained the Tia Rosita fiasco, his run-ins with his boss. He even mentioned Sarah.

"So maybe I was right to bring you down here, to let you know that Heather was around." Trevor smiled, like they were in junior high again, looking at a girly magazine some-one had sneaked out of his dad's hiding spot.

Todd didn't want to get involved with Heather, or any-one else for that matter. His focus was on getting things sorted out with his mom and getting his career back on track. He explained that most days, he was busy online looking at job sites, sending out his resumé and networking by phone. "My goal was to head to Toronto every few weeks to put in some face time. I'm hopeful something will turn up soon," he told Trevor as Phil wandered by. In fact, he had intended to go back more often than he had managed to, which was just once since he had landed in Queenston in August.

"Probably not at Christmas, though, right? Who hires over the holidays?" Trevor was right—the fast-approaching season would be a down time in Todd's search.

Todd nodded in agreement.

Trevor reverted to the earlier subject. "So you know, if this was a fairy tale, you'd fall in love with Heather, fall in love with this town again and settle down here. The old hero of the Peterborough tournament."

Todd raised his eyebrows, considering what to say. Queenston shaped people's destinies almost as if they had no control over its force. He felt the town's gentle tug on his life, just as he imagined Trevor and Heather had when they made Queenston home, but he was not ready to let fate carry him along. He wasn't interested in playing the role of the boy next door, married to the girl he'd loved and lost and living here once more.

"I think you mean *anti-hero*," Todd shot back a little too forcefully. "And I'm pretty sure I never was in love with Queenston."

Trevor had touched a nerve that had been jangling in Todd's brain since the encounter with Kenny Horton at the grocery store a few months before. "Don't shoot!" The nickname was the legacy of his failure at the tournament, a singular moment that had cost his team the title.

The Peterborough Bantam Classic drew teams from all over Ontario and beyond. It had been running since the 1950s, having established itself as the premier championship for kids ages thirteen and fourteen. The victors received the Holman Cup, named after the founder of the Ontario Minor Hockey Association. Each year, dozens of teams and hundreds of parents and fans descended on the city to contest for that trophy. The tournament's format was double elimination, so that if a team lost one game, they went to the B pool. Lose another, and it was over.

Before qualifying in 1992, Queenston hadn't sent a team to Peterborough since 1962, and they'd lost. Only a couple of people in town remembered those days, and nobody from that team lived in the area anymore. The ex-players, adults by that point, hadn't stuck around when the economy of the town started its downturn and it looked like Mackey's wouldn't last forever.

The 1992 version of the Rebels, with the town rallied behind them, managed to do better than anyone outside of Queenston might have expected. The team made it to the championship game by winning four in a row. They came out 6–1 in the first game and squeaked a 5–4 win with six seconds left in the second. Their third game had been another win, not a spectacular affair in that the final score of 4–2 was made by a goal into an empty net. Their fourth game was the toughest test, with neither team scoring until the third period. The Rebels managed to get the first goal, and then they played defensively to make it stand up.

The final game was against a team they had never played, nor seen, before the tournament. The Sarnia Cyclones were fast, and they were big, a lethal combination that made Kenora look like half the challenge they had been in the qualifier in Odessa.

Todd's team got out to a lucky 1–0 lead on a goal that had gone in off a defenseman's stick. The guy essentially scored on his own goaltender, trying to sweep the puck out from in front of his net but instead putting it right on goal, and in.

The Cyclones players sagged after the goal, halfheartedly taking faceoffs and dumping the puck into the offensive zone without bothering to forecheck to get it back. But they picked up soon after, when it became clear that they could carry the puck over the Queenston blueline almost at will.

On the bench, Bob was getting frantic, going up behind guys one by one and giving them the same pep talk. "Okay, so they're big. You're fast, and that's the counter. But first, you guys need to take them on at that blueline. All it will take is one good hit to get them off their game."

They didn't have to use the physical game often because they generally matched their opponents' power with their own speed plus skillful puck possession and accurate passing. But as he worked his way down the bench, Bob instilled confidence in them. They started to stand up at the blueline, rather than fading back and letting the Cyclones have the zone. In fact, answering the Cyclones' size didn't require them to take any good, big hits, but just a willingness to defend with guts that made it clear the Rebels wouldn't back down.

Sarnia's first goal, a dump-in retrieved by a winger, came with a minute left in the first period. The kid did exactly what Todd was supposed to do; he flew in and swooped onto the loose puck, then fed it out to center, where his teammate was cruising down the slot. He shot, the goalie's glove hand thrust out, the puck went past it, and the score was tied.

The second period was more of the same, with Todd's team pressing the attack as they kept Sarnia out of their zone. Because they were less willing to give up their blueline, they were forcing the Cyclones into making mistakes and giving the puck up more often than they had been. The Rebels quickly turned these errors into up-ice chances that proved the wisdom of Bob's experience.

On one play, Dave took the puck, carefully shoveling it ahead of him as he crossed center. Checking for his wingers as he neared the blueline, he did a head fake and a quick stutter step as he crossed the line, then fed the puck left, to Timmy. He skated it down into the corner, and instead of feeding it out front again, he surprised everyone in the arena by flinging the puck around the net.

Todd, who played like he knew that something unique was about to happen, was the only player not caught off guard. He went to the right hash marks where the puck was headed and pinned his body against the boards. When the disk got to him, he squeezed his shin pads together and stopped it. The puck dropped almost onto his stick. He picked it up and started to move forward with it, then in his peripheral vision saw Dave motioning with his stick. "Pass it back! Back!" he yelled at the same time.

Todd took a quick look behind him and saw his right defenseman poised for a shot. He dished the puck to him. Todd didn't know where the Cyclones players were positioned at that moment, but it didn't matter. He saw their legs, their reaching sticks, but he also saw the path where he wanted the puck to go, and he put it there. Then he headed for the net.

The defenseman one-timed it toward the goal. The puck slid through a maze of bodies, including Todd's. He saw it go past his right skate, and the next thing he saw was the goalie's left leg flash out. The puck hit the goalie's pad and bounced to the right-hand side of the slot as far as the hash marks, where Todd was parked.

Once again he had the puck on his stick—only this time, with a clear lane to the net. But instead of driving to the goalmouth, he hesitated. His instinct, honed throughout his playing career, was to pass. He raised his head to survey the ice, assuming that someone else had a better angle to make the shot than he did.

Bob had been working with Todd to remedy his insecurity. After their group practices on the Pond concluded in the evening, the two of them had stayed behind. Bob would set a piece of plywood in the net, with holes at the lower corners large enough for a puck to squeak through, with a little room to spare. Then he fed Todd from behind the net, or in the corner, telling him to shoot as soon as the puck came to him.

To increase the pressure, sometimes he'd tell Todd to close his eyes, then Bob would fire the pucks out double-time. He'd yell "Puck!" just before it got to Todd, who would have to open his eyes, find it and fire off the shot. The drill was designed to imitate the pressure Todd would feel with a winger on him, back-checking, or a defenseman rushing at him to block the shot.

Each time the puck came, Todd felt the same knot in his gut, the same tightness in his arms and legs, like he wouldn't be able to get the shot off. Had another teammate been on the ice at the time, he would have passed it, no question. But Bob wouldn't allow it. He was determined to make him a scorer, or at least make Todd think about going to the net as his first option. Passing could come as a second choice.

"Confidence," Bob would say. "The game is all about believing in your skills. If you think you can't do it, you can't. That's one thing for sure. When you get the puck within a certain range of the net, it's yours. You have to drive it in. You have to take that first shot."

Over the course of their drills, Todd appeared to have gained the confidence to do what he was taught, overcoming his fears and thinking of scoring before passing. Bob believed, too, that given the choice, Todd would take the shot, go after the goal.

Now, that chance was on his stick, and he held the puck, taking a second look. The goalie was shading to his left side, Todd's right, so the left side of the net, as Todd faced it, was open. It was the far side, with Todd being a right-hand shot. He double-clutched, trying to make sure he had his blade firmly on the puck, and just as he was doing so, a defender caught up with him. As Todd released his shot, which was marked for the far post, the other kid's stick made slight contact with his. It was enough to put a wobble on the puck, which didn't speed toward the open side but fluttered there. The goalie shot his stick out to cover the open spot, stopping the puck half a foot from the goal line.

Kids playing on the street would call this a "glorious scoring opportunity," in imitation of the old-school hockey commentator Danny Gallivan, and Todd had blown it. The defense picked up the loose puck after the netminder swept it behind his cage. The play went up ice toward the Rebels' end, and Todd and his line gave chase.

The play was whistled offside at his blueline, and as Todd cruised to the bench, the atmosphere in the arena shifted from excited to nasty. A voice boomed out of the crowd: "Hey, Seven! You get the memo? It said, 'Don't shoot, no matter what.'" Todd skated on, his eyes downcast, seeking the safety of his teammates, who were silent as he skated toward the door that would let him find a seat, and sanctuary.

But there was no refuge. "Don't shoot!" was yelled out again. Then in chorus, a group of spectators started to chant. "Don't shoot! Don't shoot!" they screamed as he took his seat. Whose side they represented was not clear in the din. Todd reached for the water bottle in the holder in front of him, like NHL players did. Whether they scored a goal or made a mistake, their attitude was the same—to pretend that nothing had happened, that it hadn't been them. The spectators didn't know was what was going on in those players' heads. But now, Todd knew.

Dave came off the ice and plunked down beside him. "I was there for the rebound, buddy. You should have put that puck hard on net."

Todd had sensible reasons for not shooting more quickly. The opening was to the long side. He didn't have the puck firmly on his stick. He wasn't sure if he had any support. But in truth, they were flimsy excuses for not firing the puck with all the energy he could muster. In short, the creeping lack of confidence that plagued him on the ice, even after all the extra practice, had gripped him tight in that moment and squeezed the guts out of him, making him weak. He turned to Dave, thinking he ought to acknowledge his comment, but he didn't say anything. No rationale would make his flub better.

Bob came up behind, his words sharp. "We've worked on that. A thousand times," he said. As Todd listened, the man's tone moderated from anger to disappointment. "You had that shot. You had the lane. And Dave was there to pick up the garbage in case the guy happened to get a pad on it."

Todd muffled an "I know" in response, though he hadn't known at the time that a teammate had been there for the rebound. For the split second that he paused, he thought he was making the right move by waiting and trying to get a more sure grip on the puck. He said as much to Bob.

"You don't *think*. In that moment, you just *do*. That's why we drilled it so much," replied Bob. He moved on down the row of players.

The Cyclones pressed as the game neared its finish. On the Rebels' bench, guys who had been sitting forward, looking out at the action with the belief that the game would go their way, suddenly started to hunch their backs. Their posture now signaled worry more than confidence. Todd's muff had cost more than a goal. The team had lost the feeling that, despite being outclassed by their opponent in certain aspects of the game, they could somehow win. Theirs could have been the old story of the underdog—you think you can do it, and suddenly you do. The flip side is that when you stop believing, you're toast. With two minutes to go, Queenston let in the goal that cost them the championship, and they never attacked with passion after that. Todd, who had stood there in the slot with the puck, had killed their spirit.

After the game came the trophy presentation at center ice, with each player awarded a medal and the captain of the opposition given a large silver cup with curved handles on both sides. The cup was mounted on a wood base covered in tiny silver plaques, each bearing an inscription with the year and the name of the winning team. For 1992, the Sarnia Cyclones' name would be affixed there.

As Todd was skating off the ice, he heard it one more time. "Don't shoot!" He looked for the culprit. This wasn't the same voice that had yelled during the game. That had been a grown-up. A couple of teenagers were standing next to the Plexiglas. They thrust their hands in the pockets of their hockey jackets as they said the taunt, pretending to be bank robbers with concealed guns.

Don't shoot. In some ways, this had always been his habit—pass the puck to someone with a better chance. Now this mantra was a burden he would have to carry. As he walked through the arena lobby, no excited parents greeted him. His mom and dad, apparently, had already taken off, as had the others. He got on the bus to head home, knowing he had let down the whole town.

He walked to his seat and sat down as if nothing had happened, but nobody met his eye. As the bus lurched out of the parking lot, Bob came and sat down beside Todd.

"They're right. You didn't shoot," Bob started. Todd stared at the back of the seat in front of him, its green vinyl mottled with creases. "Anybody can say that from a distance, Todd. They don't know what it's like when you're actually out there." Bob then got up and moved to the row behind, talking to each of his players in turn about their game.

Todd looked at Trevor, the memory of Peterborough now renewed in his mind. His fists were tight with tension. "We were kids, man," he said. "But you remember the hype, right? Our team was in the paper every day, practically. My mom cut out the clippings. I was looking at them the other day when I was cleaning up the basement…. Geez, what business did the whole town have putting that burden on us? I mean, what did we do to deserve it?" He relaxed his hands and leaned back in his chair.

Trevor swished the last of his coffee around in the bottom of his cup. "I don't know. Maybe it wasn't the town. Maybe it was Bob. He had something to prove, having washed out of the game himself." He glanced up at Todd, unsure whether his friend knew the guy's story.

Todd acknowledged the implied question. "Yeah, my mom told me all about it. I guess he was with Chicago in the fifties. Played a few games, then drank himself out of hockey."

"Something like that. Ended up here and tried to redeem himself by building the rink, the Shack and all that. That's one way to read it, anyway." He searched Todd's face, saw confirmation of the theory, then went on. "I guess the chance to get us qualified for Peterborough was just too good to pass up. Think about it. If we hadn't made the tournament, so what? We would have gone on, the town would have been just the same as always, nobody loses anything. But when we qualified—bingo! His hockey life was back on track. You could almost say it was more about him that it was about us, or Queenston."

Trevor's thoughts mirrored Todd's recent conclusions about his mentor's legacy, though he couldn't go along with the implication that the old guy's motivations were selfish. This would have demanded a radical reengineering of Todd's notion of Bob's character and why he'd gotten the team together and then pushed them like he had. Even if Trevor was right, Todd didn't care, because Bob changed his life. He made Todd's early teenage years bearable, Peterborough notwithstanding.

"He redeemed himself by doing things for *us*, Trev," Todd offered by way of correction. "But I just wish that team hadn't been so important around here. I mean, think about it. It's twenty years later. We're both well-educated adults, and here we are, our primary topic of discussion a weekend hockey tournament that we played two freaking decades ago." He looked around him, ready to move on in the conversation.

At the next table, a guy perked up from his pie. "Hey, I knew I knew you," he said. Todd raised his eyebrows, surprised at the man's willingness to mind someone else's business. He waited for the fellow to go on. "Sorry to burst in, but I attended the Peterborough tournament. I'm a little bit younger than you guys, but I remember you and all the fuss the town made over your qualifying for Peterborough. I'm Johnny Reid. My older brother Timmy was on your team. You're Todd Graham, right?"

Todd opened his mouth to reply, but the guy went on. "I was, like, six that year you guys went to Peterborough. I was there, at all your games. I remember that arena. The noise. The excitement. Boy, was my dad pissed off on the drive home."

"Man, we were linemates on that team!" Todd exclaimed. "Me and Timmy. He was my best friend. I practically lived at your house when we were ten, twelve, fourteen. In fact, all the way up through hockey and later. Your mom made a killer grilled cheese sandwich."

"Now that you say that, I remember you and Timmy being the wingers, right?"

Todd nodded. "What's Timmy up to these days?" he asked, deflecting the conversation away from Peterborough.

"Moved out west. He got the idea that he'd like Vancouver, so off he went. Met a girl there and got married, that whole thing. They're in Burnaby, two kids. He's selling real estate. Doing pretty well, or at least, he seems to in the boom times. He's home a couple of times a year, with the family. You?"

"I've been gone since university. I'm just back for what you might call a little R-and-R from the business world. My mom's getting physio for a broken hip." Todd tried to remember something about Johnny, who had been only a pesky tagalong kid while they were growing up. "You're still around, though?" he ventured, with the unspoken question being, "Did you get stuck here, too?"

"Yeah, my dad and I work together. Electrical contracting. I also do some projects for the city, like a certain set of lights for a certain Pond." Johnny smiled and reached over to give Trevor a fist bump as if they had planned this meet-up all along. "Sorry I didn't say hi earlier, Trev. I thought you might be in high-level discussions or something. Didn't want to get in the way."

Todd shot a look at Trevor, who shrugged. "Okay, so it took a little more than an email to Hydro. Nothing like an expert on the job," Trevor said.

Todd turned back to Johnny, sizing him up. When people get to be twenty-five or thirty, age differences don't count like they do when they're adolescents. This wasn't a kid brother anymore, but a guy with his own life going on.

"Do you have kids?" It was a sensible question in the circumstances, though not one Todd would have asked anyone he ran into in Toronto.

"Not yet. Just got married. Jessica. You might remember her older sister in school, Heather Evans."

Todd sat straight up in his chair. The family was everywhere. In a place where everyone knew everyone, there weren't many eligible people around when it came time to pick partners. He nodded at the mention of Heather's name, then moved to a new topic.

"Have you been down to the Pond? I mean, other than to hook up that electrical box? Thanks, by the way." He stumbled over the words.

"I drive by there when I'm headed to my folks' place. They bought a house out in the woods on Concession Road 43 after Tim left for university. I remember the Pond, though. I think you guys might have been the last generation to use it for serious hockey. The kids I knew skated there sometimes. We would pick teams and scrimmage, but we didn't do drills like you guys did."

So Bob hadn't tutored subsequent groups of kids after Peterborough.

Johnny went on. "I still play, though, mostly indoors now. I guess with fewer people around, fewer kids, there's less demand for indoor ice time than before. A bunch of us get together on Tuesday nights at the arena. At nine o'clock. It's pickup. No checking. If you want to stop by…."

Todd replied quickly. "I'm skating on the Pond, and it's pretty cool. Reminds me of those great times after school. But as far as suiting up and getting into a league, or I mean, a regular game, I'm not so sure."

"It's not your age, is it? Because guys play until they're seventy, eighty. You're only like, what, fifty-five?" He laughed.

"Not quite there yet, though some days, my worries make me feel like it." The confession was born of the small-town habit that made people spill the details of their lives without a second thought. Todd left the hockey invitation hanging.

"Well, I gotta run." Johnny dropped a five-dollar bill on the table to settle his tab. Not that it would have mattered had he just walked out. Phil kept tabs going for most of his regulars, without being asked. "Think about it. If you need gear, let me know. We've got a closet down at the rink full of stuff donated by guys when they upgrade or stop playing. I'm pretty sure there's enough in there to get you started."

Johnny was being accommodating, but he was too close to the truth that Todd's job situation was still uncertain and that his finances hadn't taken any favorable turns as a result.

"Yeah, I left my hockey bag in Toronto," he replied. It was taking up space in Sarah's garage, the remnant of his involvement with his grad school club team. The only hockey gear he'd retrieved on his single visit back to town in October was his gloves, skates and stick, and that was on blind impulse. "I'll keep it in mind," Todd said, offering his hand to shake.

Trevor, in the meantime, had gone over to the Bunn to refill both their cups. "You ought to do it. You're not going anywhere for a while. What's the harm?" he said as he handed Todd his coffee.

Todd looked him square in the face. "Really? You think I want to relive 'Don't shoot!' all over? With my luck, someone there would remember me. I mean, I ran into Kenny Horton at the Superstore, and it was the first thing he said."

"That guy's stoned half the time," Trevor offered by way of support.

"Right. So if he's killing brain cells and *he* remembers, how about someone *not* on the weed, or whatever his doc has him taking?"

"We were fourteen, Todd. Fourteen. So what?"

"So what? But the pictures are still up there in the lobby of your office. You know something? On the day we lost, my dad said I should forget all about it, but he used to remind me about that tournament even when I was away at university." He avoided saying the more macabre, "until the time he died."

"So what? I grew up, Trev." His voice was agitated, though he really had no beef with his old friend. "I left Queenston. I got a life that had nothing to do with this noth-ingville." He ignored the insult he was implying toward

Trevor's life only because he had a larger point to make. But what Todd couldn't acknowledge was that growing up and getting out hadn't been enough. It wasn't just that there were pictures of the team up in the city hall. It was that Todd still had those images pinned to the bulletin board of his life.

Trevor jumped in. "Yeah, I get that. And you'll get out again, Todd. Nobody's seriously asking you to fall in love with the place and stay here until you die an old man. All I'm saying is, you're here, so you might as well make the most of it. Once winter really sets in, you'll be glad for something fun to do on Tuesday nights instead of just sitting in the house and watching the snow pile up outside."

He had a point, so Todd made a promise. "Okay, I'll play, but you have to do it, too." Trevor had no recourse but to agree, since he'd tried to back Todd into the same corner.

"You know, I think I'll do that. It might be good for this." He pointed to his potbelly, which extended further over his belt than was healthy. "Having kids, you know. New studies show that it makes fathers gain weight, too, not just the moms."

Todd ignored the comment and continued. "You know how to get a hold of Johnny? I didn't think to ask him for his cell number."

"Look, Mr. Big Time. We have cellphones, too, but around here, you want to talk to someone, you do one of three things. You go up and ring their doorbell. You look them up in the phone book and dial their number. Or you hang around Phil's for a couple of lunch hours." He grabbed the check and looked at it, then pulled a five out of his pocket and waved it and the tab in the air at Phil, who was watching from the other side of the counter.

"Just leave it there, Trevor. I've got to wipe that table down really good anyway if you've done your usual number on it." Trevor smiled guiltily as he looked at the coffee rings he'd made.

"Remember that Pig-Pen guy in the *Charlie Brown Christmas Special*? I think I inherited his genes somehow."

"Of course, I remember." Todd loved that show and watched it every Christmas. "But you're nowhere near his level of dusty mess." He grabbed his friend around the neck with the crook of his arm as they walked out. On the sidewalk, he let his grip go and shook Trevor's hand, then headed to his car.

While Todd was skating after clearing snow from the Pond the following Monday afternoon, he heard an engine downshift as a vehicle eased off the road to park. The next minute, the floppy, red hair of Johnny Reid popped over the bank. He held his stick on his shoulders, his skates slung overtop of it.

"Todd!" he called out as he walked. "I thought since you were making all the effort, it might be a good idea to come down and get a skate in. These days, you never know when the weather is going to turn warm again."

He laced up on the bank, being too smart, or too scared, to trust the Shack to stand for the three minutes it would take him to get ready to play. Then he jumped on the ice, dropping a puck out of his coat pocket.

Johnny skated easily with the puck almost attached to his stick. He glided around to the end of the ice, then put on a burst of speed as he came toward Todd. When he got close, he sprayed a shower of ice chips as he stopped. "Cold out here, but nice," he said.

"I didn't know you played that much," Todd said in reference to the younger man's apparent skill. "Were you in leagues?"

"I was a kid when you and Timmy left town, but, yeah, I played minor hockey. When I was Midget age, there were rumors that scouts were interested in me for the Junior draft, but that never happened. I ended up staying in the house league because by that time, there weren't enough kids left to play Select, or not enough who were interested in buying the gear and doing all the traveling. My dad used to say that if you guys had won Peterborough, everything would have been different. People around here would have believed in hockey enough to put their last dime into it. When you guys lost, it kind of killed their spirit a little."

Todd admired his honesty, since beneath his comments were the words that everyone in town had thought at one time or another: *It's your fault*. He decided to address the issue, to get Peterborough out of the way so they could return to the present. "But they still keep mementos of the tournament around. Do you ever look at that case in the city hall?"

To Johnny, the display was just background, as it was for anyone who regularly came and went in the building. "Yeah, I guess I've looked it over before," he said.

Todd carried on. "You know how we lost, right? I didn't take that shot fast enough. If I had, and it had gone in, the game would have gone our way. Then, like you say, things might have been different around here, in terms of hockey anyway."

"And it still bothers you?" Johnny was leaning on the butt end of his stick, his chin resting on his overlapped hands.

"Honestly? Not really. I mean, it didn't bother me in the years I was away. I didn't ever think about it except when my dad brought it up. He died a few years ago." This was something Johnny likely already knew. Todd quickly glanced at him for affirmation and went on, "After that, the game was just a lost part of childhood. I'm sure everyone has that kind of incident in their past." He paused for a second, a feeling of dread welling up in his chest. "It's just that being back—when I see the pictures in city hall or look at my old scrapbook—I realize that it mattered so much to people that they still think about it—"

Johnny interrupted. "You know what, Todd? It doesn't matter. The people working at city hall are too busy or too lazy to take those shots down, so everyone has a vague memory about it. A lot worse has happened to Queenston than losing one stupid Bantam-age tournament. Anyone who tells you different just needs to wake up and get a life."

"You sound like my mother. Come to think of it, my dad even said something along those same lines after we lost, though I'm not sure he meant it."

"Maybe you needed the comfort then," Johnny replied. "Now, you know and I know that there was nothing to that tournament. You, Trevor and my brother, none of you were going to get anywhere in hockey. I mean, there was no chance of you guys making the NHL. Hockey was just a kid thing for you. It ended. You moved on. I don't even remember Tim playing hockey when he got older. In fact, I know he didn't because when I started getting serious, and remember that I'm eight years younger than you guys, I got his equipment out of the basement to see if any of it was any good, but it was so outdated, I laughed. His shoulder pads were much smaller than what players were using by then. And his gloves were hard as a rock because the

For former New York Islander Lorne Henning, the biggest problem with playing on outdoor ice wasn't the cold, but chasing the puck when it went out of play behind the net. Where he grew up in Resource, Saskatchewan, they played on a frozen lake. When it was dark, it would take at least fifteen minutes to find the puck if it went wide. He'd be the one to retrieve it, because, as the smallest and lightest kid of the group, he was unlikely to break through the ice if he got near a thin spot.

leather had dried, and they had these high cuffs on them. No one used those, either. I just threw the stuff away and talked my dad into buying me new gear."

"So you're a frustrated superstar?" Todd wasn't trying to get back at Johnny for being so blunt about his failure on the ice, but he didn't hold off, either. "You stopped playing hockey after Midget?"

"I didn't get drafted into the Juniors, but I played another two years anyway. Juvenile. Played until the end of high school."

"And now?" asked Todd as he bent to retie his left skate.

"I don't know. I watch the NHL. I play on Tuesdays, like I said the other day at the diner. Sure feels good to be out here, though. Playing on the pond, or as you guys called it, the *Pond*," Johnny said, making air quotes with his fingers to emphasize the word, "is like no other feeling. Being on outdoor ice when it's dark, a bit of a nip in the air, and maybe some flakes starting to come down. It's a hockey dream." He skated off as he finished saying this, the puck again magically doing his bidding as he flashed his blades back and forth to pick up speed.

The guy was pretty good. A lot better than any of the kids Todd had grown up with, even their superstar center.

He joined Johnny for a skate, some keep-away and a few rushes. They pretended they were beating defensemen and going in on goalies whose skills were undone by their clever puck handling and passing. It was as close to being a kid again as adults ever get.

As they started to untie their skates and get their boots on, Johnny said, "You know, that was a lot of fun. And we're not the only adults who have rediscovered the pond." No air quotes this time. "There's a tournament every year that's gotten really popular. It's called the World Pond Hockey Championship. Some of the Tuesday night guys and I have been in a few lower-level competitions as a team. Me, Andy, Steve, Gregg and Jamie. But we lost Andy when he moved to Gatineau to take an apprentice welding job. Said there was no reason to stick around here anymore."

It was a familiar story in the failed economy of Queenston.

"I wouldn't mind seeing that. When's the tournament?" Todd asked.

"Late February. Plaster Rock, New Brunswick. Tiny town. They started it to raise money for a new indoor arena. It kind of caught on, I guess."

"And when did it become the *world championship*?" It was Todd's turn to use air quotes.

"Ah, you know how it is. Like the Super Bowl champ is the 'world champion.' Or the World Series winner. They never talk about the CFL or baseball in Japan in the same sentence. I mean, not that the BC Lions are going to beat the New York

Giants anytime soon." They both laughed at the absurdity of the notion.

"Anybody can go?" Todd asked. He was intrigued—whether a world championship was at stake or not.

"Not anybody. You have to apply, then hope your bid is accepted. We put our name in. And we don't have to stick with the same guys we named on the application."

Todd narrowed his eyes, listening closely to figure out where this was going. Johnny continued, "You know what they say—'If you don't play, you can't win.' And the guys I play with on Tuesday, they can play, eh? But we need at least one more guy." He slowly wiped his skate blades with the fingers of his glove, waiting for Todd to pick up on the hint. Then, he came right out and said it. "I don't know how long you're around for, but why not you, Todd? I remember you and Timmy used to talk hockey all the time. You seemed like you really knew the game, watching you from my kid point of view. And you can obviously still skate."

Todd looked at him with a mixture of interest and disbelief. It was true. He and Timmy had endlessly discussed strategy, positioning. Bob's influence had done that. "I get that, but why would you want me? I mean, you know my history. Plus, I'm about a thousand years older than you guys. And when I said I was interested in the tournament, I was talking about watching it. From the sidelines." But that was only half true. His curiosity extended to the question of who played on the tournament teams. He didn't add that he hoped he'd be long gone before February.

"I'm not saying you'd lead the team in goals. Just be a part of it, play as much as you can and be kind of a leader. The young guys, especially, don't have much direction. I think hanging out with someone like you might be good for them. I mean, you know hockey, right?"

"I guess so. You're talking about more than hockey, though." Todd was convinced that his current situation disqualified him from being a successful role model. He'd gone to school, sure, and he knew the work world, but he'd flopped. "I'm not exactly at the top of my game these days."

The weight of failure rested more heavily on him any time he gave it a chance to seep into his head. He continued, "Though I've promised myself that I'm going to get back to the real world sometime, whether it ends up being in Toronto or somewhere else."

"You'll get there again soon enough." Johnny clearly knew his story. "But maybe for right now, this *is* the real world. You could offer something to these guys."

His frank and insightful statement compelled Todd to respond.

"I'll think about it. Maybe I'll come by tomorrow," Todd said. He didn't mention that he'd already extracted a promise from Trevor to scrimmage with Johnny's regular Tuesday group.

The nets in pond hockey are an ingenious invention. Various configurations and heights are used, including one type that has two, foot-long slots, one on either end, where the goals are scored. The ones used in Plaster Rock are not like this, but resemble miniature NHL nets. However, because they are only ten inches high, but an NHL-familiar six feet wide, they prevent players from raising pucks and eliminate the need for a goalie, thus saving cost and complications.

"When we're done with the scrimmage, we always spend a few minutes working four-on-four," Johnny said. "That's the other thing about the official version of pond hockey. It's played with four guys on each side, and there are no goalies. Just tiny nets, more like targets, that you shoot into. They're six feet wide like a normal net, but only yea high." He lowered his hand and held it between his knee and his ankle with his palm level with the ground to indicate the crossbar's reach.

Fear tightened Todd's chest as he envisioned shooting on those little goals.

Todd made good on his promise to head to the arena on Tuesday night, a routine he continued in the weeks that followed. Between that experience and skating on the Pond every afternoon, he was starting to feel the flow of the game again. The weight of the puck on his stick, the rhythm of pushing to accelerate on skates, these became familiar like they had been when he was a kid.

Each Tuesday after they scrimmaged, the guys from the pond hockey team stuck around. Aside from Johnny, there were Jamie, Steve and Gregg. Trevor and his son Brandon were also with them most nights, the boy having convinced his father to play because he also wanted to be on the ice as much as he could.

Gregg was the most enigmatic character of the bunch, though on the surface he looked like the stereotypical local. Not an ex-factory type but a farmer. Every time he showed up at the arena, he had on an old lumberjack coat and a John Deere hat. One night, he and Todd chatted as they waited for the Zamboni to finish its cleaning rounds.

"So you farm? Did your dad do that, too?" Todd asked.

"I farm, but it's hardly like what the old man did. I got an ag degree from Guelph. Came back right about the time that the Americans were changing the game. It's not about diversified crops anymore. Everyone's growing soy or corn. One crop, one huge tractor, a couple of field hands to help, and all you do all day is drive. You plow, plant, fertilize and harvest. There's no creativity in it. We got shut out about the time we realized we needed a new combine, for a quarter of a million dollars."

"So what did you do?" Todd knew the agriculture business from his time at Lydle. The grower wasn't "the farmer" in the lingo anymore; he was "the supplier." And "he" wasn't a man at all, but a corporation with suits in the office and the guys who did the real work well out of sight. A guy like Gregg, agriculture degree or not, was pretty forlorn in that world.

"I got into tomatoes. Heirlooms. Six varieties. Plus, I run some experiments for the provincial government. Checking how crops respond to fertilizers and pesticides. It's basically the same every time. You plant and spray in a controlled process. Limited access to the site. Records on everything, including every time anyone's in the greenhouse. You watch to see if whatever you're testing will end up toxic, but you already know it won't. They just have to document it. It's 'using my degree,' as they say. Not interesting, but it pays the bills. Lets me work on the tomatoes. I supply a couple of restaurants in Ottawa, plus do some farmer's markets when I've got surplus fruit in season."

"I know a little bit about that business," Todd replied. "I was in food production in Toronto. I worked for Lydle. Actually, that kind of makes me the enemy, doesn't it?"

Gregg shrugged. "Business is business, right? They taught us all this stuff in university. My dad could see it coming way ahead, though. I think that's why he told me early on that I didn't have a choice. I had to get a degree."

"What'd your dad do when he decided factory farming wasn't for him? Is he still in it?"

"Nah. Not on his own. He and my mom tried to sell out a while ago, but there's no market for a midsized plot of land anymore. So I just took it over and transitioned it to specialized crops, like I said. Built a couple of greenhouses. My dad ended up so stressed about it all that he had a heart attack. Mom's working to keep some bucks coming in. Dad helps me out where he can. He actually enjoys the farmer's market scene quite a bit. Gets to talk to people. Says he likes the idea of knowing where the product is going. *Product*—see, even he can't avoid the jargon." Gregg was clearly more of a thinker than he might have been taken for at first glance.

"And hockey. How'd you get time to develop those skills?" Todd had been taking the measure of each guy's abilities in the time they played together. Gregg was big, and not awfully fast, but he was as stable as a sawhorse and impossible to dissuade once he decided he was going to head to the net.

"I played some when I was younger. Never made an all-star team, though. But we played outside. My brother and sister and I used to skate on a pond at the farm."

Todd nodded. He'd now had conversations with each of the guys on Johnny's team. Each had played the game in his youth, like most Canadian boys do, and had continued to play into adulthood. And every one of the guys had been on organized teams for a handful of years or more. Johnny was the exception, since he'd come so close to making it to the next level. But if the guys were fair to good on the scale of hockey skills, they were missing a sense of four-on-four strategy. They had raw talent, but they needed coaching to develop it.

Sitting down in the dressing room after practice one night, Todd, Johnny and Trevor discussed the team while the other three guys looked on. "The problem with us trying to get ready for that pond tournament is that we have no Bob," Trevor pointed out. Glancing around, he realized that only he and Todd knew for certain what his reference to Bob meant. "Back when we played, we had this old guy named Bob MacIntosh who helped us grasp the fundamentals of the game. Later, we found out that he'd played in the NHL, briefly."

"I remember the guy," said Johnny. "Timmy thought he was God, practically. He used to talk about him all the time. I saw Bob out at the Pond, but when most kids stopped playing out there, I did, too. I heard he died a while back. I think I was still a teenager."

Todd chimed in. "He taught us how to think the game, showing us how to anticipate what was going to happen and act before the play developed. I think it was the only reason most of us were good enough to play at the level we did, especially those of us on the bottom rungs of the roster. Trev, do you remember the techniques he taught us? I do. All of them." Todd didn't add, "They worked—when we did them," wanting to avoid any reference to his failed goal. He had decided after confessing that moment to Johnny that he was done talking about it.

"Would his ideas do us any good now?" asked Johnny.

"I don't know. The game has changed since then, and anyway, the tournament is four-on-four, not like we're used to," Trevor replied.

"So we get online, watch what the winning teams do and adapt it," Todd said. "People learn everything from drumming to karate by watching other people do it on the Internet. I don't see how it would be any different with this. I'd be willing to bet that most of what Bob taught us is pretty much still relevant now, but it's not about the specifics. He gave us a way to *think* hockey." He tapped his right temple with his index finger. "I think that's exactly what we need. We need to be smarter than the guys we're playing."

Nobody said anything. The arena was quiet. The caretaker had asked them to lock up after they were done, and no one was left on the ice.

Todd looked from face to face. To an outsider, these twenty-somethings were typical Queenston—guys who had grown up here and been left behind when the world moved its concerns elsewhere. But to see them in that light was to deny that at least a couple of them had made the choice to remain here, which meant they believed that the town wasn't just its past but had a future. He hadn't returned to Queenston to reconnect with people, but it was happening anyway. Nor did he know if he'd be around long enough to see the team to Plaster Rock, but he decided to make them a promise.

"So after Christmas," he started, "I'll see you guys here, the next Tuesday. I'll do some studying in between, and I'll figure out some strategies. We'll use Bob's drills for precision and conditioning. Trev, you'll help me get some of those drawn up so we can run efficient practices." If they were going to do this, they needed to get a flying start. Once Santa came, there would be only eight weeks before they'd have to be in Plaster Rock.

"Better hope our bid comes in," Johnny said, referring to their application to play in the tournament.

"We made it to Peterborough, didn't we?" said Todd without a trace of irony.

CHAPTER
ten

Before his dad died, Todd had managed to get home each Christmas, if only for a couple of days. Having an adult understanding of the old man's alcoholism made it imperative not to leave his mom alone during the holidays. But for the past few years, Christmas had been celebrated in Toronto, with his mom visiting for a few days, longer if the holiday fell on a weekend. Despite Todd's best intentions, the occasion was mostly a hurried-up affair. He always hoped to get a tree early in December and have it decorated when she arrived, but he never seemed to have enough time. So they'd go out together a day or two before Christmas Eve and snag whatever was left on the lots, then decorate it together, with Mario Lanza singing carols in the background.

Usually, he went back to work on Boxing Day, so Christmas Day was celebrated quietly, with Todd's thoughts turning to his typical workweek concerns after supper. But he always felt he should put on a good show of it for his mom, so he made a point to take her somewhere nice for dinner during her stay. Once, it was Coda at the Royal Albert Hall. Another year, a new place just opened by chef-of-the-moment Mark McEwan. During these outings, she would surprise him with how much she knew about the menu items, and she would rattle on about the ingredients in the dishes. Todd was amazed that someone from small-town New Brunswick, where she had grown up before moving to Montreal and meeting Todd's dad, could be so worldly.

But this year, there would be no expensive meal out. With no hiring going on until after New Year's, Todd concentrated on giving his mom an old-fashioned, down-home-style Christmas. They might not eat at a "fancy joint," as his father would have said, but they would do quite well on their own.

Todd bought a small spruce tree, decorated it with his mom's old ornaments and read through some Christmas-themed magazines to inspire a feeling of the season. He also decided to try doing some Christmas baking, having a go at cherry bread and shortbread cookies. His mom helped him with the shortbreads because the recipe looked deceptively simple but could be hard to pull off. She had the touch that kept the dough from becoming an unworkable lump. Tasting the results as he pulled a couple of cookies off the cooling rack, one for each of them, he declared success.

"It's all in the butter," said his mom, smiling. "That's what gives them the sweetness."

He grabbed another. The cookie had a soft, almost sandy feel as it met the tongue, dissolving quickly at first, then more slowly. The temptation to crunch down on the cookie was overwhelming, and the reward was a rush of buttery smoothness. "I could taste test these all night," he told her.

It was five days before Christmas, and his other innovation was to grab the old Christmas records lying around and digitize them. Then, he put her collection of CDs on his iTunes so that they had several hundred Christmas songs to choose from. Mostly, they just let the playlist go. Bing Crosby would be followed by Amy Grant and then the Christmas Brass.

Standing in the kitchen listening to the soothing music, he felt joy at the slow, gentle pace the holiday had when it wasn't cluttered with activity. Not having a job helped maximize the mutual focus Todd and his mom had on Christmas.

"No office party to go to," he mused aloud to her. "No gift exchange. Do you know how long it takes to find a present for someone you know only because you both happen to have landed with the same company? This might be the only year I have this chance for, what? Twenty more?

For information about the World Pond Hockey Championship, see the official website, www.pointstreaksites.com/view/worldpondhockey/home. Aside from text, there's an informational video interview with the tournament's event manager, Danny Braun.

How old will I be when I retire, do you think?" He casually asked this of his mom, who was sitting at the kitchen table preparing pigs in blankets.

"Hopefully you can do it in twenty. You'll only be in your mid-fifties. Still, you probably won't be done raising your kids, at the rate you're going. University can be pretty expensive." She had taken the news of his breakup with Sarah pretty well, but she was looking ahead to another potential daughter-in-law turning up.

"I've gotta have them first, Mom. And that means finding Ms. Right and all that. Hardly high priority when I'm thirty-five and living with my mom again." He smiled, sure that she would not take offense. They both agreed that his situation would change come the new year. "Plus, it's not like there's a lot of suitable prospects, right?" He looked at her. "Unless one of your friends has a smoking-hot daughter you haven't told me about?" He felt comfortable saying this to his mom, treating her almost like one of the boys.

The World Pond Hockey Championship began as a fundraiser for a new arena in Plaster Rock, New Brunswick, in 2002. It carries on to this day, drawing nearly 10,000 spectators each year. Prime Minister Stephen Harper officially opened the 2007 tournament.

"Well, you had your chance with that Heather. What happened?"

"Oh, that. Kind of a dead-end, I guess."

Todd had gone out with Heather Evans again. They had gotten together several weeks before, but he hadn't called her since.

He had set up a date with her when he went to see Trevor shortly after they had first met up in the office. Before going into city hall, he determined to leave the past behind and just ask her out for dinner. He talked to Trevor for a while, and then he walked over to Heather's window and asked her if she'd like to head to the diner for a coffee. She tilted her head at him in a gesture that showed she was interested. He didn't say anything, but just waited for her answer.

"You know what? I'm off early. Why don't I meet you there at three-thirty?" The tone of her voice had the same embracing friendliness he felt when they had talked on the phone in high school.

"Sure." He would delay his daily trip to the Pond for this. If nothing else, it would be good to see her outside the confines of her window.

She arrived at Phil's right when she said she would, drawing a couple of glances from the regulars seated around when she took off her coat. They downed a quick cup of coffee. His agenda was simple—to get her to agree to dinner. As soon as he raised the question, she suggested a meal at her place. "There's pretty much nowhere good to eat out around here, unless you're interested in a pizza. Why don't I cook?" Her eyes danced, as if alluding to what might come. She was leaning forward, her elbows on the table, chin resting on both hands.

The date was on a Wednesday, and the evening raised considerable doubts for Todd as to what their future might be. She cooked a beef roast with gravy. He gave her credit for catching the retro food craze popular at the moment. She talked about her job, the town, the people they'd known in high school. After that, the conversation lagged.

Todd looked around the living room while she made coffee after the meal. Gossip magazines and crossword puzzle books were neatly piled up on the end tables. A giant TV dominated the largest wall. "Let me turn on the TV," she said as she came in with a tray of cookies and the coffee.

"That's okay, Heather," he replied. "I'm fine without it." He wasn't planning on making a move on her. He just had no interest in spending a half-hour with *TMZ* and its stories about celebrity goings-on droning in the background. He drank the coffee, ate a couple of cookies and bailed with the polite excuse that he needed to get home early enough to make sure his mother got to bed all right. They did manage a clumsy hug before he made it out the door.

He arrived home just before nine without a story to tell. Heather had retained her hot, high school body, and like it would for any guy, that had created a spark for him. But they appeared to have few common interests.

Age knows no limits in Plaster Rock, where adults contest for the World Pond Hockey Championship in February. At each year's tournament, the John Chadwick Award is presented to the oldest player registered for the tournament. In 2013, the winner was seventy-seven-year-old Doug Patterson of the "Hey Leafs Win" team from Moncton, New Brunswick.

Todd's relationship with Sarah had taught him that physical attraction was not enough to sustain something long term.

Now removed from the moment by a few weeks, Todd recounted the evening to his mom, after which she weighed in. "I don't think you gave her much of a chance, dear," she said. He suggested that they discuss Christmas gifts.

"Don't get me anything, Todd. I don't want you to spend the money." Typical mom reply.

"Too late. I've already ordered you a brand new Cadillac. They're delivering it tomorrow afternoon. You do like black with a leather interior, right?"

"Of course, dahling, but tell them to make room in the garage for the Corvette I got you," she replied, holding two fingers to her lips as if she were smoking a cigarette and then exhaling, old-school Hollywood-starlet style. They both laughed. "Actually, I was going to ask you to take me out to the Superstore so I could pick up a couple of items. I'm not talking about gifts, necessarily, but the traditional goodies we need for Christmas."

"Such as?" He wanted to do Christmas right, like it had been when he was growing up. Whatever she suggested, he would happily get.

"A turkey, sweet potatoes. Let's see…cranberry sauce. Stuffing. Green beans."

"I got that covered, Mom. I might even help you make the dinner if you want. I think it would be good to learn how it's done, given all my culinary adventures of the past little while. Oh, I told Trev to bring Brandon and Kathy by, to help us finish up the turkey. His family has their dinner on Christmas Eve, so I think they'd be able to polish off another one if we serve the meal later on in the afternoon of Christmas Day—"

"There's other stuff I want, though," she interjected. "Turtles, and those assorted chocolates in that black box. And bacon. You always liked a bacon-and-egg breakfast before you opened your presents." The simple reason was that sitting down to a cooked breakfast prolonged the anticipation. Todd was different from most kids. He spent weeks pestering his parents about Christmas, and he counted down the hours on Christmas Eve. But then, when the day arrived, he was all for delaying the excitement of opening the gifts.

"Do you remember that you usually left one present unopened?" she asked. "Sometimes, you'd wait a week before you unwrapped it. That way, Christmas might be over for everyone else, but it was still ongoing for you."

He remembered, but it had been a long time since Christmas had been that thrilling, though being home put some sparkle in the holiday again. He had already wrapped a few small gifts for his mom and placed them underneath the tree. He wasn't expecting any extra-big gifts from her, but if she got him a couple of presents and wrapped them, Christmas would be complete.

But if Todd was hoping that the man in the red suit was going to bring a job down the chimney, he was wrong. Neither did he experience a sudden revelation that his life was on track once more, as the holiday movies on TV suggested could happen at Christmas. Every film had the same plot elements: a guy returns to his hometown, rekindles the romance with the girl he missed out on and realizes the magic of the life he left behind when he sold his soul to move to the big city and work in corporate America. It was just like the fantasy scenario Trevor had joked about weeks ago. But for Todd, the romance segment had been at most so-so, the town itself didn't particularly inspire him and, rather than magic, he felt restlessness at how long it was taking to return to the life he'd carved out for himself in Toronto.

Still, celebrating Christmas with his mom, and later sharing dinner with Trevor and his family, made Todd feel like the effort he put into baking and decorating was appreciated. He and his mom even looked at some old photo albums that she dug out after their guests left.

As they surveyed the pictures of holidays and summer trips, Todd studied his dad's face. The old man always appeared to enjoy those times, his smiling expression giving no clue as to how his need to drink affected him.

That evening, after his mother was in bed, Todd took a walk. Snow was falling, and the streets were pure white. People weren't out this late on Christmas Day, so no vehicle had marred the perfect blanket that covered the road.

He looked at the sky, staring into the snowflakes that blinded him. He smelled the cold of the winter and kicked at the snow as he walked. The atmosphere was dreamlike. Despite the loneliness that the solitude of the night suggested, there was beauty in Queenston.

January came, and Todd restarted his job search, but it was the same slog it had been before Christmas. He did, however, have hockey back in his life, in the form of prepping the Pond and practicing for the pond hockey tournament, and this gave him reason to feel good about being where he was until late February, when they would go to New Brunswick to play. An email had arrived telling them that they'd gained a spot at the World Championship. Johnny had called Todd with the news.

At each year's World Pond Hockey Championship, twenty spots are reserved for teams from New Brunswick. Fifty teams are chosen from among squads who have competed before, and each year, fifty new teams get a spot. The organizers try to select teams from different parts of North America and the world. Some years, as many as 800 bids are submitted. More teams would be accepted, but the tournament has maxed out Plaster Rock's facilities in accommodating 120 teams.

"Great," Todd said, promising to call Trevor right away. "Gotta get that guy off the Christmas baking and ready to talk about strategy."

"Yeah, Todd, about that. I, I mean, the guys and I, we just don't think Trevor is going to do much for the team. He's not in shape like you are."

"You mean for guys our age?" Todd had anticipated this battle. Trevor sucked wind far too soon during their practices. More than that, even when they were playing together in the grand Peterborough days, Trevor hadn't been a star. He was a reserve defenseman who was lucky to be playing at the level of a rep team. The two of them were not necessary on this four-on-four squad.

"So what do we do?" asked Todd. "I mean, do you want me to tell him? Is that what you're saying? Because if it were up to me, we'd carry him." Trevor could play a few minutes a game, when they had a good lead or were far behind. He'd do no damage that way.

"Me, too, I guess, except that rosters are limited, and we really can't afford one-sixth of the squad to be deadweight. We, I mean, I, was thinking that we'd talk Andy into coming back, maybe joining us for the weekend in New Brunswick."

"Without practicing?" Todd saw his carefully worked-out plans being set aside if they made this change.

"He's good enough to fit in, a natural talent kind of guy. You'll see," Johnny replied.

"So that leaves me to be the bad guy?" Todd had a history of disappointing Trevor. When he had his Heather infatuation in grade ten, Todd had decided to change his image, and he realized that hanging out with Trevor made him look like he was a member of the nerd society. So he gave him the brush-off by working on yearbook photos during lunch hours rather than hanging in the cafeteria with Trevor and the other guys in their group. Yearbook might not have been cool, but it let Todd be invisible.

Trevor took about three days to call him on the snub, and Todd had responded with denials. Then the Heather note-on-the-locker incident happened, and Trevor had been his fallback person.

In one of the most poignant moments of father-son interaction of his upbringing, Todd had told his dad the story while they were sitting in the kitchen. It was still too early in the day for the old man to start any serious drinking.

"There are cool guys in school, Todd, but mostly, they're just putting on an act. Then there are other guys who are decent—guys who can be friends without thinking about how it might affect their image. They're the guys who like you for who you are. You tried to do the cool-guy act, but that's not you. Just be you. Trevor's a nice kid. You guys have a history."

Todd rolled his eyes as he sat across from his dad at the kitchen table. The old man had touched upon the most painful part of his son's childhood. Trevor was the first of his Peterborough teammates to talk to him on the bus as they drove home from the tournament. A couple of others approached him with words of encouragement as they shuffled off the bus to meet their parents in the Queenston arena's parking lot, but some players never forgave him, joining the "Don't shoot" crowd. But Todd didn't want this present incident with Trev to reflect the events surrounding that damn Peterborough game, which was now, happily, two years behind him, and starting to be forgotten by the people who had made his life miserable in the months following the loss.

Perhaps the best documentary on pond hockey is by Northland Films. *Pond Hockey: A Documentary Film* (2008) profiles the game, but even more, focuses on the love players have for it. From rink rats to former NHL players, they're all enthused about the purity of the game on the pond.

"I get that. But Trevor's, you know, he's kind of a social liability." Todd was using words straight from the reading in his Social Studies class. It was an effort to shift the blame away from himself.

"Do what you want, but you know who doesn't care that a girl ditches you in public? Trevor. And that's what a friend is made of." His dad's decisive tone rang of the one Bob had used when Todd had presented him with a similar dilemma while they were sitting in the Shack years before. This was when Trevor had been the only thing standing between Todd and a "D" in math.

Todd's father didn't often dispense wisdom so easily. But in this instance, he was right on. Todd left the table with a vow to up the loyalty quotient in his friendships, starting by making things right with Trevor.

Now, nearly two decades later, he would have to disappoint his friend again, though this time, he would be more honest and upfront.

"Okay, Johnny, I'm going to tell him he didn't make the cut. I'll just have to hope it doesn't bleed over into our friendship." In the years Todd was away, not maintaining contact with Trevor had never bothered him, but now he felt the renewed friendship would endure another move out of town.

In fact, his old buddy had been more or less waiting for the news, which Todd delivered the next afternoon at Phil's. "Hey, Todd, it's okay, man. I mean, I'm not the svelte teenager I was and which you still seem to be. Too many extra helpings of Kraft Dinner when the kids wouldn't clean their plates. But I want to go to New Brunswick, anyway. Maybe I'll do what the nerdy kids in high school did and act as team manager. What do you think?"

"Actually, I think *we* were the nerdy kids in high school. I also think we need someone to slice up the oranges and chill the Gatorade bottles." Todd refrained from launching into a mushy statement about what a good friend Trevor was.

They had less than eight weeks to get ready, and Todd kept his word, viewing online videos of the World Pond

Hockey Championship, as well as looking at documentary footage of four-on-four games played in the States. The strategies that unfolded focused on quick, short passes and excellent skating from everyone, especially the two men who played "up." He decided that his guys would need to work on puck movement the most, and he devised drills to practice, just like Bob would have done.

They still scrimmaged in the regular five-on-five format on Tuesday nights—ice time was ice time, after all, and playing would help their conditioning—but they also gathered at the Pond on other evenings, the four lights all working thanks to Johnny. Trevor didn't make it out every night, but he showed up at least three times a week. Other evenings, Brandon's homework demands kept him at home.

After the first couple of nights, when they practiced for an hour and then discussed strategy sitting on a snowbank beside the rink, Johnny piped up with an idea. "It might be nice to use that shed over there, where it's warm, instead of being out here, where we're freezing our butts off. There's some kind of heater, by the looks of that vent sticking out the back."

"You don't want to get anywhere near that place," Trevor said. "That's an inferno waiting to happen. The pipe isn't sealed, and it's all wonky."

"Then let's fix it," Johnny said. "I'm friggin' cold out here." It wasn't practical to drive somewhere else to debrief and discuss what they could work on next. Every place was closed by eight-thirty in the evening, and Todd didn't want a kitchen full of guys at the time his mom was getting ready for bed.

"We can do that," Todd said, "but you guys need to understand something. It's not a shed. It's *the Shack*, capital 'S,' like the pond is *the Pond*, capital 'P.' The Shack is kind of a monument to Bob." Since his name had first been mentioned, the guys had learned much more about him. Todd had filled them in, helped out by Trevor. "It might seem crazy, but if we rebuild it, we need to make sure it looks the same as it did when Bob was around. His memory deserves that much." Twenty-somethings weren't known for sharing the value of honoring the past, but Todd felt that keeping Bob's memory alive was worth the effort.

Two days later, on a Saturday, they met at eight in the morning, just after the sun had started its trajectory overhead. Their first move was to survey the Shack. Two walls were intact, but the shingled roof leaked. The other two walls, the ones that got the most sun, were bleached nearly white. Water runoff had also affected them, with the boards that touched the ground starting to show signs of rot because they were on the side of the building nearest the hill that went up to the road.

Nobody among them was a carpenter, but between Trevor's engineering experience and the common sense of the rest, they formulated a plan to replace the two weakened walls and reseal the roof. They would have to buy wood to prop up the roof while they removed the damaged boards. Steve, one of the self-named "young guns," had a pickup truck, so he volunteered to go to the lumber yard to get two-by-fours for the framing and two-by-tens to finish the exterior. The yard would do the cuts, so that all the guys would have to do on site was nail the new walls into place.

While Steve was away, the rest of them examined Bob's stove. It had to be cleaned and have its venting system repaired. There was only one heating contractor in town. Johnny called him, and Paul agreed to come over and have a look at the stove without making any promises that he knew anything about this particular installation or what could be done to salvage it. But when he showed up, he laughed out loud as soon as he entered the Shack.

"Do you guys have any idea what you have here?" he asked. Nobody offered an answer. "This is a Vogelzang 'Lit'L Sweetie.' If you'd looked, you would have seen that it says so right there." He pointed to embossed letters on the front door. "They made a bunch of models; been around probably since the 1920s. They've got a potbelly model, a standard boxwood, as well as several others. People still use them to heat their cottages. You'll also see one every so often in a family room, especially if the room was added on after the house was built. This one's probably about 1950 vintage, I'd guess."

The history lesson was interesting, but they wanted to know whether using the stove would kill them or the kids who were now returning to the Pond in the afternoons after school.

"So, can you make it safe?" Todd asked. "The town's going to want to inspect it before we fire it up," he said.

"If it don't leak and we can get that vent straightened out, you'll be good to go." Paul reached around to the back of the stove and wiggled the exhaust pipe. Noting how loose it was, he said, "Whoever did this knew how to route it. It's up to modern code, by the looks of it. But I'll need to secure it and seal it off where it exits this wall."

The only question was what it would cost to ensure the job was done right.

"You boys paying to rebuild this shed yourselves?" Paul asked. Receiving nods all around, he looked out at the Pond. "So this is the place where kids come to get in some extra ice time, eh? You're maintaining that rink yourselves, too?"

"Actually, he's doing that," said Trevor, pointing at Todd. "But we're also using it to practice four-on-four. We're going to the World Pond Hockey Championship in a couple of months. In Plaster Rock, New Brunswick." Adding the name of the unfamiliar town made their adventure seem less glamorous than it had at first sounded.

"Never heard of that, but if you're fixing this up for the kids, with your own time and money, then how can I do anything else but put this right for you?" He didn't say, "for free," but he didn't have to. It was understood.

By late Sunday afternoon, a load of firewood was sitting next to the stove, and another pile was drying in a neat stack outside. Inside the Lit'L Sweetie, a test fire crackled, the smoke wafting out of the refitted stovepipe, making the Pond and the surrounding woods smell like they had twenty years before. Although Bob was gone, the structure he'd left behind was renewed, standing like a monument to all he'd done for Todd and his friends.

By Monday afternoon, an inspector from Trevor's office had been out to the Pond to certify that the Shack and the stove were up to standard. Todd, having slapped a new coat of paint on the exterior walls, got a fire going in anticipation of the kids who would come down as fast as they could when school let out. The Pond wasn't crowded like the old days yet, but most afternoons, enough kids showed up to form two teams for pickup, with a few reserves left standing on the sides waiting their turn. Now that it was fixed up, the Shack would be their refuge.

Most nights the guys practiced drills for half an hour or so, then spent the rest of the time scrimmaging until they called it quits some time close to nine. A couple of guys from Johnny's Tuesday night men's league joined them to work on their four-on-four skills. It was a rotating crew, depending on who was free on a given night.

The team's passing was crisp, their breakouts good and their defense mostly solid. The one thing they worried about was whether they'd do well on the large ice surface of the tournament. The Pond was 40 feet shorter than the regulation 150-foot length they would be playing on in New Brunswick.

Todd concluded each evening with a chat in the Shack. He offered encouragement about what they were doing well and gently nudged guys along in areas where they needed a push.

Often, he said something like, "Bob used to tell us," and followed it with advice that he remembered. Trying to be a good coach and the leader that Johnny had recruited him to be, Todd planned these talks ahead of time, rather than just winging it night by night.

Todd's memories of Bob revealed that the man had taught them a lot of specific skills: how to pick up a puck off the boards, where to pass it when sticks were in the lanes, what a player must do when he blew his back-checking assignment. But what he really offered them wasn't hockey strategy. It was life strategy.

Picking up a puck along the boards required precision and timing, and you had to trust that the guy feeding it to you saw the player who was checking you and wasn't setting you up to get leveled. Feeding a puck to a teammate through a maze of defensive players' sticks required patience and timing. Losing the man you were supposed to be checking and having to hustle double hard to get back was about focus and intense effort. Every one of these lessons was a skill that Todd used as he made his way through university and his

MBA. The same would be true for any of his teammates who had gone on to make something of themselves in the world.

He shared his thoughts with his mom one afternoon when he was sitting at the kitchen table making notes for what to go over at practice that night. "Hey, Mom, I hope you know that I loved my dad despite everything. You know, the drinking. But if I'm honest about it, I think I learned more from Bob than I did from Dad. I hate to say that. It sounds disrespectful, but it's true."

"I think your dad understood that, Todd. And he was okay with it. You know the old saying about parents—they're pretty dumb when their kids are thirteen and pretty smart when they're twenty-three, though the parents don't change. Your dad knew that there were lessons you needed to learn that you just weren't going to get from him. He could see how important Bob was to you. That's why he encouraged you to keep playing hockey, even after you guys lost in Peterborough."

His dad had told him that he shouldn't quit because of what had happened. That one tournament didn't make, or ruin, a career. That Todd would regret it if he gave up hockey. He'd done it anyway. He didn't realize at the time that doing so would cause him to drift apart from Bob, since he didn't go to the rink anymore.

"You know, when I quit, I don't think Bob said anything to me about it. That's kind of surprising, isn't it?" He looked at his mother for confirmation. "I mean, if the relationship went both ways?"

"Bob was from another era, Todd. He didn't think like that. He gave you what he gave you, then when you moved on, that was it. I guess he kept going to that rink sometimes, though we never sent another team to Peterborough. Hockey just kind of wore off as a thing to do in this town, at least at the level you guys played it. At some point, he must have given it up, though I really have no idea when that was. Maybe he quit because kids stopped coming."

Todd was surprised by her use of "we" to refer to Queenston's Peterborough effort, but it reinforced what he'd always believed about his team's rise and fall. It wasn't just the boys who played that tournament. It was the whole town. This also explained why he quit. The pressure he felt, the embarrassment at having blown the game, was too much.

That spring years ago, he had shoved his hockey gear in the bag for the last time and put it in the basement, where it sat untouched. When he returned to playing in graduate school, he outfitted himself all over again, assuming that none of the gear from his youth would be of any value on the ice.

"My old equipment's still in the basement, right, Mom?" He hadn't looked for the hockey bag when he had rummaged around in his old boxes in the early days after his return.

"Yeah, I guess so. Unless your dad moved it to the garage. I doubt he would have thrown it away, since it was yours. I know I didn't." Her confession betrayed why there was a lot of stuff around the house that should have been pitched long ago, including his old toy chest, his wagon and a set of goalie gloves he'd used in his brief stint as a netminder in Pee Wee.

He went out to the garage. His dad had built wooden shelves along one wall, and over the years, he crammed them with old tires, multiple pairs of garden gloves, electrical extension cords and paint cans containing colors long covered over in the house. Todd rooted around, moving junk to the floor that should obviously be put out with the garbage. Nothing.

He returned to the house and went downstairs, and in the dark corner under the stairs, he found the bag.

It was canvas, black with yellow handles, and had "Queenston" lettered on the side. Below the name were two crossed hockey sticks, painted in yellow as was the team name. He picked up the bag, struck by its light weight and small size compared to a contemporary hockey bag. He carried it to the middle of the floor, bent down to unzip it and started emptying it piece by piece. It wasn't so much the equipment he was after, but what he hoped was still in the bottom of the bag. He pulled it out: the sweater he'd worn the year of the Peterborough tournament. It was a wrinkled mess, but exactly like he remembered it. Predominantly blue, with white flashes on the shoulders, it had the Rebels crest on the front and his number, 7, on the reverse side.

He stood up from his crouch and held it in front of him, gripping the shoulders between pinched fingers and thumbs with his arms outstretched. It could have been the sweater of the winning team. Disgusted at what it reminded him of, he was tempted to ball it up and throw it into the corner. Despite telling himself and others that Peterborough was behind him, seeing the sweater again brought the memories of his failure rushing back.

He controlled his anger and laid the sweater over his outstretched left arm, smoothing its wrinkles with his right hand. What happened could not be blamed on the sweater or the town, or Bob. The reason Todd was so bothered by his past was solely his responsibility. Whether the expectations placed on the team were fair or not and whether the town had made too much of the loss wasn't important. He hadn't shot that puck quickly enough, though he'd had all the drills in the world to prepare him and though the town had supported him and his teammates. His competitive hockey career had ended because of his own timidity. He needed to take responsibility for that.

Rather than rolling the sweater into a lump, he laid it down on top of the bag, spread it out flat and folded the arms in toward the crest. Then he doubled it over in a neat square, the way Sarah had insisted he fold his T-shirts, and put it where he'd remember to take it upstairs. He wasn't going to try to eradicate the past that the sweater represented; he was going to use it to motivate him. The four-on-four team needed a new outfit, and this design was still as cool as it had been twenty years ago. Tomorrow, he would take the sweater to the arena's pro shop and ask the owner to replicate it before the team headed to New Brunswick.

He put the equipment back in the hockey bag, then zipped it and returned it to the corner, sealing in its ghosts. His encounter with the past had been rich enough.

He went upstairs to finish his practice preparation, got his mom started on dinner and packed his hockey gear, which had been hanging to dry. An hour or so later, the dishes done and his mom headed into TV land for the evening, he walked out the door to practice at the Pond.

They had one month until they headed to Plaster Rock, and their strategy was pretty much set. Johnny, the best of the five of them, played with Steve up front, with Jamie and Gregg on defense. The forwards relied on speed and quick cuts to make their passes work. From twenty feet, any of them was deadeye on the net.

Todd rotated in and out on the forward line, spelling whichever of the guys was tired. He tried to mostly play Johnny full time and take Steve off to rest. Johnny never showed any signs of fading. When the defense needed a break, Johnny would shift there and take it a bit easier while Jamie or Gregg rested.

If things worked out, the basic game plan was to have his forwards pressure the other team's line, playing a skill game, forcing turnovers and wearing them down. The approach was high tempo, and the risk was that if the opposition took the same approach, it would end up being a war of attrition as rush was traded for rush. Todd feared that his defense didn't have the chops to keep the other side off the scoreboard if a team was fast and skilled with the puck. Todd's and his teammates' game was itself based on puck possession and snappy passing.

To give his squad another dimension to work with, he created a different set of strategies for the times they wanted to slow the game down. They would play keep-away, ragging the puck. That approach, which they called the "shutdown zone," wasn't intended to score but to kill time and let everyone get their breath again.

Official pond hockey games in Canada feature two fifteen-minute halves. There is a five-minute intermission at halftime (two minutes at the U.S. championships), but otherwise, play is continuous. If the puck gets buried in a surrounding snowbank, someone fishes it out while the clock runs. The team that touched it last loses possession.

Andy, who now lived in Gatineau, had pledged to join them for the tournament with no arm-twisting required, according to Johnny. The team needed his young legs, but Todd wasn't sure which linemate to match him with. Maybe he and Andy would form a second forward line to spell the top pair. The disadvantage was that Johnny would be off the ice for significant minutes.

In theory, their plans were solid, and in their scrimmages, they could move the puck well. Their single weakness was in getting back quickly enough on defense.

Todd's video explorations had showed him that on the short ice of pond hockey, it was essential for players to be able to take a few quick strides in the direction of their own net, then pivot and skate backwards so that they kept the play in front of them. The transitions were much faster than on a larger ice surface, and were required of all four players. In five-on-five hockey, seldom did a forward have to skate backwards.

Todd popped into the city hall one afternoon to pick up the equipment that would remedy his team's weakness. Trevor met him, eight orange cones of the type used in roadwork neatly stacked next to the door of his office. He grabbed four as Todd grabbed the others. They were heavier than they looked, needing to withstand wind gusts from cars as road crews did their jobs.

"You're obviously setting up for some sort of drill," Trevor commented as they got to the curb. Todd carefully placed all the cones inside his trunk, not wanting to scratch the paint on his Lexus. "You see Heather?" Trevor casually changed the subject.

"You mean just now? I didn't make a point of going over to her window, if that's what you're asking." Todd let the topic drop, returning to Trevor's earlier comment. "Bob seemed to have drills for precise needs, you remember? I was weak at turning, but he fixed it. I'm hoping to do the same for these guys in their transition from skating back on the backcheck to actually skating backwards. The best teams do this without hesitating."

That night at the Pond, Todd placed the cones in pairs at twenty-foot intervals. The guys skated toward them, pivoted to backwards, skated to the next pair, pivoted again, and repeated that sequence until they reached the last pair, and then cruised to the end of the Pond.

Todd did the drill, too, but he also watched to see how proficient they were. "We'll keep doing this, guys. It's the recipe for how not to get burned," he said to them. "There's no way we're falling on our backsides in New Brunswick, figuratively or literally." The other four teammates—Johnny, Gregg, Jamie and Steve—and Trevor, looked up from where they were hunched over, catching their breath. Nobody protested.

Playing against the guys from Johnny's Tuesday night league showed Todd that his team was going in the right direction as far as adding to their skills. But they hadn't been really tested. Todd brought this up as the group sat in the Shack after practice.

Johnny piped up first. "You know what, Todd? You've got a point. We've been doing the drills and scrimmaging just between ourselves, but that gives us only one style of play to defend or attack against. It's like the karate master who does well when he knows exactly what punch is coming because he's rehearsed it so many times. But out on the street, when the situation is unpredictable—boom! It can be disaster."

"So what do we do?" Todd asked. The team needed to play against guys who would really challenge them. Most of the Tuesday players they skated with were less skilled than they were. After all, had any one of them been better than a member of Todd's group, he would be on the four-on-four squad headed to the tournament.

"The high school team," Gregg said. "My brother says they're pretty good. They don't play a lot because they'd have to travel too much. But they get in a game or two a week, and they're always looking for practice time." Gregg's brother was the arena manager, a job that gave him an insider's knowledge of the local hockey scene.

Gregg promised to talk to his brother when he got home and to get in touch with the high school coach to set up some intense practice sessions on the Pond. They'd see if a bunch of kids younger and more fit than the youngest of their team could give them a run for their money.

The high school hockey coach liked the idea, but he said he wanted to go one better, and he came up with a suggestion: a send-off game. As soon as he heard the offer, Todd accepted. It would be a testing ground for his team's skills and their ability to play in front of a crowd. The coach suggested that they build excitement by promoting the game as a fundraiser. They'd hold the game at the Pond, and the money made from selling hot chocolate and coffee would be split between the high school's sports program and the four-on-four team.

To give the game impetus, Todd suggested that they create a slogan to put on posters that would publicize it. "Four-on-four, Peterborough No More" was his first, joking suggestion. But then one of the guys came up with "Four-on-four, Rebels Score More."

The frenzied buzz of setting up and publicizing the game occupied much of Todd's time for the following two weeks. Fliers were printed and put up, ads were placed in the local newspaper, and the St. Andrew's United Ladies Auxiliary volunteered to supply the refreshments. As the chairwoman explained to Todd, "We've done events like this a million times for schools, Boy Scouts, you name it. And our hot chocolate can't be topped." She smiled, a grandmother's twinkle in her eye.

Todd was so preoccupied with planning the hockey game that he put his job search on hold. He'd pass the table where his computer and printer were set up and feel a guilty pang. It was February. He had been home almost six months. Hiring season was coming up, and he was sitting on the sidelines. His sole focus was Plaster Rock.

CHAPTER
eleven

Todd's mom had essentially recovered from her hip injury, and she needed almost no special assistance. She was getting in and out of the tub confidently, a mark of independence that the therapist told Todd gauged her ability to function on her own. She had regained her energy; the months of resting had inspired a renewed burst of youthfulness. Todd took her along most afternoons when he was canvassing businesses to put up posters about the game. Mrs. Graham considered herself something of a good luck charm. More than anything, these excursions were a chance for her to get a different view of the world. Being cooped up in the living room for so long had allowed her to heal, but she also had a severe case of cabin fever. She was thankful for the escape.

After they'd been at it a few days and word had gotten around, people in town started to recognize Todd as he walked into their stores and offices, the posters rolled up under his arm. Most asked the same question: "You guys think you can beat the high schoolers?" Some also suggested the importance of what he was doing for the town. "Gonna go after that World Championship, eh? We'd probably get mentioned on *The National* if we won that," the woman at Canada Post said. Todd let the comment go without a remark, thanking her for letting him use the front window.

Todd and his mom would usually end up at Phil's for a coffee after they made their rounds. During one of their visits, the proprietor came over to refill their cups. "Joyce, what do you think about your boy reinventing himself as a hockey player?" he asked. Todd glanced up at the burly man, apron askew and coffeepot held at an angle that threatened to let the hot liquid escape. Phil had been the first person to let Todd put a notice about the game in his window, but the owner had shown no further curiosity about the team's pond hockey efforts.

"He's always been a hockey player," his mom replied. "He just forgot it for a while."

Todd did a double take at her comment. He was a son to her, an MBA, a business guy. He viewed himself in those terms, and it was how he believed other people thought of him as well. As a hockey player, he'd never gone anywhere, and he had never intended to. He'd laced up his skates only rarely in the time between grad school and when he started working on the Pond again. But his mom's words revealed that she, like the other people in town, was being carried along by the excitement building over Plaster Rock. Still, "He's always been a hockey player"? She had to be playing to the audience.

On the drive home, he asked her what she had meant by her comment.

"I know you've done more than hockey, Todd. But I think it's interesting that you've been so occupied with it since you got home."

He didn't remind her that he spent a good deal of time every day focused on her health. That was the "dutiful son" part of his life. He also didn't mention that as soon as he found another job, he'd be leaving Queenston for good, the occasional visit excepted.

"Everyone's a psychologist," he said in jest.

"Well, that goes along with being a mom, I guess, no matter how grown up your kid gets." From the corner of his eye, Todd saw her smile. She seemed confident in her assessment.

He stared out the windshield at the snow heaped up beside the road. February normally brought a wicked storm or two, but this year had seen only a few snowfalls, nothing major. Still, Queenston was not like Toronto, where the vibe of city life allowed residents to ignore the season other than when really bad blizzards hit. Even then, a couple of days later, the city would be dug out and life would return to normal, with clear sidewalks tempting people to walk around without bothering with boots. Todd enjoyed going out after work with colleagues and friends, hitting the Happy Hours or attending wine-tasting events. Wherever he ended up, it was an easy walk to a TTC station for a quick subway ride home. It felt odd that he hadn't given the city much thought since the frenzy of the Pond game had overtaken him.

Making a left turn and then pulling into the driveway of his mom's house, he was still absorbed by her comment about his preoccupation with pond hockey. The opportunity to go to the tournament had seemed like an accident, his involvement a diversion to overcome his disappointment at having to be home for a while. But the longer he was in town, the more he realized that he was being offered an unexpected bonus: the chance to erase the bad memories of the past.

----------⊗⊗⊗----------

Before the New Brunswick trip, Todd and the reborn Rebels calculated the cost of going to the tournament, including spending a night at a motel on the road down and back, gas, three nights in Plaster Rock, sweaters, food and a little padding for extras. They'd need somewhere close to three grand. If they were going to make any kind of a dent in that, they'd have to sell a whole lot of cups of Ladies Auxiliary cocoa and coffee.

The exhibition game against the high school squad was set for Saturday at one in the afternoon the weekend before their trip, and Todd and the guys arrived at the Pond at eleven. They cleared and flooded the rink and then set up ropes so that the spectators would not cross onto the ice surface. The day was cold and the sky bright, with the hoped-for high around minus five Celsius and a chance of snow. Perfect conditions for an outdoor game. The ice had been in for close to three months, and though the rink was used almost every day, Todd's work in repairing and flooding it had built the surface up to a smooth, hard sheen, over a base that was four or five inches thick in the lowest part.

Around noon, the ladies with the concession goods arrived. They were pros, just like their coordinator Mrs. Wallace, or "Marnie," as she told Todd to call her, had said, as evidenced by the trays of baked goods they had brought along with the vats of hot chocolate. They set up in the Shack, Marnie telling Todd that their sons would bring renewed supplies of hot drinks in large, insulated containers. "We use them at the winter carnival every year," she enthused. "Just the thing for an outdoor event."

The official version of pond hockey is played on a surface 75 feet wide by 150 feet long. Four players per side take to the ice. Instead of using a faceoff, the game begins with the centers clacking their sticks together before they go for the puck. There is a referee, but he or she watches from the sidelines, rather than skating with the players. That official also monitors timing and scoring. If there is a flagrant foul, the referee can award a penalty shot.

Todd and the team went out for a preliminary skate thirty minutes before game time. The high school kids were just arriving, and they, too, took to the ice. The teens' coach would ref the game. He was also on the ice, having donned black gloves, a toque and his hockey jacket, meant to represent the authority of a referee's striped sweater.

The players tossed the puck back and forth, familiarizing themselves with the sun's glare off the ice and the hardness of the surface. Todd looked at the sidelines. His mom was sitting proudly in a lawn chair he'd brought along for her. She never liked to leave the house without fixing herself up first. This meant a little face cream, some powder, lipstick and fiddling with her hair to get it to sit firmly, helmet-like, on her head. All primped, she looked kind of out of place sitting on top of a packed-down snowbank with a blanket around her, but the setup was better than having her stand for an hour.

He skated to the sideline when Johnny motioned him over. "Todd, you're going to flip when you see this. Remember, though, some problems are good ones." Johnny pointed over his left shoulder at the bank behind him. "You can't see it from here, but there must be a hundred cars parked out there. And more are coming. Pretty soon, they'll be backed up nearly into town. They'll have to park so far from the rink that they might as well not have driven at all."

Todd looked over at the snowbank as Johnny spoke. A flood of people was coming down the incline. Adults, kids, teenagers—everyone in Queenston seemed to think that the game was going to be worth seeing. "You know, these boys could get the better of us," Todd said to Johnny. "That would look really good, considering we're headed to the *World Championship*, eh?" Maybe his mom was right about his hockey rejuvenation having started to consume him. But nothing was at stake. This wasn't Peterborough. The worst that could happen was that a bunch of high schoolers would beat them.

"No worries. I got them paid off," Johnny said, smiling.

"Well, pay them some more!" replied Todd with a laugh. "And make sure they get the message. We win, eight-six, or else I'll see to it that they all fail a grade!" His grin betrayed the giddy nervousness he was feeling.

By game time, more than 300 people were standing around the Pond. The puck was dropped while a light snow started to fall, big flakes floating down, the kind that made you want to catch them with your tongue. The ice was perfect. The Shack was humming with people coming and going, dropping coins and bills into the jar for coffee and hot chocolate and tossing a few extra ones in the one marked "Donations." The townspeople were caught up in the excitement of the game.

To the benefit of Todd's team, the high school players were less prepared than the Rebels for the four-on-four format. Their troubles early on came about because they were used to playing contact hockey. Too often, they were caught trying to go for a check, realizing it was not allowed and ending up frozen in place as Todd's players danced around them. They played tentatively,

Players in official pond hockey tournaments are not required to wear protective gear, but many adopt the helmet and mouthpiece habit. (Helmets are required at the U.S. Pond Hockey Championships.) Shin pads are also frequently seen, and most players wear hockey gloves, partly for safety and partly because that's what they've been doing their whole lives while playing the game.

and the Rebels got out to a quick two-goal lead, both scored from in close.

Despite lacking their coach on the sidelines, the youngsters figured out their weaknesses quickly. Once they started to play the puck and not the man, the high schoolers were more proficient in stripping the puck away from the Rebels players than at first. Once they had it, they used their speed to set up scoring chances, trying to work to the front of the net for shots. Todd's team was saved by the guys' excellent positioning, which allowed them to intercept passes. Once they had the puck, they broke out toward the other team's net, zipping the disk back and forth as they worked their way up the ice.

Skating the puck, taking shots, hearing the whack as passes came and went, Todd reveled in the action, its sound as compelling as its sights. As goals were traded, he assessed his team from the sidelines, looking for weaknesses that they could still plug before they left on Wednesday. Their speed was good with Johnny's line.

Todd's rotation pulled its weight, too, with him and Andy, in Queenston for the weekend, on forward. They kept the game slow on their shifts, then let Johnny and Steve put on the quick bursts. The variation in tempo forced the high school team to continually alter their style, allowing Todd's squad to control the play. The teens were not men, like the players the Rebels would encounter in New Brunswick, but as compensation, they had the shine of youth on them that wouldn't characterize the teams at the tournament.

At one point, the high schoolers got ahead by two goals, scored on turnovers made by the Rebels' defensemen. The Rebels surged back with a renewed effort, keeping the puck away and discovering their strength in muscling through the kids.

The game ended 10–7, with the Rebels prevailing. Johnny's line accounted for seven of their goals, Todd's the other three. Todd was pleased by his one goal, because it showed that he could shoot the puck without hesitating. He wondered whether anyone watching from the sidelines had noticed and registered it as a change from the past. Todd didn't see Kenny Horton in the crowd, but there were a lot of faces huddled close together around the rink.

He gathered his players after they had exchanged handshakes with the high school team. "What I saw out there was a team that can win when it decides to win," he said. Their ability to erase the two-goal deficit they'd put themselves in remained fresh in their minds. "Good show, boys." He put out a fist, and each guy in turn gave it a bump, then they circled away to take a final look at the crowd.

Todd skated over to his mom. She'd gone to the Shack a few times to warm up and was holding a coffee in her hand. Trevor's wife would drive her home. Todd had to stay and help the volunteers load the empty coffee and cocoa urns into waiting pickup trucks. He also had to prep the ice for the kids already sitting in the Shack getting their skates on to go out.

As he changed from skates to boots beside his mom on the snowbank, she expressed her pleasure at how well they'd played. Then Todd went to inquire about how much money had been raised.

Marnie was wiping the side of an urn when he reached her. He did not get a chance to open his mouth. "You want to know the total," she said. "I know. I've been doing this sort of thing for a long time." He quickly thanked her for all her work before she got the idea that he was a hockey lout with no manners. She brushed off his thanks with a wave of her hand.

"I'll have to count it, and we've got the high school to take into account, but I'd say, looking at that jar, that you've got a few hundred dollars each. But that's nothing. The Donations jar had to be emptied, twice, and it mostly had bills in it. If you don't clear another couple of thousand dollars, I'd be surprised." The financial backing gave the Rebels the assurance that Queenston was behind them, expectations high. Todd thanked her again and told her that he'd stick around to help clean up.

As he was turning to go usher his mom to Kathy's car, he saw a flash out of the corner of his eye. It was the blur of her blue winter coat as she slipped down the bank and crashed to the ice. She lay still. He ran to her.

Quickly alert again, she was struggling to sit up, her hands sliding on the ice underneath her. He started to lift her up by placing a hand behind her head and another in the small of her back. People were already gathered around, and one of the boys was on his cellphone calling 911. Todd leaned over, his face right next to hers, and said, "Mom, Mom? You're fine. You're okay. You fell. You're fine. You need to relax until the ambulance gets here." She eased down into his arms.

Perhaps the measure of her distress was that she didn't protest. Her usual way of dealing with crisis, long honed by her dealings with her husband, was to take charge of the situation, focusing attention away from the problem. Now, she lifted her head up, wobbly, and looked around. "I'd like to go where it's warm," she said.

Todd was worried that she had re-injured her hip and concerned about whatever else she might have damaged. Protocol in such a situation, according to any basic first-aid course, always said that the injured person should not be moved. But he had to get his mom off the ice, which was slightly pooled with water underneath her where snow from skates left behind by the game was melting. Cold might net her a case of pneumonia.

Several players helped him to get her to the Shack, where she sat resting her head against the wall. Todd sat beside her, holding her hand. From her outward appearance, she seemed to be okay. He didn't ask whether she felt any pain, but he continued to comfort her and ask others around him for updates on how quickly the ambulance would arrive.

Someone who had witnessed her fall told Todd that his mom had slipped as she stood up and had grabbed the chair to steady herself. The lawn chair was perched on the snow-bank, and so was unstable. As she toppled to the ice, the chair came down on top of her. Luckily, there was no weight to it.

The ambulance, siren wailing as it arrived, parked near the edge of the Pond. Two paramedics carrying a porta-ble backboard rushed to Todd's mom and then took off with her in the back of their rig. Todd followed them in his Lexus.

In Emergency, his mom was assigned a room immedi-ately, and a doctor appeared and introduced himself as Dr. Matsuda. He was young, obviously newly out of med school, but quick and efficient in his method of assessing his patient. He examined Todd's mom and ruled out any head injury, then looked at his patient's extremities, checking her wrists and her neck particularly. An x-ray of Mrs. Graham's right arm, the one she used to break her fall, revealed no broken bones.

Todd's mom was subdued during the examination, but she spoke up when Dr. Matsuda asked if she had pain in her hip, noting from her chart that she'd recently recovered from hip surgery. She said her hip felt fine, but he ordered another round of x-rays anyway. Again, they were negative. The doctor admitted her to the hospital for overnight observation as a precautionary measure.

"You're about as lucky as you can be, given what happened," he said before he exited the examination room. Todd took the comment as a reprimand of sorts. He had been the one to perch her on top of the snowbank.

Todd was sitting in a chair beside his mom's bed when his cellphone rang. It was Trevor, who wanted to know how Mrs. Graham was doing and to let Todd know that everything had been taken care of at the Pond. "You didn't think I'd leave all that money with those little old ladies, did you?" he said. "I mean, they might be tempted to head out to the casino with that kind of cash in their pockets."

Todd appreciated his buddy's attempt to lighten the mood. Before he hung up, he thanked Trevor for calling and promised he'd be out on the Pond the next day at the arranged practice time. "That was Trevor," he explained as his mom looked at him. "He says you did it just to get attention."

His mom gave him a weak grin, the sedative they had given her to help her sleep starting to take effect. Todd leaned over. "I'm going to head home for a bit, okay? But I'll be back with an overnight bag." She nodded slightly and then turned her head on the pillow to sleep.

He zipped home and packed his mom a bag with essentials, then drove back to the hospital and spent a couple of hours alternating between the lounge on her floor and her room. As darkness was deepening outside, certain that his mom was comfortable for the night, Todd left for home.

The windows of the house were dark when he got there. The snow was still falling, and the flakes glistened in the glow of the streetlights. He pulled up behind his mom's car, back from the garage but rarely driven now, shut off his headlights and got out before realizing that there was nothing to eat in the house. He had planned to clean up after the hockey game and then head to the grocery store with his mom. He thought about driving to SuperFresh for some groceries but then realized that it would be closed. He decided that a large pepperoni pizza with extra cheese would be just the remedy he needed after the scare his mom had given him.

⸙

Todd picked his mom up the next day and scheduled a return visit Monday for a CT scan and then to talk to the doctor about the results as a final check against undiagnosed injuries. After he got her home and settled, he got in his car and drove to the Pond to practice with the guys.

The first order of business would be to go over Saturday's game, and as he drove, Todd reviewed the comments he planned to offer the guys. The kids had given them a good run for it, their speed and boundless energy the biggest challenge to the Rebels. Todd's squad had countered this by being smart with the puck, setting up high-percentage shots that could be taken from close to the net as they kept up with the pace set by the younger legs.

Whether the game predicted what would happen in New Brunswick, they could not know. The other teams might be fast, smart or a combination of the two. Maybe, a team would have invented a strategy to tilt the ice in their favor like the New Jersey Devils' neutral zone trap had in the NHL in the 1990s.

Todd's job as coach was to prepare his guys to play proficiently, countering anything the opposing teams brought to the ice. Bob had accomplished that task seamlessly. Todd's old mentor had made his Bantam Rebels squad feel like they could win, no matter the obstacles.

Bob had told them more than once that it didn't matter what the opposition did; what mattered was how well the Rebels executed their game. "They're bums, boys," he would joke. "Bums. Just do what you've learned to do."

"Bums." The word had jangled in the boys' ears, its resonance old-fashioned. But the message was clear. Their style of play had gotten them to the tournament in Peterborough, and it would be what carried them through. The other teams were skilled, but most of them, except the team that eventually beat them, relied on a couple of stars to get them their wins. Todd distinctly recalled a player with a red helmet on one of the squads. The kid could skate through everybody. He would score a goal or two every game, some-times more. He was like Gretzky was—too good for the competition. Of course, his teammates tried to dish him the puck every chance they got.

The natural defensive strategy was to put a couple of guys on the spunky little superstar. Other teams tried it and found out he could skate through them anyway. Bob's idea had been different. In the locker room before they played the team, he'd told them to watch the kid. "But don't get mes-merized, boys. He's good. He's going to score a goal or two.

He's done it to everyone. But he's not the team. Let him have his ice time, check him as close as you can, and then when he's on the bench, do what you do. Skate, pass, shoot. He might outscore the line he's playing against, but he can't out-score the whole team." Bob didn't mention that the kid sometimes could do just that, but the approach worked. Once the Rebels directed their focus away from the super-star, the rest of the ice opened up to the smart positional play honed by Bob's teaching.

The new Rebels were a more mature team, less prone to being overwhelmed by the dangles of a single opposing player. But to guard against team strategies that could undo them, they had to concentrate on their playmaking, positioning themselves on the ice to take advantage of their puck skills.

Todd parked in his usual spot, grabbed his gear and headed down the hill to the Pond. He approached the Shack with a sense of purpose, convinced that nothing else mattered but what he had to say to the guys. He reviewed plays and offered advice before leading them onto the Pond to make their final preparations for the tournament, just as Bob would have done.

Predictably, the next two days flew by, and suddenly Todd was packing his suitcase for New Brunswick. He had debated whether he should stay and look after his mom, but after learning that her CT scan was negative and hearing the doctor say his mom would be fine alone for four or five days, he decided not to interrupt his plans. But to give himself some peace of mind about his decision, Todd arranged for a young woman to come in to prepare his mom's meals and do a light cleaning. His mom protested, but with another set of eyes making sure she was okay while he was so far away, Todd knew he'd be more effective as a coach and a player.

The guys got together Tuesday night for one last full practice. Being in the arena allowed Todd a final chance to set the nets up at the regulation 150-foot interval they'd see in Plaster Rock. He needed to reassure himself that the Rebels' style was suited to the length of the surface they'd be playing on in the tournament.

Todd watched the team thread the puck to each other and work on their range in shooting at the low four-on-four regulation nets, both passing and shooting with bullet accuracy. They felt ready. As they debriefed in the dressing room one last time before they would meet, gear packed, the next morning to drive out to New Brunswick, he gave them the talk he'd been preparing for weeks.

"Boys, you've seen every hockey movie there is. You've seen the underdog team win in *Mystery, Alaska*. You've seen a trick play that saved the game in *The Mighty Ducks*, though we all know that flying 'V' formation was offside." Todd smiled, and they all laughed. "You've seen Kurt Russell as Herb Brooks give the guys that 'this is your time' speech in *Miracle*. We don't need any of that. No unlikely win, no deception and no psychology is going to get us anywhere at this World Championship."

Todd paused, scanning their faces to see if he was getting through. They were with him. Johnny's beaming grin said that he was congratulating himself for bringing Todd alongside him to lead the group. Todd continued, "You've seen Daniel Larusso beat the Cobra Kai in *The Karate Kid*, too, and if that's not a hockey movie, I don't know what is. Sure, it's about karate, but look at what happens—an old man teaches a kid to have heart and combine that with skill. And that's what it takes to win.

"You probably think I'm awfully full of myself talking like I'm Mr. Miyagi. That's not what I mean. I'm not doing this because I've got some ancient Asian wisdom that we can deploy at the right moment to score the winning goal. I'm saying these things because of what someone said to me a long time ago." He paused to catch his breath. "You guys have heard me talk a lot about Bob MacIntosh, who was one of our coaches the year we went to Peterborough." Another pause. Even though Gregg, Steve, Jamie and Johnny were six or seven when that tournament had happened, they were familiar with the story. "He was an NHLer, but we never knew that. We just knew he believed in us and thought we could win. He prepared us to win by making us smarter than everybody else. He taught us to pass the puck, to look for the opening nobody else would see. He taught us to really think our game. *Our* game, guys. Not someone else's. And that's what I've tried to do for you these past couple of months."

He looked around. These guys were not easy to impress. They were young, cool dudes, athletic, the alpha types in high school. Had they been his classmates when he was younger, they probably would not have let Todd into their circle. Adulthood, however, had changed the dynamic. All four were nodding, attentive, giving him his moment. Sitting beside Todd, Trevor also paid rapt attention.

"Let's not think about anything else but what we can do. And I have something to help you focus." He walked to the rear of the dressing room and pulled out a box stashed in the cabinet next to the showers. The carton contained team jackets, one for each guy, including Trevor. The jackets were blue, with red-and-white flashings at the shoulders. "Queenston Rebels" was stitched on the back. On the front, each guy's name appeared.

"Old-school cool," Steve said, catching the jacket Todd tossed to him. "You rock, dude. How can we lose?" Hopefully, losing wasn't in the cards, but the answer would come only when they got to New Brunswick.

Each guy stood up and put his jacket on, then they looked at one another. "Team picture," Gregg said, shaking his iPhone to indicate that he wanted to get the shot. They set up the phone on top of a hockey bag and snapped a few photos, their arms around each other, smiles creasing their faces.

On the way out of the room, Todd grabbed Andy's jacket out of the box to take with him in the morning.

CHAPTER
twelve

Plaster Rock was more than ten hours by car from Queenston, and that was true only when the weather was clear and the roads not snow-covered. Because of the unpredictability of conditions in midwinter, Todd had suggested they take off early Wednesday so that they could be through Quebec that day. If all went well, they would stay in Edmundston, New Brunswick, that night and move on to Plaster Rock Thursday morning in plenty of time to get settled into their motel before registering for the tournament.

Andy had gone back to Gatineau after the game against the high schoolers so that he could work Monday and Tuesday. The rest of the gang—Todd, Steve and Jamie in Todd's Lexus and Trevor, Gregg and Johnny in Trevor's family-sized Chevrolet Impala—took off early Wednesday morning. By ten o'clock, they had collected Andy. When they pulled up in front of his apartment, each guy was wearing his Rebels jacket, but they had agreed to act like they had no idea they were outfitted in matching team gear. Andy's first words, "Hey, what about me?" broke their silence. Gregg burst out laughing and went to Todd's trunk. "Hit that remote, and let's put this guy out of his misery," he called out to Todd. The trunk popped, and he grabbed Andy's coat and threw it to him.

They quickly found the Trans-Canada highway and headed through Quebec. The weather posed no obstacle.

Thursday morning was equally clear and dry, and Todd followed the GPS directions in the Lexus toward Plaster Rock's Settler's Inn and Motel on Main Street with Trevor right behind. The outskirts of the town looked similar to Queenston's, mostly small farms in the outlying areas and some industrial buildings and warehouses closer to town, along with what Jamie said was the Fraser sawmill, the largest employer in town. He had done a little online research on Plaster Rock before they'd left.

As they approached the city's center, the traffic picked up. Soon, they were almost bumper to bumper. "It's probably their only traffic jam of the year," Jamie commented from the back seat of Todd's Lexus as they crawled toward a four-way stop one car-length at a time.

According to the GPS, the motel was just a couple of minutes away, but Todd's attention was diverted when he saw the crowds on the sidewalks and signs hanging from every light pole.

Main Street was festooned with banners stretching over the street from side to side. In every restaurant and store window, there were "Hockey Players Welcome Here" signs, and "Go Team Go" banners hung at the gas station adjacent to their motel. They jumped out of the cars when they reached the Settler's Inn, anxious to check in and take a walk to the ice rinks on Roulston Lake, a few blocks from the center of town.

It takes a month to prepare Roulston Lake for the World Pond Hockey Championship. First, the snow is removed, and then the ice is groomed daily until the first puck is dropped for the opening game, which takes place on a Thursday in February.

Todd and the guys had expected the town's welcome, given the sheer size and importance of the tournament. But seeing the enormity of twenty ice surfaces lined up two deep and side-by-side overwhelmed them. The area where the outdoor rinks were located was so large that the layout of the rinks would be visible from the windows of any passenger plane climbing westward out of Moncton or Fredericton on its way to Montreal.

Since they had a lot of time before their first game, Todd and the guys walked back to the center of town, fascinated by the people—everywhere, there were guys with hockey jackets. Team names went from one extreme to the other, from serious to silly. The "New York Shields" was in line with expectations. "Ratty Ass River Boys" was something else. The "Philadelphia Warriors" might be a group that could get under an opponent's skin, given the reference to the roughshod nature of Philly's NHL teams in the Bobby Clarke era and since. Against all of these, the jackets Todd had bought, and the Rebels name itself, were points of pride, uniting them as a group in search of what ought to be at minimum a couple of wins.

Once they had their bearings, they walked once more down the street from their motel to the registration tent set up beside the rinks. With 120 teams in the tournament, Todd and his teammates were not likely to see any of their future opponents, but as the group lined up to sign the release forms, he looked around to get a general sense of the players. Many of the guys seemed to be the same age as his Rebels, mid-twenties, but that was by no means a rule. Men in their fifties had team jackets on. He assumed that they weren't all spectators or managers, like Trevor was.

Most of the guys looked less like professional athletes than the truck drivers, accountants, painters and teachers that they likely were. They were fit, but the occasional potbelly could be seen bulging behind the hockey jackets a lot of them wore. So size and uber-athleticism weren't going to be factors. Nor would meanness, he decided as he surveyed the scene. Players kiddingly shoved ahead of teammates in line or grabbed their wallets out of their hands as they tried to display their IDs. The atmosphere was relaxed, a contrast to the experiences Todd had when he played organized hockey as a kid.

Always one of the average-sized, and never very aggressive, he had his heart in his throat every time he saw a big guy walking into an arena with his teammates when he was a kid, thinking that the boy's laser gaze would pick him out of his team and target him for lining up with a cruncher during the game. Of course, his fears never materialized in that way, but fear was a part of hockey for him all the same. But not today. With no boards, there was nothing to smash into, even if contact had been allowed. He signed his release form, excited anticipation churning his stomach thanks to the pre-tournament buzz.

After Todd's group was handed their schedule, he and the guys gathered to see their draw. "Not that we know who any of these teams are, eh?" Trevor said. But it was natural curiosity to wonder who was going to be on the other side when a team might give itself a name like "Puddle Jumpers."

Before they had left Queenston, the tournament had started to take on heightened significance for Todd, with the town's excitement reminiscent of 1992. Now that they were in Plaster Rock, he thought the levity with which team names were chosen betrayed a lack of pressure among competitors, which was a relief to him. He took a look at the list of teams they'd play. "'Has-Been All-Stars.' Anybody wanna bet that one of those guys thinks he's Guy Lafleur?" he said, looking at the guys for affirmation but getting blank stares in return. Todd's new Rebels, except for Trevor, had been little boys when Lafleur retired in 1991. He corrected himself to make reference to a player familiar to them. "Or maybe Mario Lemieux?" A couple of the guys looked at him and smiled. Lemieux's exploits on the ice had been highlights of their childhood.

Their first game was on Thursday afternoon, with two more on Friday and two on Saturday. If they were one of the thirty-two teams to make it to the playoffs, they'd face single elimination on Sunday. But that was a long way off in their eyes.

They headed back to the motel and got their gear ready for game one. Todd packed his hockey equipment and an assortment of snacks. Before they left Queenston, he had put together a supply of power bars, nuts and sports drinks. He never felt good eating hamburgers at fast food places, so he brought food that would give the guys a nutritional charge in case McDonald's was all the choice they had. When he met the team in the motel lobby, he suggested they eat a decent meal before their game. They went down the street to the diner they'd seen as they drove into town, seeking something hearty to charge them up for their first contest. The sign on the roof said "Daniel's." "Must be a relative of Phil's," Trevor quipped. Nobody laughed. "I'm just saying," he added.

The team names at pond hockey tournaments can go from sublime to silly. For example, you might find the Boston Danglers playing Operation Slap Shot, or the Green Mountain Boys up against The Fernie Griz. Other unique monikers are the New Blue Stars, Maine WingNuts, California Rat Beach Reds, Beaver Barley Kings and Boiled Owls. You might think about what you would name your team if you got the chance to compete. Here's a good one: the Goaldiggers. Sorry, though; it's already been taken.

They ate and chatted, trying to decipher the names on hockey jackets they spied out the windows. "Get Back Jack," Gregg said. They threw out other names: "Glowing Worms," "Fried Already" and "St. Catharines Donut Kings."

"Oh, here's a normal one," said Johnny. "'Ottawa Senators Light.' Well, almost normal."

Todd walked in the middle of the group as they went to retrieve their equipment. It was not the time to give a big Bob speech, but he wanted to get it in their heads that they needed to get a quick start in their first game. "Ignore the surroundings, guys. It's like that movie *Hoosiers*. The rink's the same size we've been expecting it to be." He congratulated himself for marking off the 150-foot distance with the cones to replicate the scale of the rinks in Plaster Rock when they played indoors on Tuesdays. "What's going on around us has nothing to do with us. We play our game, pass like mad, shoot when the shots are clear and try to win the first one."

As the afternoon unfolded, that was precisely what happened. The Winnipeg Puck Bombers did not have a mentor like Todd to prepare them to play hard right from the first minute. As a result, they came out slowly, fumbling the puck and not getting their game going until the Rebels led by two goals.

While waiting to go on for a shift, Todd observed their opposition's confusion. Their nervousness was amplified because they had a few fans cheering at the sides of the rink. The Rebels, by contrast, had no one. There had been some talk around Queenston of a caravan getting together and heading down to watch. Todd couldn't have stopped townspeople coming if they wanted to, but he didn't encourage it. He had no interest in having firsthand witnesses should they lose.

The Bombers picked up their game in the last half of the thirty minutes of regulation time, getting a few goals, but the Rebels traded for several more. By the end of the game, the Puck Bombers were desperately rushing the puck, flinging shots from everywhere as well as watching Todd, Johnny and the others pick up pucks and charge back toward their net. Todd didn't instruct the guys to pace themselves because it was the only game of the day. On the contrary, near the buzzer, his guys increased their clip while they were leading 10–6. The Rebels won the game 12–7, with a couple of the goals by Todd, and Johnny scoring a hat trick. Todd would use their performance as a reference point for how to start the next day's game.

In the evening, after the guys ate dinner at a Chinese restaurant, Todd and Trevor returned to the room they were sharing, vowing to get to bed early. It was only nine-thirty, so Todd decided to call his mom before she turned in for the night.

"How are you managing with the woman who's helping you out?" he asked her. She was in the middle of her answer—which worked its way from the proper method of cooking meatloaf to what people ought to wear to work, especially when

The World Pond Hockey Championship has helped build recreational facilities in Plaster Rock, but it is also a huge economic boost to the community. The population swells during the weekend of the tournament, and hotels and cottages are full in town and as far away as Edmundston.

they were working with the general public—when another call came through on his cellphone.

"Can I call you back in five minutes, Mom? I've got a second call." He looked at the number that appeared on his screen. The area code was Toronto, but the rest of the digits were unfamiliar. Sarah was in Toronto, and she knew he was at the tournament. It wasn't her number, but she could be at a friend's or using someone else's phone.

"Hello," he said cautiously. "This is Todd Graham speaking."

"Todd, Russ Hoffman here. Empire Foods. I don't think we've met. I'm VP in charge of operations, and your name came across my desk a couple of weeks ago. Actually, I was having lunch with someone and the topic of underutilized MBAs came up."

The format of the Plaster Rock tournament allows 120 teams to enter, and forty teams play at any one time. Each team plays at least five games, one on Thursday, two on Friday and two on Saturday. The playoffs are held on Sunday, with a single-elimination format reducing thirty-two teams to two that vie for the championship trophy. The winners will have won five games on Sunday and logged ten games in the tournament overall.

Todd looked at Trevor, who was lying on his bed, staring at the TV. Todd put his index finger to his lips in a *shhh* sign and then replied, "Hi, Russ. I'm pleased to hear from you." But his first thought was, "If you want to talk to the poster boy for underused graduate degrees in business, you've got the right guy, pal."

"Let me get right to it, since it's eight-thirty at night." said Russ. Todd had forgotten that Toronto was an hour back. The call wasn't as late as it had initially seemed. Still, if the conversation moved in the right direction, Hoffman could call at two in the morning and it wouldn't be an imposition.

"We've been a little light in terms of financial oversight since we lost a guy to retirement. I'm looking for someone right now, and we think you might be a good fit." Hoffman went on, using the common business jargon of "matching skill sets," "drive to succeed" and "outcome-based performance."

Todd in his reply found himself slipping into the same lingo, frequently used among people in management-level positions. He was starting to close the conversation with, "I'm looking forward to meeting you, Russ," when the man interrupted him.

"Call me Rusty," he said, adding an encouraging level of familiarity.

Todd jumped in. "I'm not available until the early part of next week, though. I'm…." He hesitated. It would be so easy to say something evasive like, "I'm tied up in meetings all day tomorrow," and Hoffman wouldn't ask for further explanation, though he might wonder how busy someone was who had been out of work for the better part of a year. Todd decided to just spill the beans. He raised his eyebrows at Trevor and gave him a wry smile. "I'm competing with my hometown team in the World Pond Hockey Championship. You actually caught me in New Brunswick."

"Plaster Rock."

The speed with which it shot out of Hoffman's mouth took Todd by surprise.

"Right."

"You're about to ask me how I know."

"Right again." Todd felt encouraged by their common ground in hockey.

"I saw a story about it on TSN last week, then watched a bunch of videos on YouTube. Looks like a pretty great opportunity," Hoffman said, sounding like he was about to close a deal or squeeze out a couple of million dollars of venture capital from a potential investor.

"I don't know about opportunity…." Todd said, then cringed. You never contradict the interviewer, and as far as he was concerned, this was a preliminary interview. "But it's cool to be a part of something."

"Kind of maximizing your break, I'd say," Hoffman replied.

It may have been meant to get the "you're not working right now" topic out in the open, or maybe he was probing to see whether Todd had another pending opportunity, which, of course, he didn't.

"Actually, it's a chance to reprise a loss the town's team took in 1992, though it wasn't pond hockey. I was in Bantam back then." The words connected Plaster Rock to Peterborough explicitly. Todd winced, looking over at Trevor, who was keeping his attention politely focused on the reality show he was pretending to watch.

"Redemption. The theme of every great novel, and many a great playoff series," Hoffman replied. He then shifted gears, saying, "If you're going to be back in Toronto next week, maybe we can meet. Ten Tuesday morning okay with you?"

"Sure, Rusty. Ten's fine. Can you shoot me an email with the location info?" Todd gave him his email address.

"No problem," said Hoffman. "If you need to contact me, you've got my number on your phone, right? If not, then I'll just see you next week. Oh, and good luck. I don't think it can hurt your chances if you show up here on Tuesday a World Champ."

Todd signed off, then panicked. Hoffman's comment might have been intended ironically, but he assumed Rusty meant what he said. To a Canadian, even a pond hockey tournament had to be respected when it billed itself as the best of the best. Todd's low-expectation lark by a bunch of overgrown kids had now turned into something that would come up when he met with Rusty on Tuesday.

He turned to Trevor after looking at his phone to make sure the call had been ended. "My ticket out, maybe," he said. "Guy from Toronto who's big in the food business.

Heard about me and, well, you got that I have an interview next week, right?"

Trevor nodded to indicate that he'd heard. "You've got the world's best timing, eh? Right when we're about to get to the thick of the tournament?" he said.

"It does add some pressure. He knows all about Plaster Rock," Todd replied. "Trevor, do you honestly think there's any way we could manage to win this tournament?" He was shaking his head "no" as he said it. "I know we practiced as if we could do it, but that's not really why we're here, is it? I mean, this is just for fun, right?"

"I don't know, buddy. But we won the first game, which is the start you were hoping for. Let's just see what happens tomorrow."

Todd called his mom back to say goodnight. He detailed their game but didn't tell her about his call with Hoffman. Superstition didn't allow it, though he'd have to say something before he left for the interview.

As he got ready for bed, he rationalized that Rusty's comment about being a World Champion had been a throwaway. Their performance in Plaster Rock would have no relevance to someone at a huge food production company. Still, it was better to have a goal than not, and if winning was now on the radar, albeit as a long shot, then so be it.

However, if they did manage to make the finals on Sunday, making it to Toronto in time for the interview was going to be nearly impossible. But he'd face that problem if they got to the playoffs.

None of the guys slept well that night, according to the reports given at breakfast on Friday morning. Nerves weren't so much the cause as noise. The motel was replete with players and fans of the tournament coming in throughout the night. They acted like kids at a little league baseball meet all sugared up on Cokes, and they kept up their racket while they walked down the hallways to their rooms.

The Rebels weren't scheduled to play until later that afternoon. It meant that their two games for the day would be relatively close together, which would be a disadvantage. Fatigue wasn't something a bunch of twenty-five-year-olds thought about, but as their coach, Todd would help them deal with it so that they'd be as strong for the second game as they were for the first.

Their first game was against a team from upstate New York, the Orangemen. Their sweaters resembled those of Syracuse University, with bands of orange and blue around the arms, and orange letters outlined in blue. They were not as youthful as the Rebels, which Todd immediately thought might be an advantage for his side, and their approach was to tomfool their way through games. Before the first ten minutes of the game had gone by, the Orangemen had drawn a couple of penalties as a result of careless play with their sticks.

Todd shouted encouragement from the sidelines when the Rebels' other line was on. "Who are you, Punch Imlach?" an Orangeman player barked in his face as he skated by. Punch had been the Leafs' coach in the 1960s, a fact known by most people who lived near Toronto or who were fans of the team.

Todd went out for a faceoff, and across from him was that Orangeman. "Well, if it isn't Punch himself," the guy said, a smirk on his face. Todd held his head level, staring at the guy without acknowledging his comment.

Had they been twelve and on the schoolyard, or in a league where "chirping" was a common tactic to get under an opponent's skin, the guy's outburst might have been appropriate. In pond hockey, his behavior was absurd. Todd watched for the puck to be grabbed after the two centers clapped their sticks together. When the play moved, Todd felt a burn across his calves. He turned around as he skated away and saw the guy, his stick still held out at an angle in midair. "Watch it, Punch. Some people don't like you."

Maybe this was just the guy's game. Maybe it was a joke, though the slash, which was designed so the referee who stood on the sidelines would not see it, wasn't funny. Todd's skin burned where the stick had made contact. His stomach churned, partly with the old feeling of intimidation that he equated with hockey, and partly out of indignation. Plaster Rock was supposed to be a fun tournament, the "World Championship" title notwithstanding. The guy's actions violated that spirit. Todd was suddenly returned to childhood times when he reported to his mom that something wasn't fair. There was no remedy available now, however. A return slash begged for a penalty, and he was not going to disadvantage his team.

Bob's advice would have been to outplay the guy, rendering his idiot comments useless. Todd grabbed the puck with his stick and skated right toward the bigmouth, then shifted his weight to his right as he got near to the guy. He held the puck on his backhand, then pitched his weight back to center and teed the puck up, shooting from twenty feet and ringing it in off the short post. He raised his arms as if he had just won the Stanley Cup, embracing his teammates as he jumped into their arms when they got to him. The teammates of his rival went past the name-caller, pushing him on the shoulder in what was jest but also derision. The Orangemen all took the same goof-around approach to the game.

The Rebels picked up their play, putting on a show of puck handling and scoring twice more. At 8–2, with a few minutes left in the game, it was inevitable that they would win. Johnny decided as the time wound down that he was going to give the Orangemen a taste of his skills, and he played a keep-away game, holding the puck for what stretched into more than a minute before firing it into the net again.

"Punch! I'll show you Punch!" he yelled toward the Syracuse side as the puck went in.

Todd put a hand on his arm. "I got it, Johnny. I'll do my own fighting." He didn't mean it literally, but it was still gratifying to have someone stick up for him, even if it was

Johnny Reid, the little redheaded kid who used to stand in his playpen while Todd and Timmy watched *The Price Is Right* in the Reid living room.

Johnny was still agitated, anxious to show the Orangemen that his team wasn't going to take their crap.

"It's cool, man," Todd said to Johnny as the clock wound down to zero.

"No, man. It's like the NHL. The veterans get the protection." Johnny didn't mean to call him old, though it came out like that. They both laughed. The game ended 9–2, and the Rebels agreed that with any luck, they wouldn't encounter another squad as ill-tempered as this one.

The Rebels' record was perfect so far, but their second game of the day was in an hour, so Todd prevailed on the boys to find somewhere to sit inside while they ate something instead of watching another game, as they had been planning to do. The energy of the games was absorbing, with most teams standing on the snowbanks and critiquing the other teams when they weren't playing. Actually, most did more cheering than looking for errors. The spirit of the tournament was friendly and supportive, the game with the Syracuse team being an exception.

Todd's guys were upbeat about how they were playing, complimenting each other as they finished off the hot dogs and fries they bought at a food truck and took into their motel's lobby to eat. He observed their confidence from an outsider's point of view, occasionally joining in on the conversation, which covered topics as diverse as girlfriends to how to fix doors in an old house so they shut firmly. It wasn't what they said so much as how they were talking—loose, free, with no pressure. Todd felt as though something magical was going on, even at this early stage in the tournament.

They'd won two games, and they looked good doing it, but the unpredictable draw, which assigned the first five games randomly, and the impossibility of pre-scouting opponents given the number of teams, made guessing the outcome impossible.

Mystery, Alaska (1999) is the most famous film that features pond hockey. In the movie, a group of guys who played on a frozen lake takes on the New York Rangers in an exhibition game. It sounds a bit far-fetched, but "barnstorming," where professional teams would tour around in the off-season, sometimes taking on local amateur players, was very common in the days before players made a lot of money from their NHL contracts. Even today, NHL old-timers' teams do some barnstorming. Imagine being on your local rink when the Edmonton Oilers old-timers showed up with a challenge!

Todd looked at the clock behind the check-in desk. "Less than half an hour, guys. Let's get turned around in five minutes and head to the rink." He meant that they should head to their rooms, use the bathroom and be back ASAP. He handed each one of them a power bar. "Take these with you. Eat them between now and game time," he instructed.

They needed to make up for the greasy hot dogs and fries and get some proper nutrients.

Game three was not much of a contest. The other team was slow, and their puck movement was restricted to short passes. Once Todd's guys figured this out, they backed up and let the play come to them, then broke the game open by skating around the other side. The game was 8–3 before half of the time had elapsed.

The Plaster Rock tournament is entirely run by volunteers. Most are local residents, but people from as far away as Calgary have served to keep the tournament organized over the four days. Local volunteers work on the event year round, and in the time leading up to the tournament, many take a week's vacation to devote their time to the WPHC.

"Certainly not what I expected," Johnny said to Todd on the sidelines as he waited to go back in. It was the rare occasion when they were both off the ice at the same time. Because the Rebels were winning easily, Todd was playing him less and giving Andy first-pair minutes with Steve. "How'd these guys get here?"

"There was a bidding process, remember," Todd said. "Almost anyone could get in if the cards fell their way. There's Exhibit One right there." He grinned and started to spread his arms wide to indicate the other team, then decided the gesture was not very sportsmanlike. "Maybe there's a reason they call themselves the 'Has-Been All-Stars,' eh?"

Johnny smiled. "But *we're* okay, right? We belong here." He was referring to their being first-timers, notwithstanding the local tournaments the guys had played the prior year, before Todd had joined them. None had been on the scale of Plaster Rock, though the competition, mainly teams from smaller towns in the eastern part of Ontario and from Quebec, had been tough.

"We belong here, Todd," Johnny repeated, with assurance this time.

Neither of them could dispute it. "Do you think we ought to invoke a kind of silent mercy rule?" Todd asked. "I mean, it wouldn't be cool to beat them 15–4, which is about the pace we're on right now."

"Yeah, it wouldn't, but it would establish our reputation as ass-kickers." Johnny said proudly. Then he reversed course. "Okay, I'll spread the word to take it easy on them," he said. He signaled with his hand to indicate to Steve that he wanted to get back onto the ice at the next break in play. The game ended 11–4, with the added benefit that the Rebels didn't have to expend an all-out effort. The two games on Saturday would be tougher because by then, all the teams would have found their stride.

That evening, while the other guys went into town for *one* beer, Todd's orders, he settled down with his iPad and did some research.

Empire Foods was run as a satellite to their American parent, Southern Cooking, though their websites indicated that the two weren't interconnected in terms of the products they offered. Southern Cooking brands were not sold in Canada, meaning that Empire had its own lines. Some of them were similar to Lydle's. He also noticed that Empire did a lot of business in store brand condiments.

He grabbed his phone and gave his mom a quick call. She had many of the same complaints as the day before, although the main issue this time was that the girl had roasted a chicken the wrong way. His mom's cantankerous and feisty responses reassured Todd that she was feeling fine.

Then he called his ex-girlfriend, seeking information about Russ Hoffman and hoping she might have some ideas about how to approach the interview. The first question he asked after greeting her and filling her in on Hoffman was, "He told me to call him 'Rusty.' Do you think that means anything?"

"I don't know much about him, really," Sarah said. "He's been around for a while. I've seen him at the trade shows and other industry events. I'm surprised you've never run into him." It was a subtle rebuke that he hadn't done more to get himself known among the players in the food world. "I get the impression that Empire's kind of in a stall right now. They lost the Metro contract for store brand ketchup, I think it was."

"Good to know." Todd could have dug up the information himself had he had time to check out the food industry trade mags, but given that his interview was on Tuesday, he was unlikely to be home in time to do much reading, even if the Rebels bombed their Saturday games. "So do you think I'd be jumping on board a sinking ship?" he asked her. She was savvy about such matters, having landed a VP position before she turned thirty.

"I think you have to do something, Todd, and if that means jumping aboard and then heading straight to the life-boats, well, so be it. You get work when you're working, they always say. I mean, it'll look better to know that someone took a chance on you. You can't control what the higher-ups do."

They chitchatted for a while about his mom and the tournament, which she was more interested in than he expected. After they hung up, he took a walk. On the main street, hockey jackets outnumbered other winter coats by a huge margin. Couples strolled arm-in-arm. Although it was early, some of the guys were showing the effects of the beer that flowed in Plaster Rock's pubs. He hoped that they'd be the ones the Rebels would play tomorrow.

He walked down a side street away from the bustle of the bars and found a quiet spot to stand and look at the sky. It was a clear night, with wispy streaks of white cloud illumi-nated by the full moon. The view wasn't much different from the night sky he saw on any winter evening in Queenston, though he found it puzzling that his life seemed more mean-ingful here, and less lonely.

On the face of it, Plaster Rock was much like Queenston. The welcome packet all the teams were given told the typical story of a small town—a population of just over

1100; 20,000 total residents in the county; the major industry potato farming. Not a place where someone with big-time ambitions would end up by design. The tournament, though, infused energy into streets that, like Queenston's, normally rolled up their sidewalks most nights shortly after it got dark.

He stuck his hands in the pockets of his Rebels jacket and kept walking. A year ago, he was in Toronto, with crazy amounts of stress coming at him every day and the last gasps of Tia Rosita starting to spell doom. Hockey had been moved to the margins of his life. Six months ago, the thought that he'd be playing in a tournament that actually meant something, at least to the several thousand people participating in or watching it, never entered his mind. But now, being a part of it called into question his long-held belief in the corroding effects a small town could have on a person. It struck him that meaning in life came from what you were doing, and not where you were doing it.

He got out his cellphone out and dialed Trevor's number. If the guys weren't in their rooms by the time he got there, he intended to go out and drag them back to their motel.

By Saturday, when the last two qualifying games would be played, a buzz had started to develop about some of the better teams, the Rebels included. When Todd and the guys went into the diner for breakfast, heads turned. On the way to their table, Todd heard someone say, "Rebels, eh? Good luck today." He turned and sent a thank you in the general direction of the voice.

The day had dawned colder than the prior two. The snow crunched underfoot on the sidewalk as they headed to the rink an hour later. The air felt heavy, the way that bitter cold can. It was the heart of winter.

The sun was bright, as it often is when temperatures reach levels of minus ten. No snow was forecast, and the ice surface was hard and chippy because of the freezing temperature. Before ten minutes of the Rebels' first game had elapsed, snow covered the rink, and some ice-cube-sized chunks that had come out of ruts where skates had dug in hard had to be cleared.

"Slow it down, boys," Todd advised on the sidelines as the game progressed. Their passing game was not working because of the ice conditions, the puck skipping all over the place as it hit gouges in the surface. Their strategy was to skate the puck. And the Orillia Otters responded by doing the same. The two teams seemed to mirror each other, skill-wise.

Neither team scored early, and about halfway through the game, they were tied at two. Todd was on the ice, still playing the patient game he had prescribed for his team, when he heard a cheer. "Go Rebels! C'mon guys! You can do it! Do it for Queenston!"

On Saturday afternoon, the tournament in Plaster Rock takes a three-hour break for ice resurfacing.

He didn't look over, but he recognized the voice. He carried the puck in, dropped it for Andy and skated toward the net to look for the redirect. Andy zipped it low along the ice between Todd's legs, and he got a stick on it. It went wide.

Todd picked up his man on the back-check, and then headed to the side for a player change, finally having the chance to survey the crowd for that familiar voice. Behind a group of spectators stood Heather. Her face shone with redness as a result of the cold, but she looked sporty in a blue ski jacket and thick retro faux-fur hat. Beside her were a couple of other women Todd recognized from the city hall and several guys, including the coach of the high school hockey team. The coach's son, one of the players who had been in the exhibition four-on-four game, was also in the group. Todd waved, contemplating what it meant to have them in Plaster Rock and the additional pressure it might put on his Rebels. He then turned his attention to the ice again.

The game went back and forth, one goal at a time. It was 3–2 for the Rebels, then, near the twenty-minute mark, it was tied. The Otters went ahead by a goal, then it was 4–4. Behind the subs, Trevor was pacing. "Come on, guys," he said. "You've gotta win. It's going to take five to get us to Sunday." Perfect records were called for in order to make the playoff round.

As the clock wound down to the last five minutes, Todd's emotions started to ramp up, his stomach churning in hopes of the win. He watched his guys play, his fists clenched in anticipation of possible goals, and he yelled at them and waved his arms to indicate when their positioning could be adjusted.

In the end, it was a game that might have gone to over-time in the NHL, so closely was it played. The difference was a bounce, with the puck skipping over the stick of one of the opposing players and landing straight on the tape of Gregg's. He skated it alone to center, thought of shooting long, and then recognized that the Otters had anticipated this move. They had backed off, which gave him a lane up the middle of the ice. He carried the puck some more, barging through the slot until he was almost at the goalmouth. Once there, with defenders converging both left and right, he tucked it in for the 5–4 win. The Rebels killed the last seconds on the clock after that.

Plaster Rock is not the only place with an important pond hockey tournament. Many take place in the U.S., and there's even one in Beijing, China. The U.S. Pond Hockey Championships tournament happens each January on Lake Nokomis in Minnesota. It has been contested since 2007 and even has a division for players who wear boots rather than skates.

After the game, Todd and the guys said hello to their fans, who came over in a group. The first question he asked was when and how they'd decided to come to New Brunswick.

"Well, as you know, my sister Karen is helping out your mom this week," a woman named Leslie told Todd.

"Mrs. Graham was all excited about the win after you called her Thursday night, and she told Karen on Friday morning. Karen called down here and found out that you guys had won the second and third games, too. We had talked about it beforehand and decided that if your record looked promising, we'd jump in our cars and come down, as long as the weather cooperated. So we took off in the middle of the night and just got here now. By the time we found your game, it was almost over."

Neither offside nor icing rules are enforced in pond hockey. Players must score from the offensive side of center, however.

As Leslie talked, Todd listened for a hint that would indicate the importance of the tournament back home. If folks were viewing it as a reprisal of Peterborough, this added a layer of pressure that he hadn't prepared the team for. Nothing of the sort came up, and Todd's worries were lost in the hubbub of his players explaining how they had won all four of their games. Steve described their goals and the energy of the host town, and their friends complimented them on getting as far as they had with their record intact. Then Todd told them they had to regroup to prepare for their fifth game.

The Rebels won their final game on Saturday in front of the now-vociferous crowd. The competition, a group of firefighters from Searsport, Maine, who called themselves the "Blazing Boys," were big, but they didn't skate as well as the Rebels did. Johnny rose to the occasion, playing his best game of the tournament and leading Queenston to a perfect record with four goals. By the time they sat down at a pizza joint with their fans that evening, the team knew who their first playoff matchup would be.

Beside Todd sat Heather, her hat perched on the empty seat on the other side. He made a joke about it being so grand it needed its own throne, then grimaced at the boos he got from his friends. Someone wadded up a paper napkin and threw it at him. He fended it off and turned to her. Despite having spent most of the night on the road, she still looked fresh, mascara outlining her eyes, lipstick giving her mouth the perfect pink accent. Being in a group made it possible to talk to her without worrying that there wouldn't be enough to say, but as the meal progressed and the conversation rolled, he realized that he might have been hasty in his earlier judgment of her. As they parted at the end of the meal, she squeezed his arm. "Good luck tomorrow," she said with a wink.

thirteen

If Saturday had been cold, Sunday was a deep freeze. The Rebels played four games that day, with the threat that a single loss would knock them out. For whatever reason, their luck held, and by late that afternoon, they had just one obstacle between them and a replica Stanley Cup, plus the title "World Pond Hockey Champions." The Lethbridge Stingers, a group of guys who had won the tournament the year before, were their next opponents.

Todd gathered his guys around him prior to the start. He rubbed his bare hands together, then put on his hockey gloves. With his stick blade, he banged the ice in front of him. "There's the old cliché about having been there before, guys. They have. We haven't. They probably think that gives them an advantage. But I think it puts them at ease. They don't need this. We do. I don't want to build it up too much, but look over there." He pointed his stick toward Heather and Leslie, who were holding up "Go Rebels!" signs while the other Queenston fans huddled next to them. "And you'll see something. Those people represent Queenston. Maybe we didn't think we'd get this far, I don't know. Maybe we did this for a lark. But despite the reasons, our efforts have gained significance. You don't think that they aren't texting, tweeting and posting photos of everything we do?" He had seen their thumbs flying on their BlackBerries ever since the group arrived.

"So to go back to my earlier speech, there's no mantra that's perfect, but let's just say that we can do this. We can do this. And if we do, it's forever."

He looked around at their faces, earnest, with their eyes focused on his, and went for his final push. "I'm being completely honest when I say that I had no idea Plaster Rock existed six months ago. I came on board because I thought I could help, and because Bob did the same for me years back. But along the way, something changed. Pond hockey might be a simple game, but there's a world championship at stake. Why shouldn't it be ours?" He paused, then took in an enormous breath and shouted, "Why?!"

Todd put his hand out in front of him, inviting the others to pile their hands on top of his. It was a gesture familiar to them from a lifetime of playground games. Their hands went out, and Todd said, "On three, 'Why not Queenston?' One, two, three..."

They threw their hands up in the air as they yelled the cheer, "Why not Queenston!"

As the guys took their last pre-game loop on the ice, Trevor came up beside Todd and gestured to the crowd. Their group of friends was cheering wildly in anticipation of the start, but they were dwarfed by the mass of people around them. Banners reading "Stingers" were held up. People were shaking tin cans with coins in them, replicating the arena atmosphere. Everyone was acting as if they were indoors, warm, at an NHL game.

"I don't know what you're thinking right now, Todd. Well, I kind of do, knowing you and your habit of analyzing things."

"Losing is forever, too," Todd jumped in, offering an alternate ending to his pre-game speech to the team. He hadn't intended to confess this to Trevor, and he would never have said it to his players.

Trevor responded without hesitation. "Well, you've got them pumped up, all positive. You've just gotta let that fear go, man. Whether we like it or not, this has gotten bigger than we probably hoped it would. The people who came out here from Lethbridge want this. And our gang does, too, small but mighty. So get your butt out there and get it for them. And remember, what happened in Peterborough only matters if you use it to your advantage."

Trevor might have grown up in a small town and gotten stuck there by his life's circumstances after he'd escaped to university, but his ability to help Todd focus his thinking revealed the true wisdom Queenston held.

Todd gave him a high five. "You know it," he replied.

The game began furiously, with both sides fighting for the early lead. The ice was hard, like it had been all day, but it was gouged from being used for hours on end. The rink had been flooded, and the water had taken, but old ruts reappeared. Still, the skaters ignored them, charging up and down the ice and reaching to get their sticks in front of shots. It quickly became apparent that the rapid transitions Todd had taught his guys using the cones were the key to defending against this hard-skating team. Guys who came to the sidelines for changes were winded, no matter how short their shifts.

Early on, Todd scored a goal that electrified the Queenston fans. He took the puck from Steve going through center and moved it up the ice. A defensive player skated backwards, keeping pace with him. The guy's skating skills demonstrated why Lethbridge had won

No slap shots are allowed in pond hockey.

the cup the prior year. He moved with the fluidity of someone with Major Junior level talent. His teammates were similarly skilled. But Todd did not let the player's smooth backwards strides alter his plan of attack.

When he got within thirty feet of the net, he faked a shot, forcing the D-man to drop to one knee to block it. As he did, Todd flipped the puck over the man's stick and charged past him. The guy hadn't gone down all the way, and he was on his skates and pursuing as Todd picked the puck up on the other side of him, nothing between him and the tiny net. Todd carried it in, hearing the guy's skates cut into the ice as he chased him. When he was about ten feet out, Todd shot the puck. It headed straight to the center of the net and went in. They were ahead, 2–1.

As he waited on the side after the goal, hands on his knees, trying to suck in some air, he felt the bite of the cold, the freeze in his nostrils and mouth. He raised his head.

The Queenston fans were still cheering, looking around at the people surrounding them as if saying, "Yeah, that's us." He caught a glimpse of Heather and noticed that she was sporting a different ski jacket and hat combo than the one she wore Saturday. He was tempted to flash her a smile, a signal that maybe he wasn't as uninterested in her as their first date had indicated, but the game called his attention to the ice again. The Stingers' skating skills were starting to put Todd's team back on their heels, the play more in their end than the opposition's.

The strategy he had developed during the tournament was simple: alternate two forward pairs hustling all the time, play an offensive game but drop back low when the other team had the puck. Naturally, this meant the forwards would have to skate a lot. He had stuck with Johnny and Steve, and he paired himself with Andy. The defensemen were Gregg and Jamie, and they stayed back and fed the puck up but were also expected to join the rush.

Early in the games, Todd had rotated the forward duos but given preference in terms of ice time to Johnny and Steve. Johnny was the best player on the team. In fact, he was the best on the ice in almost every moment of every game they played. And he and Steve had played together for a while, including all the time that they had spent practicing since Christmas.

As the game progressed and the guys on D got tired, Todd would drop Johnny or Steve back and rest a defense-man. For these top-two forwards, being on the backline was as good as sitting out. They were fit enough to play the whole thirty minutes anyway, and when they were on defense, they had the sense to rest their legs, unless a golden opportunity came for a rush.

When either Johnny or Steve was on defense, Andy would go in at forward to pair with the one who remained up, or he and Andy both would be on, taking their regular shift.

The scheme had worked for the team. The only problem with the plan was that Andy, a player of considerable skill himself, had not been happy with the ice time he was given rotating in and out at forward. Now, he leaned over to Todd as they watched the Rebels and Stingers trade rushes.

"Coach, I really want to get out there on defense. I think I could make something happen," he said. Todd scanned the clock. The game was halfway over. Andy's approach had not occurred to him, but it was time to start adjusting his strategy. Having another good skater on D to complement Johnny and Steve up front might be what the Rebels needed to regain offensive momentum.

The decision was made for him when Stingers put a couple of goals in and set up the need for a late charge from the Rebels. Luckily for Todd, the other captain called a timeout.

"All right, guys, we're down by one," Todd said, stating the obvious in the way that coaches do. "We need a goal right now, or these guys are going to shut it down on us." The score, at 3–2, was unusually low for pond hockey, which was a testament to the even skill of both squads. "Let's go with Steve and Johnny up, Jamie and Andy back. Andy will carry the puck."

He looked at Gregg, searching for any sign that he was ticked off at the switch. Gregg seemed okay with the call.

The Rebels responded as play resumed. Steve grabbed the puck at center and, instead of heading straight toward the Lethbridge net, he wheeled back in a tight circle with it, letting his three on-ice teammates catch up with him. The Stingers waited, four across side by side, ten feet on the other side of center ice. Steve dropped the puck to Andy, who quickened his pace with short, chopping strides and drove right down the center of the ice. He flipped the puck to Johnny, skating on Andy's left, and got it back as they reached the Stingers players. They, in turn, started to skate backwards in defense against the rush. Andy bypassed one Stingers forward. Then he swept wide left with the puck as a Lethbridge defenseman tried to angle him to the side. Stopping short, Andy let the guy go by him and pulled the puck toward him, backhanding a pass to Johnny.

Instead of driving straight toward the net, Johnny swung with it to the right side of the ice, then realized his mistake. There had been only one man between him and the goal. He glided toward the corner and shot.

From that odd angle, he was unlikely to score, but the puck was redirected by Andy, who had driven to the net after his pass. It bounced across the slot and in. The Rebels raised their hands in joy, enormous grins on their faces.

"Amazing!" Gregg said beside Todd. Both were incredulous at the trajectory the puck had taken. "But that's okay.

That's okay." Neither of them would have given back the goal. Pretty didn't always win games.

The game went down to the last couple of minutes tied at three. By this point, the tournament director had brought the trophy out, setting it up on a table beside the rink in imitation of—or homage to—the NHL. Todd watched as time wound down, as did the crowd. A goal would decide it.

Todd waited for a stop in play, then he called his timeout. The guys skated over. He was on the spot for something to say to inspire his players.

The moment paralleled the end of the final Peterborough game. He had blown the chance to score and was sitting on the bench. Behind him, Bob was pacing, tapping kids on the shoulder when it was their time to go out. He kept the shifts short.

Todd, his failure fresh, should not have had another chance, so when he felt Bob's tap, he looked around, convinced that someone was playing a joke. If he jumped over the boards when he wasn't supposed to, they would get a too-many-men penalty. But Bob nodded to say, yes, it was Todd's turn on the ice. "Play for now, not for then," he said as he moved to the next guy.

Todd could not think about the goal he'd blown. He had to go out and do what was needed given the current circumstances. He did just that, playing his heart out, and hoping that something would happen to reverse the mistake he'd made. Of course, nothing did.

Play for now. The advice was as relevant in Plaster Rock as it had been in Peterborough. So with five sweat-glistened faces staring at him, he repeated what his mentor had said to him many years before. "Play for now, guys. This is it." And then he made a make-or-break decision. "All forward lines from here on out, boys. Johnny and Andy up front, me and Steve behind."

Everything rode on this chance, this shift. "Play for now," he said again, exhaling a vapory breath as he lined up for play to resume. Peterborough didn't matter. Heather didn't matter. Nor did Rusty Hoffman. Todd gripped his stick through his hockey gloves, feeling the smoothness of the carbon fiber as he prepared to accelerate if the puck came to him.

He took the puck from Johnny after the draw, then zipped it forward to him through center ice. Johnny lost the puck skating laterally toward the left side of the ice, and a defensive player for the Stingers was about to head back up ice when he muffed the puck and it bounced on him. Johnny, who had stayed with the play, saw the bounce and whacked at the loose puck. It flew directly to Todd, who had moved up parallel to him, all pretense of playing to protect against attack forgotten. Without being conscious of it, he was following more of Bob's advice. "There's always the chance for another chance," the old man had said. "Back-check only after you're sure the hope of scoring is over."

Todd took the puck on his forehand and pushed it ahead of him, the net in clear sight. From his right, a defenseman was coming. Todd paused, letting the guy go by, and headed to the left corner to set up.

As he got there and wheeled around to survey the situation, a Stingers player was on him. Todd deked around the guy and moved the puck away from the snow bordering the rink, his head up all the way. Johnny and Andy were in front of the net, each with a man on them. Just behind the group of bodies, Steve was poised for the puck. Todd skimmed it out to him, and he let fly with a wrist shot. It snaked through the tangle of legs in front.

Todd headed to the net in case the puck bounced off someone, his stick down. If it came to him, he would not hesitate. This was his shot.

The puck never did arrive on his stick. The net was barely tall enough to contain it, but Steve's shot found its way to the cage and in. The Rebels had done it. They just had to kill off the last thirty-four seconds. As the time ticked on, the Queenston fans made a rabid noise; the Lethbridge spectators slowly went quiet, their hopes for victory fading with the seconds.

Todd put Gregg and Jamie in on defense once more, instructing them to sacrifice any part of their bodies necessary to secure the win, and he let Andy and Johnny play out the time up front, with the expectation that they, too, would sacrifice to defend the lead.

Todd didn't hear the buzzer go to conclude the game, so loud was the crowd's "five-four-three-two-whooooo" countdown. As time got to the end, he threw his arms into the air, dropping his stick and shrugging off his gloves. They'd won it! He pumped his fists above his head. All around, heads bobbed up and down as people clapped and shouted at his guys.

The Rebels took turns holding the trophy after the presentation. The crowd was thinner than during the game, but several hundred people were still standing around the rink, including the Queenston contingent. The light was turning toward evening, and the air was changing into the kind of bitter, windy gusts that drive people indoors.

The winner of the World Pond Hockey Championship in Plaster Rock is presented with a trophy roughly resembling the Stanley Cup but carved out of wood. In both 2012 and 2013, the trophy was won by the Acadian Boys of Tracadie-Sheila for the men's side. The women's trophy in 2013 was taken by a team from Maine, the Bud Light Lushes. They beat out a squad from Greenwood, Nova Scotia.

Photographers took pictures of the Rebels, and, as unlikely as it might have seemed, a small crowd of reporters with recorders approached the Queenston players for comment.

When it was his turn to speak, Todd was so caught up in the moment that he didn't care that his words would be printed in the papers and online the next morning. He hated the clichés that hockey players used after games to avoid saying anything real.

The Rebels were asked about their skill and their strategy, but one question had the most impact on Todd. "You guys came from nowhere, both literally and in this tournament, to win. Did you surprise even yourselves?"

"I don't think I would say 'nowhere,' and it's no surprise," Todd replied. "I've been preparing for this tournament for more than twenty years." When he was asked to explain his comment, since the tournament was only about a dozen years old, Todd said, "All hockey's pond hockey really, right? I mean, which one of us hasn't been doing this his whole life? I just didn't realize until now that playing after school all those years can get you somewhere."

Todd avoided uttering the words "Bantam" and "Peterborough," though he would have used them had the reporters pressed for details.

He grabbed the cup and skated it over to where the folks from Queenston were standing. The guys were right behind him, and when they got there, Todd held the trophy over his head, then brought it down and cradled it like a baby before handing it to Johnny. When Todd turned around, Heather was in front of him. "You guys were amazing," she said. "I'm so glad we came down."

"Yeah, me too. Unexpected but great, the whole tournament," Todd replied.

"So we'll see you at home?" The tone of her voice and the gleam in her eyes suggested a deeper meaning than just "see you around."

"Gotta celebrate the win, right?" he answered, leaving the implications of the invitation unstated.

The Rebels thanked the Queenston fans before the group trudged off to their cars to head home in hopes of getting to work the next morning. They'd be lucky to get two hours of sleep after arriving in Queenston, and that was if the roads were clear all the way.

The excitement at the rink complex had died down. Todd carefully set the trophy on the ground and packed his gear. Beside him, the team also stowed skates and helmets, then they put on their hockey jackets and headed back to their rooms. Their plan was to spend a few hours wandering around town with the trophy, Stanley Cup–style. They calculated that the beer and snacks would be free wherever they went with the trophy in tow. After their celebration, they would try to get some sleep. The two guys who didn't drink would be designated to drive the first leg home the next day. They had ten or twelve hours in the car to face, but the trip would have to be done in one day. Todd's name was on Hoffman's calendar for Tuesday morning.

As they rolled out of town at one on Monday afternoon, Todd called his mom and told her all about the win and his appointment in Toronto.

CHAPTER
fourteen

Todd and the guys drove into Queenston close to midnight on Monday, expecting to drop everyone off to enjoy a quiet bedtime. The town had a different idea. The team's first clue was when they turned off the highway. "Check that out," Steve said, pointing ahead. "It looks like the old town isn't bundled up in bed for the night." A bright shine of lights was reflecting off low wintertime clouds. Normally, by this time of night, the only light would be from the few streetlights on King Street.

If you want to see the World Pond Hockey Championship for yourself, you'll be pleasantly surprised to know that admission is free!

"It looks like a road crew's out with the floods going full bore," Jamie added. They were in Todd's Lexus. Behind them, Trevor blinked the headlights of his Chevy. They'd seen it, too.

They continued driving toward the center of town, curious about the bright lights. Maybe it was road repair, though the only reason for them to be out late on a Monday night would be a water main break.

As the two cars got closer to the town's main street, the lights shone directly into their windshields. Temporarily blinded, Todd put on his four-way flashers and slowed down, throwing up a hand to shield his eyes. Behind him, Trevor slowed also. Each driver rolled down his window, oblivious to the blast of cold air. Music blared, and as they coasted to a stop, their cars were mobbed with people pounding on the hoods and roofs and pulling the doors open. Before they knew it, the six of them were herded toward a makeshift stage set up in front of Phil's.

As they were trying to process the fact that the whole town had turned out to welcome them home, they started to notice individual faces. "Wow," Trevor said, "it's everyone in town. Man, is Andy going to be ticked off that he missed this." They had dropped him in Gatineau on their way.

"I'm not sure I see my mom," Todd responded. He kept scanning the crowd. Friendly hands slapped his back and gently pushed him and the others toward the stage. Kathy grabbed Trevor as he walked by and gave him a quick kiss.

They climbed the couple of steps to the platform and shook hands with the mayor, who was sporting a grey winter coat and leather gloves. Behind him, a banner reading "Queenston Rebels—Pond Hockey World Champs" flapped in the wind, one corner no longer tied to the pole used to secure it.

The mayor was on loudspeaker, a mic in his hand. He was in the same jovial spirit he would be on July 1 or Labor Day, glad to be the center of attention, despite it being almost midnight. As he started to talk, the crowd united its energy in a chant. "Hock-ey, hock-ey, hock-ey!" they yelled. Then "Reb-els, Reb-els!" When Todd was handed the mic, the yell switched to "Cap-tain, cap-tain." He tried to say something, but the chants were so loud that he had no idea if his voice was being projected. All he heard was the crowd.

Someone retrieved the trophy from Trevor's car and brought it to the stage. The mayor grabbed the cup and presented it to Todd, in the same way the tournament guy had done the day before. "Everyone's a Bettman," Todd said as he turned and grinned at Trevor, not realizing the mayor's mic was open. The crowd picked it up. "Bett-man, Bett-man," they started, defying the typical Canadian cynicism about the much-unloved commissioner of the NHL.

Each of the guys was introduced to a crowd who had known them all their lives. Everyone standing around grew hoarse as they chanted the players' names and watched each one take a turn raising the trophy above his head.

Todd scanned the crowd once more. He felt the townspeople's sense of familiarity, the possessiveness mixed with their excitement. The crowd displayed the same emotion an NHL city would for its players who had won a Stanley Cup. The flip side of such enthusiasm was obligation. Todd and the guys had done something for their town, something to be proud of, and now Queenston was reminding them that they were home. Maybe, in his case, they were offering forgiveness.

What he saw came straight from a Christmas movie, one where the final scene would end right at this moment. The small-town go-back plot becomes complete as the hero suddenly realizes everything that he has lost in moving to the big city. He then gives up his glamorous urban lifestyle for the values that the local people and place offer. Only that wasn't Todd, and the movie of his life wasn't about to stop rolling.

His resistance to the emotional pull that the rally represented was related to his even-keeled nature. This wasn't a failing on his part; it was a fact, a reaction to the turbulence his father's alcoholism had brought to Todd's childhood.

Todd rarely cried. It wasn't that he didn't want to at times. When his dad died, he felt a weight on his chest that he thought would be released in the form of tears, but even at the funeral, he didn't weep. He sat with his head bowed during the eulogy, willing a sob, almost feeling it burst out of him. In the end, he just let out a long breath and squeezed his hands into tight fists. The moment passed. He slowly relaxed his hands and rested his palms on his thighs. He returned to Toronto a few days later, and he and his mom rarely talked about the funeral again other than as an aside.

When he and Sarah had split up, his reaction was similarly banal. No big scene, no desperate attempts to win her back or despairing weekends trying to put her behind him. They just talked calmly, deciding to go their separate ways but agreeing to remain friends. The closest he had come to experiencing an overpowering emotion was the moment when

Mrs. Reimer called to tell him his mom had broken her hip. In the second it took her to go from saying hello to telling him what had happened, he ran the gamut from panic to sadness. Maybe his feelings were a precursor to what might come when his mom did have more serious health issues. He wouldn't know until that moment arrived.

Todd picked up the trophy to take it with him, the energy of the celebration having started to dissipate into the early morning air. He stepped off the stage. Heather was standing there.

"Well?" her eyes danced at him, that intense gaze saying more than her words might have.

"You planned this?" He was curious how it had come about.

"Cheesy, right? I mean, cool to do, but too much a clone of every bad Christmas movie you've ever watched," she responded. "'Small town celebrates its heroes' kind of deal."

He put the trophy down beside him on the sidewalk. "Funny, but I was just thinking thoughts along those same lines, and I'm not sure where I fit in that story, but thanks. The boys appreciate this." She raised her face toward his as if she was hoping for him to lean in. He quickly added, "Me, too," feeling a grip of warmth around his heart that came from somewhere he couldn't trace.

She leaned forward and opened her arms, saying "good night" as she did so. He hugged her, her body unfamiliar to him but fitting perfectly with his. He watched her walk away, noticing that she was wearing the same stylish jacket she'd had on the first day the fans had turned up in Plaster Rock.

"Not bad, eh? Though it's not right for a married man to say." Trevor was next to him.

Todd nodded his assent, then added, "Yeah, it's going to make things kind of tough when I get the offer that springs me free of Queenston. Speaking of which, I gotta run." It was only hours until he needed to head for Toronto and Rusty Hoffman. "Looks like most of the excitement is over, anyway." He shook Trevor's hand with the promise that they'd catch up again when Todd got back to town after the interview.

"Goaltending," defined loosely as being stationary in front of the net, is not allowed in pond hockey. Players can block shots, but only while they are moving through the area in front of the goal. They are not allowed to sprawl to the ice to block a shot, nor can they lie in front of the net.

He drove home to his mom, who had made the wise decision to watch the presentation on video the next day rather than braving the crowd. She'd called Kathy and made her promise to record the whole event on her iPhone.

When he arrived at the house, he found that the lights were off. He went in. Hearing her stir and noticing that her bedroom door was open, he stuck his head in. "Did you know that rally was going to happen when I called you from the road this afternoon?" he asked.

"Everyone in town knew, Todd. Did you enjoy it?"

He wasn't one to be the center of attention or to feel comfortable as the focal point of a public ceremony. "It happened so fast, I hardly knew what to do. We ended up on stage, with everyone chanting for us." He retold the events as he remembered them.

"I'll see it for myself tomorrow. I won't see you before you go, but let me know what happens after you see that fellow for your interview. You're coming home tomorrow night, aren't you?"

Todd said that he was. "Goodnight, Mom," he said as he backed out and closed the door.

"Goodnight, champ." The words rang in his ears as he walked down the hall to his room.

He didn't get the opportunity to process the celebration further. By the time he got a shirt ironed and a suit ready, packed his briefcase with extra copies of his resumé and stuck a few toiletries in a bag so he could freshen up when he got into Toronto, it was after two in the morning. He had to leave for his interview around half past five to be sitting in front of Rusty Hoffman at ten. Todd hoped that the story he had to tell Rusty would make up for the bags under his eyes.

CHAPTER
fifteen

A week later, Todd's life was looking altogether different than it had before the tournament. He was scrambling to pack so he could return to Toronto to take the job Rusty Hoffman had offered him. His mother supported the decision. His potential relationship with Heather would have to be long-distance while he got his career back on track.

Following his mad dash to the city for his interview with Hoffman, Todd and the guys celebrated their win properly again. They took the trophy to Phil's so that everyone could see it up close, in the daylight. The locals, in turn, endowed it with a Stanley Cup air of importance. Some of them held the cup above their heads as if they'd won it themselves; others hugged and kissed it. Had the bowl been metal rather than wood, they would have poured Phil's bad coffee into it and had a sip. Before the day was over, the cup had appeared on Facebook several hundred times via photos posted by people in Queenston. Even Todd's reclusive neighbor, Hugh Alexander, turned up to experience the fun.

Todd ran into people he hadn't seen in years, and he found himself enjoying being in Queenston for the first time since he had left for university. Everyone wanted a recap of the games in Plaster Rock. He told them how happy the team was to see the crowd welcome them back. Although they spent the day talking about hockey, nobody brought up the Peterborough tournament. It was a first.

That evening, he took the trophy home, his mom having demanded to see it apart from the crowds. He placed it on the kitchen table and sat down with her there, the teapot and two cups between them as well. Todd laughed. "Look at that thing," he said of the two-foot-high brown tower. It resembled the Stanley Cup, but in such a way that its designer wouldn't get sued for copyright infringement. "Now I know what Miyagi means in *The Karate Kid Part III* when he tells Daniel-san that he's not going to help him 'defend plastic-metal trophy.' When you look at it, it's just, well, it's just a block of wood, really."

"That's where you're wrong, Todd. It doesn't matter what the cup's made of. What matters is the meaning behind it. It's the same concept in business, though you don't get a trophy. You sell more than the next person. Your company outdoes another company. Nobody's headed down to the trophy shop for a plaque. But you won, and you know you won. That's what gets people up in the morning. I would think they'd have taught you that in an MBA program." She was smiling now, pleased with the irony that she was teaching him about something that should have been obvious to him.

"So do you think this will finally erase Peterborough?"

"You're well past that, aren't you? I mean, how many of those boys have gone on to a life as good as yours?" He'd heard this kind of pep talk from his mom before, but he never got tired of having it repeated. "But if it makes you feel better, you know what I heard when I got my hair done the other day? They're working on a new window display for the city hall,

"And the winners are...." These are the winners of the Pond Hockey World Championship over several years, in random order: New York Boars, Boston Danglers, Wheat Kings, Tobique Puckers, Progressive Planning.

and you guys will be there, probably forever." She placed her hands together on the place-mat in front of her. He noticed the veins, sharp and purple, standing out through her thin skin. Todd had never concerned himself with her age before, but having lived with her for the past six months, he recognized that she was getting older. He brushed aside the fear that he'd lose her some day.

"Mom, I wonder...a hundred years from now, will some anthropologist look at those displays at the city hall and realize that one player was a part of both teams? And would he, or she, recognize that winning the pond hockey tourna-ment was vindication for the loss in Peterborough?"

"A hundred years from now, neither of us will be around to care," she offered.

"I know, but I still think that something's changed, now that Peterborough is...I mean, now that we have Plaster Rock."

Coming to this realization didn't tie Todd to Queens-ton, despite the vindication he felt. Staying in town and recounting the Rebels' glorious moment for the rest of his life wasn't an existence that would satisfy him. Sooner or later, people would get tired of reliving the tournament. And even if they didn't, Todd didn't want to forever be known as the guy who came back after escaping once. In Toronto, he could be who his education had prepared him to be. Now all he had to do was convince his mom to move down there so he could look after her better. In time, as things developed, maybe Heather would be able to make the adjustment as well.

At least that's what he thought when he left Queenston to take his new job. Six months down the road, though, a new revelation came to him. Empire had hired him because he was a sharp moneyman, but they also wanted someone to direct the launch of their new line of salsas, Tia Yolanda. It was essentially his Tia Rosita idea, but the salsa would be made with entirely local, organic produce.

When Rusty pitched him the idea, Todd laughed. His first reaction was to say, "I invented that, you know," but as the words were forming in his head, the light bulb flashed. "So that's what you wanted when you hired me," he said. "You knew I had the passion to do that launch."

Hoffman raised his eyebrows and cocked his head at Todd. "Why, whatever could you mean, my friend?" he said, then added, "Of course that's what we wanted. We were surprised as heck that Lydle dropped the ball on it and left the market wide open. Now that you're on board and have proved yourself to us, I've been able to prep the ground for you. Our upper-level guys are pretty keen on the line. It seems that someone's wife, or maybe his mistress, who knows, has spent a lot of time in Mexico. When we brought it up at the board meeting, he knew exactly what we were talking about."

As his boss talked, Todd's mind churned. A product launch couldn't happen without inventory, and that involved manufacturing. Tia Yolanda had to produce her salsa somewhere.

"What'd you have in mind as far as a production facility?" Todd asked. "I mean, how long do we have to tool up?" He kept his tone inquisitive, letting Rusty talk.

"Tooling's no problem. We bought the equipment Lydle was using for a song. If we had to, we could set up in your garage and be bottling by late in the week." He was joking of course. "But only if you had a 50,000-square-foot garage. And if you did, then you'd certainly have some house."

"Really?"

"We actually do have the equipment already, and we're going to set up in Markham. They're scoping out property right now."

"Markham's expensive. And last time I checked, they didn't grow tomatoes there. Or onions. Or anything else that you'll need if you're going to do the local and organic thing. Are you going to bring it all in from afar?"

"As you know, 'local' is kind of a flexible term in this business. So yes, Markham. That's what we have to do. And it's not that far from the field. We'll probably get the produce in Leamington. What else?"

Todd looked at Hoffman, settled comfortably in his chair, where he generally spent twelve hours each day. Behind him, the Toronto skyline poked up, the trees in the distance once again starting to lose their leaves. Hoffman's desk was the desk of a powerful man. There was a brass holder for business cards and an expensive Mont Blanc pen, plus his Mac laptop. On the shelf opposite, a boxing glove was displayed in a glass case. It had been signed by Muhammad Ali. The key fob sitting on the corner of the desk would start the Jaguar XF parked in the underground garage. The office was devoid of family photos.

Todd leaned forward, resting his elbows on the desk in front of him. "I'm going to shock you, but here's what I'm thinking. Why not a factory in the heart of farm country, in Queenston? We can contract with local growers. There's a lot of empty industrial real estate, so setting up the plant wouldn't be a problem. And the workers are dying for jobs up there. The last of the auto industry was gone around a decade ago."

He looked at his boss, whose raised eyebrows indicated he was skeptical but interested, and continued. "We could retrofit a building with no trouble. Getting it up to code would be easy, too. The heavy electrical's all there, as are load-approved floors." He knew that Hoffman liked to deal in details. "And the guys at the city hall are more than willing to work with anyone who can bring jobs in."

"Sure, Graham, stick me with a factory far off the beaten track, filled with disgruntled ex-union assemblers, and expect me to like the idea. And even if the numbers make sense and I decide to do it, who's going to run the place?"

"The people I have in mind want to work, and the financials will work out, Rusty, I can promise you that. And as for someone to run the plant and keep the suppliers happy, how about a local hockey hero who swore he'd never go back, but who now sees the wisdom in taking on a great project like this?"

"Someone with the moxie to win a pond hockey world championship, you mean?"

"Something like that."